Kindred Spirits

Also by Lynn Eldridge

Kindred Spirits

LYNN ELDRIDGE

WOLFPACK
PUBLISHING
— EST 2013 —

Kindred Spirits
Paperback Edition
Copyright © 2023 Lynn Eldridge

Wolfpack Publishing
9850 S. Maryland Parkway, Suite A-5 #323
Las Vegas, Nevada 89183

wolfpackpublishing.com

Paperback ISBN 978-1-63977-390-9
eBook ISBN 978-1-63977-389-3
LCCN 2023946613

Kindred Spirits

Prologue

JANUARY, 1776—ST. AUGUSTINE, EAST FLORIDA

"Philip, please do not risk your life."

"There's no other way." Philip Burke saw in Camilla Johnson's green eyes a fear so soul-deep it strangled his heart. "I've only signed onto Captain Bledsoe's ship for a year," Philip reminded the lovely eighteen-year-old blonde who had been his neighbor all his life. He warmed her delicate hands in both of his as they stood on the small, St. Augustine pier at dawn. A winter wind cut through his navy coat and fluttered the baggy legs of his gray britches. Another chilly gust nearly stole the wool cap off his head and billowed the hood of Camilla's forest green cape. "Only aboard such a ship as Bledsoe's can I earn the amount of money your father requires before he will grant me your hand in marriage."

"Papa is being harsh because of his increasing debt," said Camilla, or Cammy as Philip affectionately called her. With tears in her eyes and voice, she continued, "Philip, even though East and West Florida are the only two southern colonies remaining loyal to England's King George III, if you're caught by the British for supporting the American rebellion, you'll be hanged."

"Nay, I'll walk the plank." That jest, because it was all too true, did not lighten the gravity of the situation. "Your father says at twenty, I'm unproven as a man who can provide for a wife."

"My father is not one to talk."

"Still, if it were not for the long friendship of our families, Mr. Johnson would not have granted me this opportunity to prove my worthiness."

Shaking her head, Cammy said, "My father's wealth, like your father's, plummeted due to the Continental dollar losing two-thirds of its value. While your father opened your fine home as a sailor's rest, mine is selling me to the highest bidder."

"C'mon, mate. It's quite a row out to the *Sea Phantom*." A crusty old sailor in a dinghy motioned to Philip, who nodded. "The cap'n waits for no man. I don't want to be the bloke left on the breadline here in port, do you?"

"Nay, Higgins," Philip called to him and turned back to Cammy. His heart absorbed her pain as he wiped a tear off her cold, pink cheek. "I detest leaving you, but we both know I cannot come near Striker's offer for your hand in marriage unless I board that ship."

"I do not wish to marry that decrepit old, self-titled lord who favors the British over the colonies," Cammy cried, her arms twining like ivy around Philip's neck.

"I will not let that happen."

"I fear for your safety, Philip," she said, peering up at him. "The *Sea Phantom* is a pirate ship. Everyone says so."

"The *Sea Phantom* is a privateer ship, not a pirate ship. As Commander-in-Chief of the Continental Army,

George Washington needs Captain Bledsoe and other privateers to sail against enemy ships. I've seen the captain's manifest. Thus far, his ship has seized or destroyed a vast fortune of illegal cargo. I will earn my share, and we can marry." Cammy shook her head, not convinced. "I have a gift for you." Philip eased her back and pulled a small brooch out of his coat pocket. He placed the brooch in her hand. "A cameo for my precious Cammy."

As Cammy gazed upon the pale pink stone carving of a man and woman embracing, she sobbed, "Philip, let's elope. Please"

Philip heard the desperate edge of hysteria in her soft voice. "We would forever be outcasts. Your family and mine would never forgive us. Our children would be shunned by their own flesh and blood, as well as society."

"I do not care. Please, stay. I beg you," Cammy wept. "Fate will not be kind to us. I feel it deep in my soul. This will be the last time I shall ever see your bright blue eyes. Never again will I run my fingers through your soft brown hair. 'Tis the last time."

Philip followed Cammy's gaze to the two-mast wartime sailing ship. Looking at it made him already feel a thousand miles away from the woman he could scarcely bear to leave.

"Cammy, the tears of sadness on your pretty face will be tears of joy as I lay a pile of coins at your father's feet. We will marry, raise a family, and be happy."

"Goodbye forever, my love," she whispered.

Philip clasped her to his chest. "Nay, only farewell, until I taste your lips in greeting on this very dock. If I stay, I would have failed to win you without ever competing. I would indeed see your wedding to Striker."

Cammy touched her lips to his. They were as salty as the sea. "'Tis our last kiss for all eternity." Her chin quivered, and her tears spilled. "Remember how much I love you."

Philip's voice shook as he said, "Each morning, the birds will sing of my love for you. Every afternoon, the ocean waves will echo the heart that beats only for you. And each star in the night sky will be my promise to return to you, Camilla Johnson."

A raspy voice called from the dingy, "Farewell, Burke."

From an inside pocket of her cape, Cammy pulled a tiny bouquet of bright blue flowers. "Forget-me-nots symbolize true love and respect." She pressed them into his hand. "Godspeed, my sweet Philip Burke."

It was gut-wrenching torture for him to leave her. Before he could change his mind, Philip turned and ran to the end of the dock. The old sailor dipped the oars into the choppy waters as Philip lowered himself into the dinghy. As soon as he was seated, Philip swiveled around and looked at Cammy.

She stood a forlorn figure at the edge of the Atlantic Ocean. The cape hugged her body as Philip wished he could do one more time. The days must pass quickly, or he would surely die of missing her. He waved to her, and she raised her delicate hand. In her wave, he read resignation and defeat. Her choked words resounded in his ears, *Good-bye forever, my love.*

"Never forget me." Cammy's voice floated to him on the breeze as though an angel had whispered in his ear.

"I will return to you," Philip shouted against that same wind whipping up whitecaps on the water. Cammy shook her head. Did she not believe him, or was she saying she couldn't hear him? "Wait for me." She made no response. Did she not intend to wait? No, she was simply unable to hear him with the building tempest hitting them from all sides. Philip's throat ached as he whispered, "I will not rest until you're back in my arms."

One

JUNE, CURRENT DAY—ST. AUGUSTINE, FLORIDA

The man at the dormer window was naked!

Sydney Crane snapped her head away from the imposing Victorian mansion she had just admired. It was an elegant, light gray house with a round tower, decorative royal blue trim, a brick walk meeting up with the wide concrete steps leading up to a large porch, and a big oak door. Though somewhat stark without flowers, the otherwise well manicured grounds were surrounded by an ornate, black wrought iron fence.

Could the lovely estate be the home of a lunatic? Or worse?

Sydney quickened her step along the wrought iron fence. Upon reaching the white picket fence which took over where the wrought iron left off, she didn't stop until her hand was on the gate. The wrought iron fence belonged to the corner-lot estate on her left. Maybe that dormer window was made of stained glass. Perhaps she'd mistaken its design for a naked man. Sydney squinted against the June first sun to focus on the window high in the roof's attic.

The glass was clear, and the man was gone.

"What's the matter?" the woman at Sydney's side asked.

Sydney was too unsure of what she'd seen to say. "I think I have jet lag, Patricia."

"Let's see this house and then resume my prearranged listings," the woman replied.

Patricia Hudson, Sydney's rental/real estate agent, stepped in front of her and shoved open the gate of the picket fence. Sydney followed the pretty brunette down a cobblestone walk leading to a slightly smaller but equally impressive Queen Anne home. Sea green with hunter green shades of decorative trim and matching triangular gables, the house boasted a fancy, white wraparound porch. In the center of the porch was an old-time, white, wooden screen door over a heavy oak door inlaid with cut glass. Floor-to-ceiling windows were framed by hunter green shutters matching the hunter green roof.

"The shutters look as if they can actually close over the windows," Sydney said as she climbed the steps to the tiled porch. "In California, shutters are often plastic and pretend."

"Isn't everything out there?" Patricia unlocked the door.

"Not in Redlands, where I'm from. We have our share of homes like these, if not quite as large," Sydney replied. She thought of herself as friendly and had done nothing to offend the realtor. Yet the woman had soured the moment Sydney had spied this Queen Anne house for rent. Though puzzled by her attitude, Sydney followed the woman with the upturned nose and attitude into the furnished home. "Oh wow," Sydney sighed in wonder.

The two-story ceiling of the foyer boasted a crystal

chandelier. A wide staircase rose on Sydney's right, and a hallway lay to her left. She walked into the living room, where white sheets draped the furniture. Despite the pinched expression on Patricia's face, Sydney removed the sheets, revealing a Martha Washington-style chair whose fabric coordinated with a Chippendale sofa. Plush carpets decorated oak floors. Sydney ran her finger over a marble-top coffee table and saw the dust she'd collected. She could hardly wait to dig in and make this house seem like hers.

"The next house on our prearranged list which I spent a good deal of time compiling, will be much more suitable for you," Patricia said, starting for the door.

"Is there a problem with this house?"

Patricia pursed her lips and said, "This is way too much house for one person. It typically goes for five grand a month."

"But didn't you say when we were in the car that the rent and house were shared by five renters, somewhat like a bed and breakfast but without the breakfast? And it rents for a thousand a month per bedroom?"

"Yes," Patricia looked at her phone as if losing interest. "But the owner doesn't want a bunch of renters over here this summer. The landlord said, and I quote, 'Rent to one or none.'"

More to herself than to the disapproving realtor, Sydney defended her desire for a big house. "I worked my way through grad school and saved my money. To live in a dream house like this with an ocean view for the next three months would be unbelievable." She walked to one of the front windows and pulled open the heavy, velvet drapes. The sunny day outside brought its cheer into the magnificent home. Looking out across the porch was a view just as breathtaking. The thick lawn was vivid green, the picket fence pearly white, and bordering the sidewalk lay a red, brick-lined road. Beyond the charming, old-fashioned road—

Patricia broke into her thoughts with, "If the owner has his way, the local historical society may soon be viewing and researching this place along with the other houses on the block. What an inconvenience that will be. Not to mention vacationers and their kids running along the beach and pier."

Sydney loved kids. And beyond the red brick street, a white sand beach swept one's eye to the bluest ocean imaginable. But it was the narrow, weathered pier that captured Sydney's attention. There was something forlorn about the little pier that ventured away from the shore to bravely stand against the mighty ocean's waves. Staring at the pier, Sydney continued in a whisper, "The moment I saw this house, I was drawn to it. It's the home I want to live in for the summer. I'll take it."

"Don't say I didn't warn you." The snap of Patricia's pen onto a round table in the foyer under the chandelier jolted Sydney out of her daze. Patricia said, "I'll need first and last month's rent for a total of two thousand plus the cleaning deposit when you sign this lease." Patricia tossed a lease onto the table and checked her watch. "The family on the other side of you went north for the summer to avoid the humidity. But a real prize from New York will be moving into the mansion on the corner lot."

Sydney crossed the room and, recalling the nude man in the window, said, "I think he's already moved in."

Patricia raised a haughty brow and flicked an invisible piece of lint from her tailored pantsuit. "I strongly advise you avoid him, even though he's your landlord."

Sydney planned to avoid him, but her curiosity was more than peaked. "Why? Because he's—odd?"

With a smart aleck ring in her voice, she replied, "Uh…because he doesn't want to be bothered?"

Sydney'd had enough of the woman. Flinging her purse over her shoulder, she said, "I'm sorry if you're not making as much money renting this house to me as opposed to me buying one. But if it will save you time and trouble, let me write you a check for the full three months' rent and cleaning deposit now. I'll sign the lease, and you can be on your way." As she wrote the check and signed the paperwork, Patricia scrolled on her cell phone. Upon receiving the money and lease, the woman turned on her heel. "What about my house key, Patricia?"

"When you're ready to *buy*, give me a call." Patricia snapped a key along with her business card onto the table, clipped across the foyer and out the front door.

"Right," Sydney said, picking up the key. "I'll be sure to do that."

Two

ar keys in hand, Jack Malone crossed the living room of his family home. Through the window, he glimpsed a woman. The sight of her stopped him like a freight train. Meandering past the wrought iron fence along the front of his yard, she was munching an apple and reading a book. The scowl Jack had worn for the past two years worsened as it occurred to him that she might be his new tenant.

But no, his tenant's name was Sydney. A man. Right?

The ponytail, centered high on the woman's head, fell past her slender shoulders. Her hair was shades of light and dark blond, and as the ponytail switched back and forth, the sun danced among its golden streaks.

"Keep your nose in that book and keep going," Jack muttered.

As she neared the end of his fence, she threw a glance over her shoulder, directing it at the attic floor of his house. All he had time to notice about her face were the oversized, green-rimmed glasses perched on a dainty nose. Then, just as quickly, she buried her nose back in the book. Jack lowered his gaze, straining to see the rest of her through the picket fence slats of the Queen Anne house. Clad in a red tee shirt and snug cut-off blue overalls, her hips had a saucy sway, and her rounded fanny was as sexy as all get-out.

From cold ashes, warm embers stirred.

Jack was honestly surprised that she'd caught his eye. No problem. His mind ruled his body, and his heart was too broken to vote. Yet, he wondered if he were open to new friends what kind she'd make. Would they have fun if he took her to dinner or to the movies? If they embraced to kiss goodnight after a casual date, would she slip the tiptoes of her probably size six red tennis shoes between his size twelve black leather boots?

No. He had no desire to romance any woman, especially one who had an aura of untouched innocence about her.

"Damn," he growled as she stopped. "I said keep going."

She wiped something, a smudge of dirt maybe, off the gate of the picket fence. Then she opened the gate and walked into the yard.

"Great, she *is* my tenant, Buster," he grumbled to the black Labrador retriever. The dog barked. Just what Jack didn't want, a bespectacled bookworm bugging him all summer. True, a tenant could keep an eye on the inside of the house, but right next door?

As she moseyed down the cobblestone path to the porch, Jack was limited to her profile, which was somewhat obscured by the glasses. However, her neck was fully visible due to the ponytail. It was a slender neck ripe for nibbling...or, if she tried to befriend him—for choking.

Halfway to the house, she stopped and faced the ocean. She stared as if mesmerized by the sand and water. One strap of her overalls draped a graceful shoulder, but when she'd turned, the other strap had slipped to her elbow. That afforded Jack a view of the curve in the front of her red tee shirt. Her breasts were perky. Each one a perfect, perky handful.

Jack groaned irritably as his palms itched.

He clenched his fists and then plowed his fingers through his hair. The tragedies he'd faced had torn him to shreds. Even now, those raw emotions threw him on a roller coaster. One minute he wanted to date this tenant, and the next, he wanted to strangle her for breaking into his self-imposed isolation, his much-needed summer solitude. Instead of telling Patricia Hudson that he didn't want to be bothered by tenants, he should have told her not to rent the place, period. He could check inside, regulate the AC, and turn on the water once a month or so.

Loneliness and grief made him feel empty and mean. He'd left New York City partly to give his employees a break. He barked at them constantly and criticized himself at every turn. The people in the office hadn't complained. In fact, they'd offered their support. But he knew he was getting worse, not better.

As his new tenant gazed out to sea, Jack thought she looked a little lost, almost vulnerable. In his present state of mind, he was sure to rub her the wrong way. Unlike a co-worker, she wouldn't cut him any slack. And what if he liked her? He had to avoid that at all costs because he couldn't live through another loss.

Jack's eyes stung, and he blinked hard. The deaths he'd suffered had left him without the people he'd loved and respected more than anything on earth. His throat ached with sadness. Hopelessness twisted the knife in his broken heart. This pain was unbearable. Jack silently vowed for the hundredth time never to care about anybody again. Never.

Next door, his tenant twirled on her heel, breaking

Jack free of the fresh wave of despair. This girl was bound to pay him a visit sometime during the summer. Damn. There had to be a way to protect his shell of seclusion.

Hands on his hips, he grumbled, "The best defense is a good offense."

He thought a minute, narrowed his burning eyes, and nodded. As his tenant skipped up her wooden porch steps, Jack regretted that making friends with her was not an option. But he knew the best thing for him was to make her a quick and sure enemy.

Three

The roar made Sydney jump. Earlier, it had rained, and thunder had rumbled across the sky and ocean. The storm had ended around noon, but apparently it was back. Again, a booming roar split the quiet of the sultry late afternoon. Sydney nearly dropped the bottle of cleaner she'd just sprayed on the cut glass in the front door. She turned just inside her foyer and realized the ear-splitting racket, this time, was that of an engine.

A man on a motorcycle rode into view. The front tire barely touched the ground as he ripped down the driveway at the far side of the Victorian mansion on the corner lot.

"Well, well, Ichabod, that must be our perverted landlord," Sydney told the fluffy, white cat grooming himself at her feet in the foyer. "At least he has his clothes on today."

Inside the wrought iron fence, a black Labrador retriever, wearing a red collar, loped alongside the motorcyclist. The man had to stop and cool his heels as a long van with Flagler College printed on the side neared his driveway. He reached a large, square hand over the top of the pointed iron bars of his fence and petted the enormous dog's head. Then, gripping the handlebars of the motorcycle, he revved the engine. Ichabod was oblivious, but Sydney was annoyed. She hoped this wasn't a sample of more to come this summer.

The man wore sunglasses and a helmet, so Sydney couldn't clearly see his face or hair. But his body was undeniably magnificent. Having glimpsed only a flash of his bare skin the time he'd appeared naked at his window —since she was currently concealed by her screen door— Sydney took a longer look. The man's broad shoulders strained against his black tee shirt, and the short sleeves were tight against his well-developed biceps. Blue jeans were molded to his thick thighs, and black boots encased his feet.

Sydney mused that this muscular man would be harder to handle than any motorcycle on the road. She had no desire to try to handle him, of course. She preferred the scholarly kind, not this tough-guy type. No. Romantically speaking, she preferred neither. The studious ones tended to be boring, and the unruly ones were too unpredictable.

She told herself the flip-flopping of her heart at the sight of this man was because his motorcycle had startled her. She watched as two females leaned out the window of the passing college van. One playfully reached for the man on the motorcycle, and the other puckered her lips and tossed him a kiss.

Straddling the powerful machine, he did make a sexy picture.

Sydney huffed and told Ichabod, "Like all cocky guys, he's a heat-seeking missile in search of one thing." Sydney's cheeks flamed as she imagined herself in the sinewy arms of her muscle-bound landlord. "You watch, he'll torpedo that bus so that he can meet those two girls."

Surprising her, he didn't respond to the flirts on the bus. Instead, he turned in the opposite direction of the tour bus. "He's coming our way, Ichabod."

Ichabod continued his grooming as Sydney hopped into the shadow of the foyer and peeked around the oak door. The man rode close to the curb in front of her house. Then, turning sharply away, he caused the back tire of his motorcycle to splatter the gate of her white picket fence with black mud from a rain puddle. Sydney trembled with anger. "And to think I'd hoped for some peace and quiet this summer."

As the man roared down the red brick road, Sydney opened the screen door and stepped onto the porch. Planning to inspect the damage to her gate, she and Ichabod were halfway down the cobblestone walk when the big black dog spotted them. Barking savagely, the dog charged across the landlord's yard. Thank God for the wrought iron fence. Still, with the dog bearing down on them, Sydney scooped up her cat.

As the dog vaulted the wrought iron fence separating the properties, Sydney broke into a run down her cobblestone walk. In her peripheral vision, she saw the dog cutting through her yard as she scrambled up the porch steps. As Sydney tore open her screen door, the dog bounded up the steps. Sydney slammed the heavy front door. But before the screen door could close, the huge dog smacked muddy paws onto the cut glass that Sydney had just cleaned.

"Fine," she seethed, clutching Ichabod and gasping for air. Glaring at the blurred image of the barking dog through the dirty glass, Sydney vowed, "If it's war he wants, he's got it."

Four

Two days later, Jack reached into the mailbox by his front door and pulled out a letter. Walking through the house with the high ceilings, dark trim, and wood floors, he spoke to his dog, "Let's read my email first, Buster. The snail mail is addressed to *Resident* and has no return address. So it's probably junk."

Before reading anything, Jack took ham and cheese out of the stainless steel fridge. Grabbing a loaf of bread, he plunked down on a ladder-back chair at the kitchen table, and Buster rested his head on Jack's knee. As sunlight streamed in the windowed alcove of the breakfast nook where he sat, Jack checked his email and nodded. Good, his clients were being well taken care of during his absence. Another email told him three grand plus a cleaning deposit, minus Patricia's rental fee, had been deposited into his bank account. Opening the plastic container of ham, he tossed Buster a slice and then slapped together a sandwich. Taking a bite and chewing, he opened the letter and read.

"Hell." Jack sat up straight and nearly choked. "That new tenant had the guts to send me a list of repairs she wants made. Not only that, she's registered several complaints."

Buster whimpered sympathetically as Jack swung his head in the direction of the Queen Anne house. His back yard and that of the house next door shared a large, round courtyard encircled with brick. When Buster was out back, an invisible fence kept the dog on Jack's side of the courtyard. He noticed now that her half of the courtyard displayed some newly planted blue flowers. His half boasted dirt. In the middle of the joint courtyard was a worn, wooden bench. His eyes returned to her letter.

"This tenant, named Sydney, says I play my music too loud, my bike is too loud, and you bark too loud." Jack registered the deep remorse in Buster's soulful, brown eyes. "Don't worry about it, pal." He patted the dog's head. "She says if you jump over the fence in the front yard again, she's going to—I didn't know you could jump that high. With the pointed tips of the wrought iron, I need to do something about that." Buster barked and placed a paw on Jack's knee. "She says her sink doesn't drain fast enough, her shower isn't hot enough, and her air conditioning isn't cool enough. Dammit. Talk about junk mail."

Jack looked up and saw Sydney emerge from the back of her house. Facing away from him, she squatted on the ground and moved as if stirring some kind of pot.

"She's probably whipping up a magic brew she plans to poison us with, Buster. It's a cinch she's not mixing up a love potion." Jack ignored a fleeting sense of disappointment.

Sydney wore a crop top which displayed a tiny waist. She stood, and her short shorts took Jack's gaze to her shapely bottom. All her attributes, right down to her small, bare feet, screamed femininity. Even from a distance, she pushed his male buttons. He pictured himself walking over to her with a smile on his face, instead of a frown, and apologizing for the noise.

"No, she might accept my apology and offer to be friends," he told Buster.

Watching her ponytail switch, he craved a good look at her face. As if by his silent command, she turned and walked toward the courtyard. Bangs and florescent sunglasses covered almost half of her face. She pushed the glasses up her nose, and he noticed a paintbrush in her hand. In her other hand was a can of paint. Jack decided the sassy bounce underneath her crop top meant she wore no bra. When she stopped at one end of the wooden bench, a longhaired, white cat pranced across the tops of her feet.

"Let's go scare this Sydney person off once and for all, Buster."

Five

Sydney heard the back door of the Victorian house slam shut with a loud bang. Though she continued to spread white paint on the bench as the man and dog approached her, she secretly snatched glances of the stranger through her mirrored sunglasses.

He was Hollywood handsome.

The dog stopped before reaching the courtyard. The man was built like a quarterback for the Las Vegas Raiders, the football team formally from her neck of the woods in southern California. And he'd proven he was just as ornery as they were reputed to be.

To Sydney, he was one big package of brute force, probably six foot three and at least two hundred ten pounds of raw bone and sinewy muscle. In the way he swaggered, with no hurry in his stride, was the air of a man confident of his masculine appeal. Well, he needn't think she was going to fall at his feet.

As she stood to face him, she wished she'd worn a bit more makeup.

His blue jeans were snug and low around his waist, and a white tee shirt stretched tightly across his broad shoulders. She couldn't tell what color his eyes were yet, but he had slashing black brows. He combed his thick, black hair with his fingers and squinted his eyes against the sun. He stopped in front of her and folded athletic arms across a muscular chest.

"Didn't the rental agent tell you to contact her office with any and all complaints?" the man asked, towering over her.

Sydney was captured by an icy gaze obviously meant to intimidate. How ironic that those piercing eyes were the same ocean blue as the flowers she'd planted. Above his brows was a high forehead. She'd always thought that indicated intelligence. His cheekbones and nose were so perfectly sculpted that he could be a model. When he clenched his strong jaw, she knew her letter had angered him. She squared her shoulders and raised her chin.

"Patricia Hudson advised me not to contact the man in the house next to me. However, I don't always do as I'm told."

"Obviously. The rental agreement stated no pets." He glared at Ichabod, who had his back up over the dog's nearby proximity.

"I signed the lease rather hurriedly and didn't notice the no-pet part until after I'd moved in, but Ichabod won't damage your property. In fact, this bench—"

"Who gave you permission to paint my bench?" he broke in, pointing at it with what Sydney could tell was her letter.

"As I was about to say, Ichabod likes to sleep on it, and I'm afraid he'll get splinters. I'll paint only my half. Let's back up. I'm Sydney Crane. Nice to meet you." She put down her brush and extended her paint-free right hand. He hesitated, apparently reluctant to shake. Then, his large hand, with long, thick fingers, engulfed hers. She shivered at the feel of his firm grip.

"Jack Malone, your landlord." He released her hand as if she'd stung him and waved her letter. "Whatever's wrong in your house will be fixed. As for my dog, Buster won't hurt anyone unless I tell him to." In the background, the dog snarled as if on cue. "I will have an invisible fence installed in the front yard, like the back yard, so don't threaten me with the dog catcher."

"Thank you," Sydney said quite pleasantly. "Now, what about the music, the motorcycle, and Buster's barking?"

Ichabod hissed at Buster, who barked. Jack snapped his fingers, and the dog sat as silently as a statue. As Ichabod ran toward her house, Buster appeared the picture of innocence. Sydney knew better.

"I'll ask Buster to tone it down," Jack grumbled.

"Fine, please do the same with your music."

"What's wrong with country? Don't you like Tim McGraw and Jason Aldean?"

"It's not your choice of music. It's the volume," Sydney explained patiently and splayed her hands. "I like pop music. But I don't play it full blast."

Jack's brows drew together, and he delivered her letter to her open right hand. "I like Chesney and Shelton full blast," he said. "In case you don't know who they are—"

"Kenny and Blake." She watched him nod as she shoved the letter into her back pocket. "Play them a little softer, please."

"Soft isn't my style." There was a challenge in his deep voice. "If it were, I wouldn't ride the Harley."

Sydney pulled her sunglasses to the tip of her nose, planning to scan his body with disdain. She rolled her gaze down his chest to his waist. Passing over the wide black belt, she reached the area of his jeans where his personal equipment was stored and lingered. The denim there cradled a generous bulge. She stared, trying to recall ever seeing anything so intriguing, so thrilling, so... she felt his heavy gaze. Her heart thumped as she shoved her glasses up her nose.

"Maybe if you revved your engine less, you'd be easier on the ears," she said.

"My engine runs *hard*."

When Sydney gave him a flippant flick of her fingers for him to leave, Jack stepped forward and grasped a handful of her ponytail. He tilted her head back, took off her sunglasses, and locked eyes with her. His glare might have knocked her over had he not been holding her in place. As his eyes closed, his lips touched hers.

Jack's mouth was tightly shut. Planning to yank his arm away, Sydney cupped a hand over his biceps muscle. Futile. The man's arm felt like a slab of lumber with skin wrapped around it. He smelled fresh from a shower, and his natural scent was utterly male. When Jack skimmed her lips with his tongue, Sydney stood stunned in his embrace. Then he retreated, leaving her lips slightly parted. She spied his smug smile and clicked her teeth together.

"If that kiss was meant to scare me, it...it—" she began.

"It succeeded."

Jack was not just gorgeous, he was swoon-worthy. From the second he had burst out of his house, Sydney had felt the animal magnetism this man exuded with his every masculine move. But not wanting to appear subdued, and with no thought to consequences, Sydney grabbed the front of his tee shirt and jerked herself to him. Standing on tiptoes, she cupped her other hand to the back of his head, pressed, and planted her lips on his. Jack didn't touch her. Feeling she'd proved her point that he hadn't scared her, she broke off the kiss with a peck to his lips and took a step back.

As Jack stood his ground before her, Sydney noticed he, too, was barefoot. His feet were strong in appearance, with fine black hair lightly sprinkled atop his toes. She raised her eyes, but avoided a certain area of denim. His hands clamped on his waist, indicating he wasn't easily backed down. Her gaze continued up his washboard stomach to his broad shoulders. Her landlord was the stuff dreams were made of, except when the glowering anger on his handsome face was directed at her. Challenge blazed in his eyes as power radiated in his body.

Jack Malone was as untamed as a hurricane and just as stormy.

Six

S ydney Crane was a siren luring him to crash his ship upon her shore.

Her mouth had been warm and supple. When she'd placed a gentle hand to the back of his head, he'd cooperated by lowering his lips to hers. As he'd stood, his body burning and arms aching to embrace her, she nibbled his lips, catching them on fire too. But her tongue had remained elusive, never touching his. She'd ended the kiss sweetly, then backing away from him, she raised an eyebrow and grinned victoriously.

Damn, he'd been better off not getting a look at her face because Sydney was stunningly spectacular. From long blond hair to sparkling green eyes to those full pink lips, she was a heart-stopping beauty. Her perky breasts had molded to his chest, and his palms had itched to cup them. When she'd taken a step back, on her flat tummy, the cutest belly button he'd ever seen peeked at him from between her crop top and shorts. He pictured her slender legs wrapping around his waist, and—he gave himself a mental shake.

Straightening his stance, Jack squared his shoulders,

emphasizing the difference in their sizes. He flattened a hand to his chest, smoothed the wrinkles she'd put in his tee shirt, and ignored his thudding heart. He'd set out to frighten her, but instead, she'd frightened him by stirring up yearnings that had lain dormant.

"In case you didn't know it, kisses aren't meant to scare people, Jack. I've dealt with guys as big and tough as you." Sydney poked her finger in his chest and gave her ponytail an impertinent shake. "And I learned not to tuck my tail and run." She put delicate hands on those saucy hips of hers and looked him in the eye. "So what do you say about that?"

His abrasiveness hadn't worked, in fact, it had royally backfired on him. He hoped arrogance would do the trick and replied, "Your bed or mine?"

"You," she laughed as though incredulous, "wish."

Jack pulled a piece of paper out of his pocket and thrust it into her hand, "Here are the phone numbers of a plumber and an AC guy. Call them, and I'll pay for it, but don't bother me again." With that order, he swiped a bead of sweat off his brow.

"Glad to know you're hot and bothered."

"Hey, baby girl, if you wanna get me hot, you'll have to—"

"To thank you for these numbers," she cut him off as she casually glanced at the piece of paper, "I'll bake you a sweet treat and leave it on your back steps." Sydney squatted and dipped the paintbrush into the paint. "Do be a good boy and run along now."

"A good boy?" Jack laughed. "Hell, *you* wish!"

"Oh, one last thing, Jack," she said as she painted her half of the bench. "I consider standing naked in a window an indecent proposal."

"What the hell are you talking about?"

"You know exactly what I'm talking about."

To dismiss him this time, Sydney gave him a wave with her brush. He dropped her sunglasses next to the paint can, pivoted, and stormed toward his house.

"C'mon, Buster," Jack called. Reaching the back of his house, he stomped up the steps and let the door slam after his dog was inside with him. "Damn," he muttered in the kitchen.

Jack leaned forward and placed his hands on his thighs. It had taken every bit of his willpower to keep his body from betraying him to Sydney Crane. He groaned with an ache of longing. Turning his head, Jack stared out the alcove window at her. He should have referred Sydney's grievances to the realtor's office. He'd have been a lot safer never knowing there was a drop-dead beautiful woman *right next door*.

From pink toenails to pink lips, she was spirited sass, wrapped up in about a five-and-a half-foot, hundred-and-ten-pound body. Kissing her kindled the very urges he'd hoped to ignore a whole lot longer. The guys she'd mentioned had taught her well.

An unexpected knife twisted in Jack's gut as he wondered what else they'd taught her. Hell, he should be grateful to them because they'd turned Sydney into the best little kisser he'd ever found. But finders didn't have to be keepers. He wasn't ready to deal with the depths of desire and anger she'd aroused in him.

"Maybe if we maintain one hell of a low profile, that green-eyed nutcase will leave us in peace, Buster."

With a glance at Sydney's house, Buster whimpered his assent.

Seven

Three days of quiet passed. At least where Jack Malone was concerned. Sydney had called the numbers he'd given her, and thus, a plumber had unclogged her sink and replaced the hot water tank. The air conditioning man had repaired the AC, and the house was cool. Therefore, she'd put a cake in the oven for Jack as she'd promised.

Sydney was rinsing the shampoo out of her hair when she realized the cake was done. Hurrying to finish and then hopping out of the shower, she threw on a short robe and rushed downstairs to the kitchen. Taking the cake out of the oven, she hoped Jack liked chocolate. While it cooled, she checked her email and took a load of laundry out of the dryer. After sending a text back home, she iced the cake. Giving the creamy chocolate a final twirl on top of the cake, she heard a *whoosh*, like the sweep of a broom, behind her.

"Good morning, Ichabod," Sydney said without looking. She licked the icing off the spoon and picked up the cake platter. Not a bad-looking cake if she did say so herself.

When Ichabod didn't meow for his breakfast, Sydney turned. A nude man stood at the far end of her kitchen. Sydney froze, holding the cake at waist level. She stared, transfixed. No, the man was not naked, but his solid bronze tone gave that impression. He was slightly out of focus, yet his form began to suggest clothing. Fuzzy feet floated an inch above the tile floor.

Like a rock in a slingshot, Sydney's body was taut, tensed for flight, but held back by stark terror. She stared, her mouth opening in a silent scream as fear pumped adrenaline throughout her body.

"I believe in ghosts," she whispered, sounding like the cowardly lion from the *Wizard of Oz*. She heard the lion in her head and thought he may have used the word *spooks*. Her voice still quivering, but desperate to convince the apparition not to kill her, Sydney said, "I do, I do believe in spooks."

The image vanished. Clutching the cake, Sydney shot out of the kitchen. She raced across the courtyard and ran up the porch steps to Jack's back door. Shaking violently, she dropped the cake on the top step and pummeled the door with both fists.

"Jack!" she screamed as Buster ran up behind her, barking at her heels. "Jack!" She glanced down at Buster and noticed her state of undress. Afraid to go back into her house alone, she removed Buster's collar. "This is one time you're going to be helpful."

Eight

J ack rode his bike down the drive to the rear of his
house. As usual, the first thing he did after
dismounting was remove his helmet and hang it
over the padded sissy bar at the end of the Harley
seat. Walking toward the back door, he saw a chocolate
cake, half on a platter and half on his porch steps.
Buster's collar, which kept him inside the invisible fence,
lay a couple feet away. Jack looked across the courtyard
to the Queen Anne house. The back door was wide open,
and he clearly heard Buster's bark from inside Sydney's
house.

"Oh hell," Jack grumbled. Sydney had brought the
cake, and Buster had lost his mind. He hoped Sydney
didn't own a shotgun. Jack cupped his hands around his
mouth and yelled, "Buster!"

Buster and then Sydney, carrying her cat, bolted out of
her back door. They stumbled over each other in their
frantic flight toward him. With a glance at Sydney, Buster
took the lead.

"Jack!" Sydney called and waved.

She wore a white, sleeveless top. From what he could

see around the cat, cradled on her shoulder, the blouse looked haphazardly tied above her waist. The jean shorts she wore were buttoned, but the low waist displayed her cute belly button and showed him that her zipper was down. Something had scared her half to death. Otherwise, she would not be trampling through the blue flowers she'd recently planted on her side of the courtyard. Darting out of her yard into his as she neared him, Jack automatically opened his arms. When she threw her curvy body against him, he closed his arms around her. She trembled uncontrollably and gasped for air. She roped his neck with one arm and held tight to her cat with the other.

"You're squashing your cat," Jack said. Sydney loosened her grip, and the cat bailed over her shoulder. Landing behind Sydney, the cat spat at Buster. Buster barked, and Sydney screamed. "Buster, sit. Sydney, calm down." Buster sat and blinked his eyes. The feisty cat hightailed it home. Sydney trembled against him. "Tell me what's wrong."

Sydney looked sideways at her house. She gripped his shoulder and bunched his tee shirt in her fist. Cupping her chin, Jack turned her head toward him. Her green eyes stayed on the house as long as possible before she finally looked up at him.

"There's a ghost in that house, Jack."

"You wanna run that past me again?"

"There is a ghost in my house."

Jack chuckled as he splayed his hand on her back. She wore no bra under the sheer white blouse, which was not only haphazardly tied at the waist but buttoned up wrong.

"So a ghost was the reason for the wild jig you danced through your blue flowers. Did the ghost dress you in this dance costume?"

"I came to tell you about the ghost, dropped the cake, took Buster, and raced home to change my robe for clothes."

"Sorry I missed the robe part."

"I grabbed the first two things out of my clean laundry basket. Then I heard you call for Buster and ran, forgetting all about my flowers."

"I thought you didn't tuck your tail and run. I guess those guys you know didn't teach you as much as you let on."

"I've never faced a ghost before."

"I'm flattered." Jack patted her slim hip. "But, the fact you'd claim you were scared by a ghost, instead of a burglar, to get my attention only adds to our personality clash. If an analytical guy like me didn't steer clear of an emotional lady like you, she'd drive him crazy." Her chin quivered, and there was the slightest hint of a pout on her full lips. "Logic and impulse don't mix. However, I'll admit that a ghost story is an original pick-up line, and coming from New York City, I've heard 'em all."

Sydney yanked herself out of his arms. Apparently, the quivering and pouting were the onset of spontaneous combustion. Sure enough, her temper exploded as she shrieked in anger and shoved his shoulders. He stayed his ground, but Buster growled.

"Maybe I'll do my wild jig on your closed mind," Sydney threatened as Buster barked.

"Buster," Jack said, quieting the dog.

Sydney clenched her fists at her sides. With her ponytail switching, her nipples beaded against her catawampus blouse, and her jeans shorts unzipped, she made an outrageous picture.

As tempting as hell.

Her cheeks and neck red with fury, Sydney fumed, "I

come from California, the state which is king of pick-up lines. Believe me, a ghost story isn't one of them."

"If you say so," Jack replied. She was as livid as lightning and sizzling with sex appeal. Jack told himself he should be happy she was mad at him. So why wasn't he?

"You gave me phone numbers of people who fixed what was wrong in my house. You'd better have the number of someone who can get rid of a ghost or get ready to refund my money." She folded her arms under her breasts, giving him an eyeful.

"I don't have Dan Akroyd or Bill Murray's numbers." Jack smothered a grin and added, "But isn't that why you took my dog with you...so he could be your *ghost Buster*?"

"Oh, I get it now." Sydney's green eyes flashed, and she nodded. "I don't know what kind of parlor tricks you rigged up in my house, but this is your latest effort to scare me off."

"No parlor tricks."

"Why do you want to get rid of me so badly?"

How could he answer that? "You have my word that I'm not responsible for you thinking you saw a ghost."

Sydney took a calming breath and said, "Then I think the naked man I thought I saw in your dormer window was the ghost I saw in my kitchen."

Jack shook his head. "I think your noggin's as baked as your cake." He tapped an index finger to his temple.

"Baked as in crazy?" Sydney seethed through her straight, white teeth. "I think you're a rude, uptight New Yorker."

"Better than being a nutty, laid-back Californian." Jack was mad at himself now. She'd come running to him as a scared little girl, and he was being a big jerk when he wanted to be nice. He flinched as she whirled away from him. Throwing caution to the wind, he grabbed her elbow and turned her to face him. She glared at his hand, and he released her. "Sydney, come inside with me. I'll fix you a cup of coffee...decaf," he added with a grin that made her squint her eyes and purse her lips. "If you can be neighborly enough to bake a cake for me, I can be neighborly enough to share what's left of it with you."

"Fine. I'm in no hurry to go back into a haunted house."

Sydney flounced ahead of Jack and bent over to pick up the cake platter. Her bottom was outrageously cute. He tore his eyes off it and opened the door for her. Buster followed Sydney inside as if she were his new best friend. Buster might be an easy mark, but Jack could resist Sydney's allure. He had to. Friendship meant caring. It didn't take much to remind himself that losing those you cared about resulted in unbearable pain. He forced his thoughts back to what had brought Sydney running into his arms.

"I'm going on record as saying the Queen Anne house is not haunted."

Nine

"**L**et's agree to disagree," Sydney said. Thinking non-nutty conversation might erase the scowl on Jack's face, she changed the subject. "I love galley-style kitchens like this one."

She did find the airy room comforting with its pastel colors and glass-front white cabinets. Two ceiling fans slowly twirled high above a hardwood floor. Wainscoting trimmed the walls, and a colorful padded mat lay in front of a porcelain sink. Jack swung a hand toward a round table fitted beneath an alcove window facing Sydney's house. When she'd settled herself in a ladder-back chair, he placed approximately half the cake on the table and gave Buster a dog biscuit.

Sydney jumped up. "Ichabod's all alone."

"Ichabod Crane," Jack said, making the connection between the cat's name and that of Washington Irving's schoolteacher, who, in *The Legend of Sleepy Hollow*, believed in all things supernatural. "That's some additional insight into you, Ms. Crane." Setting a mug in place on the coffeemaker, Jack asked, "Did your ghost have a head on its shoulders? As the legend goes, the headless horseman was carrying his head when he chased ol' Ichabod across the valley on horseback. He threw the head, knocking Ichabod off his horse and into oblivion."

"Or the headless horseman was really the bully of the valley, Brom Bones, who threw a pumpkin at poor Ichabod, knocking him out of the saddle, out of Sleepy Hollow, and out of the competition for the fair maiden Katrina Van Tassel's hand in marriage," Sydney said as Jack splayed his hands and grinned. "The ghost I saw had a head on his shoulders." Worried about the ghost hurting her cat, she walked toward the door. Reliving, in her mind's eye, the fuzzy phantom she'd seen, Sydney shivered and explained, "I need to go look for Ichabod."

"Your cat is sunning himself on my half, the unpainted half, of the bench," Jack said, looking out the window. "Sit down and have some cake. You'll feel better."

Sydney followed Jack's gaze to the bench where Ichabod lay grooming himself. Still more than a bit shaken, she was happy to return to her chair. "I could use the time it will take to drink my coffee to build up enough courage to go back into that house." Not commenting, Jack served her mug of coffee and fixed one for himself. He brought a powder creamer and sugar to the table.

"Creamer, sugar?" he asked with an infectious smile.

"Just creamer, sugar," Sydney replied. Jack brought out a flirty side of her personality that she hadn't known existed. She worried her lower lip as she creamed her coffee. "If Ichabod's going to sleep on your half of the bench, I'd better paint it. Since my half is as white as Ichabod, I'll paint your half as black as your dog, your hair, and your attitude."

"Don't forget my black boots and black bike." He

fished forks out of a drawer and sat down across the table from her. "As your landlord, I'll buy the black paint. Maybe I'll pour it into your white paint and see what happens."

"Gray happens." Sydney's heart pounded as he looked her straight in the eye. "Like the gray area of ghosts."

She broke away from his gaze and took a sip of her coffee. Staring into her coffee mug, her thoughts were consumed with how attractive the man on the other side of the table was. Though she was certain of what she saw, she didn't want him to think she was nutty, so she once again steered away from the ghost topic. At least for the moment. "This kitchen has a woman's touch." She nodded at the pretty, flowered wallpaper.

Jack nodded and glanced around the room. "My mom decorated it twelve years ago, the summer I graduated from high school."

"That makes you...thirty?"

"Yes," he said. There was a sad tone in his voice, which he covered up when he said, "I like this kitchen because it reminds me of her."

"Does your family live here in St. Augustine?"

Jack lowered his head for a moment, and when he looked up at her, he answered, "My mom and dad were killed in a car accident in New York City two summers ago." Stoically, he added, "Soon after, my younger brother, Alexander, took his own life. I have no other family."

"Oh no." Sydney couldn't imagine such tragedy. "Jack, I'm so sorry for your loss."

He frowned as if surprised or maybe angry that he'd revealed so much. He shifted in his seat and grumbled, "I don't want to talk about them."

"Of course. I understand," Sydney said. She wanted

to reach across the table to him, but the scowl on his handsome face kept her from doing so. Like he'd said of her, Jack had given her additional insight. Whether he'd meant to or not, he'd revealed a probable reason for his orneriness. "Is New York your permanent home?"

"I was born here in St. Augustine but mostly raised in a Manhattan brownstone." He took a swallow of his black coffee. "This summer, I'll decide which place to make my permanent home." Jack picked up one of the forks and dipped it into the cake. He chewed, swallowed, and cocked his left brow. "You do make a sweet treat."

"And tart ones. You should taste my cherry cheesecake."

"I'd like to." He looked down her body until the table edge cut off his visual pursuit. When his gaze met hers again, he said, "If cooking at your house causes you to see ghosts, you're more than welcome to cook with me in my kitchen."

Sydney huffed over the ghost jab and was unsure if his expression reflected a smile of innocent generosity or a grin packed with risqué suggestion. Not wanting to show her naiveté, she shifted the conversation back to him. "What kind of work do you do in New York City that you get the whole summer free? Are you a teacher?"

"No."

"What then?"

"After high school, I enrolled in New York University." Jack took another bite of cake as Buster lay down at his feet. "I went to school full time, worked part-time, and wound up with a Ph.D. in finance the summer before last."

Sydney knew New York University was a private school, far more costly than the graduate school she'd attended near her home. After receiving a master's degree, a Ph.D. usually took another four to seven years to complete. To have earned his doctorate in finance two years ago meant Jack was nothing short of brilliant inside his brooding exterior. "So you were Dr. Malone at the age of twenty-eight. That's impressive, Jack."

"Thanks." He scooted back his chair, laid a booted foot over his knee, and stared at the floor. "The car accident happened the night of my graduation. My brother and I stayed out with friends, and our parents headed home." Raising his head and squaring his broad shoulders, he said, "I went from broker to owner overnight at the brokerage house on Wall Street."

Sydney smiled with a compassionate shake of her head at what all he had endured. He'd buried his entire family. Since he'd said he didn't want to talk about the accident, she asked, "Do you enjoy your work?"

"In New York, being a stockbroker is an *uptight* business." This time, his grin meant he was conceding a point to her.

"How so, Jack?"

"Short hair." He plowed his strong fingers through his thick hair for emphasis. "Long overcoats, designer suits, shirts, ties, and Italian dress shoes." He glanced at her blouse, and for the first time, she realized it was buttoned wrong. Since she usually avoided bras, there hadn't been one in the clothesbasket. But she needed one with a blouse as thin as the white cotton top she had thrown on in her kitchen. "Stuffy meetings, power lunches, constant crowds, and cold weather."

In her mind's eyes, Sydney could visualize him walking down a New York City sidewalk. Yet, the description he'd given was a far cry from his tee shirts, jeans, and boots. "Did you go, umm...what do they call it —belly up?" she asked, genuinely interested as she swiveled in her chair and, with her back to him, buttoned her blouse correctly.

"No, I didn't go belly up." He laughed, and when she turned back to him, amusement played in his blue eyes. This time, his laughter seemed authentic and not at her expense. "I almost always buy low and sell high. I think I inherited my dad's good instincts for stocks, bonds, options, and all that goes with the business."

"Instincts based on logic or impulse?"

"Both." His eyes narrowed, letting her know she'd made another point. He hesitated and then grumbled, "But, I don't like the work anymore."

Sydney placed an elbow on the table edge and rested her chin on her fist. Intrigued by the motorcycle hood-turned financial wizard, she asked, "Why don't you like it?"

Ten

J ack gazed out the window. He'd once been hungry
to prove what he could do on Wall Street. His dad
had wanted him to finish school before hiring him.
But Jack had talked him into part-time. Then disaster
had struck as soon as he graduated, and even in his
grieving, he'd been successful almost in spite of himself.
Professionally, he took excellent care of his clients, but
personally status quo was okay. In fact, he'd not felt challenged until meeting Sydney. Maybe that's why he hadn't
cut her visit short today. As he knew he damn well
should.

"I used to love my work. My dad took over the firm
from my grandfather when he was thirty-five." Looking
from the window back to Sydney, he said, "That's why
figuring out if I want to stay or leave New York is so
tough."

"What are your alternatives?"

Jack rubbed his forehead. "One would be to follow
through on my dad's dream of opening a branch office of
the brokerage house here locally. If I did that, I guess I'd
stay in the business and also work on my mom's goal.

She always wanted to return the five houses from yours to the one at the other end of the block to their former glory. She said the house at the opposite end of Magnolia Road would make a good house for a museum."

"The white and yellow Queen Anne." Sydney had walked past it several times. "Queen Annes are known for their multicolored decorative trim, asymmetrical design, and wraparound porches like mine. Victorians, like this one you live in, have more of a gothic influence with pitched roofs, round turrets, and towers."

"Very good," Jack said.

"I love the style. I knew I wanted to rent the Queen Anne next door as soon as I saw it from the street," she told him.

"My mother said the trolley tours of historic places would bring people to walk along Magnolia Road the way they visit St. George Street in the Spanish Quarter of St. Augustine. She felt knowing and staying in touch with American history was important, and that's why she wanted to turn the house at the far end of the block into a museum."

"St. George Street is where the oldest wooden school-house in America is located."

"Yes, how'd you know about that?"

"I read a lot." She shrugged, and when Jack tilted his head in question, she said, "I just received my MAT, which is the Master of Arts in Teaching, with an emphasis in history, from the University of Redlands. Since I plan to teach, I wanted to visit the oldest school-house which is here, since St. Augustine is the oldest, continuously settled American city."

"Have you made it to the schoolhouse yet?"

"Yes, I went there right away, even before I found the Queen Anne house. I was surprised at how tiny the schoolhouse is."

"It was made completely by hand of cypress and red cedar and is held together with wooden pegs and hand-made nails."

"That makes sense. The records on it date back to 1740." She nodded thoughtfully and added, "The schoolmaster and his wife lived upstairs above the single classroom below."

"Their kitchen was separate from the schoolhouse to avoid the danger of fire and in order not to add heat to the building in the summer," Jack said. "So speaking of schools and masters, if you just got your master's degree, are you...twenty-three, twenty-four?"

"Twenty-four," Sydney replied.

Eleven

J ack studied the gorgeous female as she took a bite
of cake. Her full lips closed around the prongs of
the fork, and a surge of reckless craving shot
through him. When she licked her lips, he recalled
her kiss, which had aroused an ache inside him that had
yet to subside. "So, are your parents out in California?"

"Yes. I was born and raised in Redlands. It's east of
Los Angeles in the midst of orange groves at the base of
the San Bernardino Mountains." Sitting forward in her
chair, she said, "The Kimberly Crest House and Gardens
is a Victorian Chateau on a six-and-a-quarter acre estate
not too far from where I grew up on Highland Avenue.
And much like your mother envisioned, there are public
tours on Thursdays, Fridays, and Sundays."

"Are you missing home?"

"I was ready for a change of scenery, but," Sydney
raised her right shoulder. "I am missing my fam—home."

He'd caught her compassionate change of word. Jack
wondered how many California guys were missing
Sydney's delicious kisses. However, her leaving California for an entire summer might mean there were no

current men in her life. "Will you go back to Redlands when summer's over?"

After a sip of coffee, she said, "That depends."

"On what?"

"I've applied for a teaching job here at Flagler College and at the University of Redlands. Both have positions teaching history opening mid-year in January. I'll know if I landed one, none, or both on September 1."

"I'm guessing Flagler College is your dream come true, since you're here."

"Half of a dream," Sydney said wistfully. "I like the city of St. Augustine's history as well as the curriculum and small class sizes at Flagler. I think the college is beautiful with its Spanish architecture and Tiffany windows."

"I do too. The college was founded in 1968, but it was originally built as a hotel in 1888 by a railroad magnate named Henry Morrison Flagler."

"Not many colleges can make the claim of starting out as a hotel," Sydney said with a soft laugh. Waving her fork, she added, "Stanford University in Stanford, California, officially Leland Stanford Junior University, was also founded by a railroad tycoon, Leland Stanford, with help from his wife, Jane."

"You're right. I remember hearing that somewhere," Jack said, thinking how smart Sydney was and how easy conversation flowed with her when he wasn't being mean.

Sydney nodded and said, "You told me your parents' dreams. But, what's yours?"

Jack couldn't put a finger on his dream. Yet, he needed it, wanted it so badly he was slowly starving to death for lack of it. "My dream's doing nothing all summer."

"I shouldn't have asked. I've been told I'm an outspoken chatterbox." She raised her right hand, held it as if it were a puppet, and moved her fingers to and away from her thumb. She lowered her arm and smiled. "Thank goodness not everybody's a motor mouth like me."

"Thank goodness not everybody's a loner, like me." He wasn't a loner, was he? Staring into Sydney's sultry green eyes, his urge to kiss her surfaced again. She'd tasted as sweet as chocolate cake, and her unpredictable personality was just cherry tart enough to make her mouthwatering. He shook his head and chuckled, trying to throw off his irrational urges. "You know I had you pegged for a timid bookworm."

"Before or after you pointed out that I ran from the ghost?"

He tapped his fork to the table as though deciding how he wanted to answer. He laid the fork down and said, "Before."

"Now you've decided I'm a timid, soon-to-be schoolmarm."

"You're unconventional, not timid." Jack shook his head as she took another bite of cake. "I like that about you. I'm sorry I've been such a jerk." What the hell was wrong with him? He hadn't planned on apologizing. He scowled self-consciously.

"Jerks don't treat dogs the way you take care of Buster."

Sydney reached across the table and placed her soft hand over Jack's clenched fist. Her smile was filled with understanding. Sydney was a sweetheart, which meant she could also be a heartbreaker. Even so, Jack wanted to turn his hand over and hold hers. To keep from doing that, he pulled his hand out from under hers. She sat back, laying her hands in her lap.

"Buster's four years old, so he's been through a lot with me."

"Jack, you could open a branch of your dad's firm in the Queen Anne house next door. The parlor could be a reception area-slash-waiting-room for clients, the dining room could be a boardroom, and the den could be your office. You'd have the kitchen as needed. All five of the huge bedrooms could each be made into one or more offices. And you could furnish the house with touches of the way it was when the houses on this block were built."

"The living room could be a bullpen; one big office for the less experienced, new hires." Jack could see it all along with the picture Sydney had painted and replied, "Something like that might be the start of Magnolia Road staking claim to its historical origins."

"Word to the wise, I'd consider finding a new realtor before trying to buy the other houses. Patricia Hudson wasn't friendly. Actually, she came off as calculating. I tell you this because I'm not sure she has your best interests at heart."

"Patricia and I have known each other since we were kids. I told her I didn't want to deal with any tenants. And the houses are no problem. I inherited all six."

"One problem solved," Sydney said then splayed her hands.

When his cell rang, Jack answered it. "How are you, Patricia?" he grinned at Sydney, then turned sideways in his chair. "Dinner?" He shook his head. "I can't. I've got other plans this evening. But, thanks anyway."

The expression on Sydney's face said she understood now why the realtor had not been friendly to her. Patricia treating Sydney inconsiderately didn't sit well with Jack. Hell, who was he to talk? Saying goodbye to Patricia, Jack thought maybe, without getting too involved, he could make it up to Sydney.

"I won't keep you any longer since you have other plans," Sydney said.

He placed his right arm on the table. "I hope my plans include you." He rolled his hand palm up, fingers pointing at her. "Stay a while, and I'll make lunch for you." With that and a lopsided grin, he closed his hand. "What do you think?"

Twelve

"Hmm—" Sydney thought this man could charm the pants right off her. Today, that could be particularly dangerous as she not only wore no bra, she was pantiless as well. She'd have to watch it. She didn't want romance complicating her summer plan. And he didn't want that either. She sensed that the loss of his family had wrapped some hard-to-break chains around his heart. "What can you make for lunch?"

"Ham and cheese sandwiches?"

"So the financial wizard doesn't actually cook?" Sydney asked and laughed.

"Rarely. It's not my strong suit." He chuckled and said, "Nor were history and research my strong points in school. So, for me, the problem with including the houses as historical sites is that I don't have a lot of information on them. My mom was researching the backgrounds with the historical society before she died."

Sydney nodded. "As you might guess, I thrive on history and research." She flattened both hands over her heart for emphasis. "I love digging up buried facts about the past. My plan for the summer is to doing dissertation research for my doctorate in history."

Jack tilted his head. "So you'll be Dr. Crane someday?"

"That's the other half of my dream. I want to be a professor of history at Flagler College for a year or two, and then I'll go home to California and finish up my Ph.D." She sat back in the chair and rubbed her temple. "My problem is I can't start my dissertation until I decide on a previously unpublished, historic topic to research."

"I admire your ambition."

"Right back atcha." Wheels whirled in Sydney's head, and she clasped her hands. "Hey, what do you think of bartering my research time in exchange for a ghost-busting landlord's protection...if needed?"

Jack sat forward with interest. "If you could dig up interesting histories on my houses, I'd pay you to help me."

"That sounds like you don't want to barter services."

"It wouldn't be a fair exchange for you." He crossed his arms over his chest. "There's no ghost in your house."

Sydney bristled. "I know what I saw, Jack. And how can you say there's no ghost when you admit you don't know the histories of any of the houses? How do you know they aren't haunted?"

"Because I don't believe in ghosts."

"Ooh!" Sydney squeezed her eyes shut and turned her head away from Jack. When she opened her eyes, she glanced out the alcove window. A lanky man with blond hair falling across his forehead and a cloth satchel in his hand was fiddling with the latch on the gate of her picket fence. "Oh, no. There's Leslie Bowen." Sydney jumped out of her chair. "I completely forgot I invited him over for coffee."

Jack stood and looked out of the window. "Who's he?"

"A part-time archeology professor working on his doctorate. I met him at Flagler College the other day," she replied of the bespectacled man as she crossed the kitchen. "He's bringing me a book on dissertations." She placed her mug on the counter. "Thanks for the coffee. I can let myself out."

But as Sydney neared the back door, Jack stepped in front of her. Blocking her exit, he put his hands to the bare skin at her waist. Sydney's pulse raced, and her flesh caught fire. Jack's touch was seductive, dominating, and weakened her knees. As he slid his hands to the front of her shorts, he looked over her head and out of the window.

"You don't want your back pockets to fall off when you serve up his coffee," Jack said, his expression a cross between flirty and accusatory. "Do you?"

When he zipped the zipper Sydney hadn't realized was down, she figured that nailed her as being nutty in his view. Jack, though, was anything but nutty. His masculine touch felt protective with a smidge of possessiveness. Momentarily taken aback, she stood still and didn't answer his question. He frowned, stepped away from her, and opened the door. Sydney ducked past him and avoided the chocolate cake on her way down the steps. Buster followed her out of the house and wagged his tail.

"I'll come back and clean the cake off your steps," she told Jack over her shoulder.

"Don't worry about it." All tanned muscle and brooding good looks, he leaned against the door jamb, crossed his ankles, and cocked a black brow.

Buster followed her into the yard, and Sydney said, "Thanks for your help, *ghost* Buster."

"I guess Professor *Bones* can take up where Buster left off," Jack said with a cocky grin, jamming his hands into his front pockets.

Sydney put a finger to her lips to shush him. "I said Bowen, not bones."

"Hell, he's as pasty white as a skeleton's bones." Jack was not about to be shushed, but he had lowered his voice. "Maybe he's Ichabod Crane. Maybe he teaches in Sleepy Hollow. Maybe he showed up early, and you mistook him for the ghost bully."

"Surely you know Sleepy Hollow was twenty-five miles north of New York City," she said. Jack shrugged. Sydney ventured quietly, with a suggestive smile, as she walked backward toward her house, "Skeletons and ghosts go together just like baking and cakes."

Jack smiled back. "Your kitchen or mine, Doc?"

"I haven't earned that title yet, Doc."

"You will." Jack looked past her to Leslie, ambling down the cobblestone walk. "You want him for his book or his body?"

"Maybe both." She watched Jack's eyes narrow appraisingly. "Leslie is very studious." She grinned impishly. "Even if he's not—" she ran her fingers over her mouth, "like you."

"What was that?" he asked. Sydney swiveled away from him and jogged toward the courtyard. "Sydney!" he shouted. "What did you say?"

"Exciting!" she called over her shoulder. Leslie had spotted her and been drawn around the side of her house. He glanced at Jack and stopped on Sydney's half of the courtyard. He pointed a long, knobby finger at the little blue flowers and asked what they were. "Forget-me-nots, the flower of friendship." With a quick grin at Jack, she plucked Ichabod off the unpainted half of the bench and walked with Leslie toward the back door of her house.

"Friendship?" Jack sounded stunned. Buster barked. Before Sydney entered her house, his voice drifted to her. "Buster, you don't want to be friends with a cat lover. Do you?"

Thirteen

The next week passed with Sydney catching only glimpses of Jack Malone. The last few words she'd heard him say to Buster echoed repeatedly in her head. Did he not want to be friends, or did he want to be more than friends? She came to suspect he wanted way less.

At first, Sydney expected Jack to drop off paint for his half of the bench. He didn't. Mid-week, she thought he might stop over to ask if she'd started researching the Magnolia Road houses. He didn't. By the end of the week, she hoped he'd come tease her about the ghost. He didn't. So he didn't want less, he wanted none.

The sun was setting as the roar of Jack's motorcycle drew her off the Chippendale sofa, where she had been skimming Leslie's book on dissertations, to a floor-to-ceiling window. Across her pretty porch and over the green lawn, at the end of the red brick road, she glimpsed the back of Jack's powerful body riding away. She sighed and wondered where he was going. Then again, this was his town, and he had plenty of places to go, people to see, dates to make.

Since the day she'd run to him, there had been a languid quality in the sultry days and nights. It was as if something were hanging in the air, waiting to happen.

Turning away from the window, Sydney tossed the book onto the sofa. She strolled past the beautiful staircase and down the hallway to the kitchen. She fixed herself a Cobb salad for dinner and gave some of the turkey to Ichabod. After she and Ichabod had eaten, she opened her laptop at the kitchen table and researched St. Augustine history while Ichabod snoozed in his favorite kitchen spot on the wide marble window sill.

Her mind wandered. Back to Jack. She had to admit the sensual weather was the only element of romance in her life since Jack wasn't giving her the time of day. She was glad. She had too much studying about her dissertation to get sidetracked with a man. Still, she kicked herself for the comment about the forget-me-nots and friendship. Since the trampling, she had lovingly tended the little flowers, and they were thriving.

"I gave Jack the opening he needed, Ichabod," she told the cat who slept on undisturbed. "And he closed the door on friendship."

Turning off the laptop, Sydney gently petted Ichabod. Then she wandered back to the living room, with Ichabod following along behind her. She plopped down on the sofa, and Ichabod made his way to his favorite living room napping spot on the Martha Washington chair. Even if she and Jack weren't friends, they were still neighbors. Couldn't one neighbor invite another to dinner? After all, Jack had invited her to lunch. Sydney's stomach lurched as she remembered how flatly he had refused Patricia Hudson's dinner offer. How would he react if she took him that cherry cheesecake? This time, she wouldn't drop it on his steps. From what she could tell, standing on her half of the courtyard, he'd long since cleaned up the cake. Dogs weren't supposed to have chocolate, so he'd taken no chance of Buster eating any of the cake.

Just like she'd pointed out to him that jerks didn't care for their dogs, like he did Buster, she'd glimpsed his vulnerable side. When Jack had talked about his family, his hostility and aloofness couldn't camouflage the fact he had the ability to love.

Sydney pushed her reading glasses up her nose and tried to focus on Leslie's book instead of thinking about Jack. Near midnight, she was simply staring blindly at the pages. She took off her glasses and rubbed her eyes. One thing she had firmly decided.

No dinner invitation and no cherry cheesecake.

Too bad she wasn't going to get to know Jack. Not only handsome, he was smart and well-educated, which made him all the sexier. Sydney pressed her lips together. Jack's kiss had left her breathless and her heart thudding. Her fingers tingled, reminding her how soft his thick hair was as she'd stroked the back of his dark head while kissing him. She hugged herself as she recalled slipping into Jack's strong arms after she'd seen the ghost. How would it feel to hug him back with both her arms? If she did, would he trap her in a cocoon of muscle and hold her to the length of his hard body?

What did Jack normally do with women after a kiss and hug? Did he leave them wanting more, as he had her, or sweep the woman off her feet and carry her upstairs to...

Upstairs. She heard a noise upstairs.

"Ichabod?" Sydney glanced at the Martha Washington chair. Sure enough, Ichabod lay curled up in a fluffy ball.

Sydney listened. The noise in the kitchen the previous week had been...what?

Whoosh.

The sound was louder. Was it coming closer?

The hairs on Sydney's arms and the back of her neck rose. Her heart thumped, and her throat grew dry as she pictured a fuzzy form waiting for her at the top of the straight staircase.

Call Jack. No, he didn't want to trade research for protection. He was a loner. He'd be flattered at what he'd suppose was another pick-up attempt. Besides, it was midnight. She had no place to run. She was on her own. Well, except for Ichabod. Sydney glanced back at the chair. Ichabod was sitting up and staring in the direction of the staircase.

Quietly, Sydney placed the book on the sofa. She stood and soundlessly padded across the room. Avoiding the squeaks in the hardwood floor, she reached the archway between the living room and hallway. As usual, Ichabod followed her. Taking a breath, Sydney peered around the corner. Nothing but the foyer under the dimmed chandelier. She crept forward.

Whoosh.

Sydney froze in the middle of the foyer. Chills… silence…determination. Slowly, soundlessly, she tiptoed to the bottom of the stairs.

Whoosh.

With goosebumps prickling her skin, she looked up the dark staircase. There he was at the top, on the second-floor landing. A fuzzy, bronze glow. Ichabod hissed. Sydney was sure she'd either awaken from this nightmare or die in her sleep. She did neither because she was wide awake, and this was all too real. Terror knifed her heart, cutting off all mobility. Her arms hung at her sides like the dishcloth draped over the kitchen faucet. Her feet were as rooted in the floor as her forget-me-nots in the courtyard.

The apparition floated in thin air. As she stared, his

hollow eyes took on a distinct shape. Sydney wanted to scream for help. Meeting a ghost in daylight was terrifying enough, but at night, it was horrific. She thought maybe her mouth opened and closed. No shriek sounded, so she wasn't sure. Ichabod hissed again.

The phantom hovered in place. Watching her. Waiting…to kill her…kill them. Paralyzed and speechless, Sydney was the spirit's unwilling prisoner, his defenseless victim.

Whoosh.

Instantly, he was halfway down the stairs.

With escalating fear and fresh goosebumps, Sydney was only vaguely aware she was still standing upright with some semblance of cohesive thought. Ichabod's back curved as he growled between hisses. Hovering above the step, the specter's eyes turned blue as his facial features sharpened. The bronze glow began to dissipate, indicating he was young, maybe twenty. Caucasian, his brown hair became visible under a wool cap. A navy coat stretched across broad shoulders, and baggy gray britches covered his legs. Blurry feet became roughly tooled footwear with buckles across the top. She guessed he was about six feet tall.

Whoosh.

He was on the foyer floor, face to face with her. And this time, it was he who spoke.

Fourteen

J ack got out of the shower and shivered. The usual, steamy weather had evidently taken a day off due to a storm heading their way up the coast. Putting on an undershirt, he tugged a lightweight, forest green hooded sweatshirt over it. He stepped into dark blue jeans and black leather high tops.

After walking Buster out of the house to the back yard, the dog barked at him. "I said I'd ask her," he told Buster, since he'd run an idea past him in the kitchen. "Why don't you take a nap in your doghouse? I'll be right back."

Crossing his yard, Jack recalled how sexy Sydney had looked scampering away from him, calling him *exciting* over her shoulder. He'd not laid eyes on her since. As he walked toward the courtyard, half filled with forget-me-nots, Jack wondered if Sydney had changed her mind about being friends.

He had. After a week of inner turmoil, he'd decided he could be friends with a tenant without getting emotionally involved. He'd keep the relationship strictly platonic. No more kissing or hugging. No matter what.

No romance; no risk. Besides, the summer had just begun. What was he supposed to do the next two and a half months, lock his door and pull the shades?

Hearing the front door of the Queen Anne house close, Jack turned and headed down her side yard. Rounding the corner of the wraparound porch, he spotted her locking the door.

Jack liked what he saw so much, he inwardly groaned. It was the first time he'd seen her golden-streaked hair worn loose. Waving halfway down her back, it was sensuously feminine, and he knew from having grasped her ponytail it was silky soft. He wanted to plow his fingers into it, kiss her, and have her smile up at him.

"Hi," Jack said, walking to the bottom of the porch steps. Sydney jumped, gasped, and swiveled to face him. Her hand shook as she stuffed her keys into her purse. "I didn't mean to scare you. Sorry."

"That's okay," she said, descending the steps. "Nice to see you."

"Good to see you too." He smiled at her as she came to stand in front of him on the cobblestones. "Since we didn't get to have lunch the other day, I was wondering if you might be free to have dinner with me tonight. I'll barbecue some steaks, old-school on a charcoal grill, or we could go out."

"I can't." She shook her head and started down the walk. "But, thanks."

Jack fell into step beside her. "I'd like to repay you for the cake you baked for me. You have to eat dinner sometime today, right?"

"Maybe. I have to work on my research tonight."

As they came to her gate, she placed her hand on the latch, but Jack held it shut. "Research for your dissertation?"

"No…yes…maybe. I don't know. I have to go."

"Where?"

"To St. Augustine City Hall."

Jack grinned, holding tight to the gate. "Are you researching the history of the six houses on this block after all?"

"Kind of," she said, flinching. "Not exactly."

Jack wasn't accustomed to a brush-off from a woman, but he was sure that's what Sydney was giving him. "We're *kind of* like the weather."

"We are?" She tilted her head and looked at him. "How?"

"We run hot and cold. I think you're the one responsible for this chill in the air today."

Her eyes narrowed. "And you're a heat-seeking torpedo after one…never mind."

"You seem a little preoccupied. Is it because I make you hot and bothered?" He chuckled as she pursed her lips at having her line thrown back at her.

"I'm bothered, not hot."

"Oh, you're hot, all right," he complimented her. "What exactly are you researching?"

"You wouldn't understand. Please, Jack, open the gate."

Reluctantly, he opened the gate. She stepped onto the sidewalk and turned right along the sidewalk toward his house. "City hall is all the way downtown. You'd get there faster if you'd let me give you a ride."

"I've seen the way you ride your motorcycle. I'd like to arrive at city hall in one piece. I'll walk, thanks."

Coming up beside her, between the white picket fence and curb, Jack asked, "What happened to the girl who liked *exciting*?"

"She's had enough excitement lately."

"Does that mean you're going out with Bones?"

"No, not that it's any of your business." Sydney glanced at Jack and shook her head. "I haven't seen Leslie since he stopped by my house for coffee."

"Did you tell him about the ghost that day?"

"No," she answered, staring straight ahead.

So she hadn't run to the guy, clung to him and confided in him about her ghost. Why did that make Jack happy? As they left the picket fence behind and started down the wrought iron one, Jack urged, "My bike's parked in the garage at the back of my house. I'll give you a safe ride."

"Here comes the city shuttle bus. I'll take it." She lifted her hand to signal the bus, but Jack grabbed her wrist. She glared up at him. "You don't take no for an answer, do you?"

"And you do? Like there's no ghost in your house?" Jack slid his hand into hers. Her hand was soft and warm. "Come on. Without your glasses, you might get lost."

"I only wear them to read."

She tugged her hand from his, but when he opened the wrought iron gate, she followed him into his yard. From a side gate, they emerged onto the driveway leading to a four-car garage. Jack opened the garage door and listened to Sydney speak to Buster, who was lying half in and half out of his doghouse.

"Buster says he missed you," Jack said as Buster trotted to the fence.

"I meant to tell you the other day, Buster, that you have a nice doghouse."

Buster barked his thanks.

"Dad and I built it for him right after I adopted him," Jack offered as he backed the motorcycle out of the garage.

"Did you and your dad install the basketball hoop?"

she asked, pointing to the state-of-the-art backboard attached above the middle of the garages.

It occurred to Jack that Sydney was making small talk. Her perfunctory remarks convinced him she was preoccupied with something. He wished he knew with what or with whom. Using the garage door remote, he closed the door and turned the bike around.

"Yeah, we installed the hoop."

"The hoop looks regulation height."

"It is. How did you know?"

"You aren't the only guy I know who plays basketball."

Pride kept Jack from asking who the other guys were. He handed her a helmet and helped her make sure it was snug. He put his helmet on, and then, swinging himself onto the bike, he started the engine. "See ya later, Buster." Jack gestured with his chin to bring the lovely girl to him and, at the same time, prodded, "Come on, Syd."

"Syd?" she huffed, hands on her hips. "Do I look like a man to you?"

"No." Jack eyed the curve of her breasts under her snug, hot-pink top. Around the bottom of the tummy shirt, fringe draped over bare skin to the low riding white shorts clinging to her hips and tops of her slender thighs. Her small feet were encased in white sneakers. When his gaze returned to Sydney's emerald eyes, he saw a stain the same color on her cheeks as her sexy shirt. "Men don't blush. Step onto the foot peg and hop aboard."

Putting a dainty hand on his shoulder, Sydney did so and then threaded one leg between his back and the padded bar on the seat. Jack tightened his fingers around the bike's handlebars as her spread legs molded around his hips and thighs. He saw her right hand come to rest on her right knee.

"Ready," she said.

"Hold onto me."

"I won't fall off. The brace is behind me."

"It's a sissy bar."

"Does that mean you think I'm a sissy?"

"No." He laughed.

"I have to hold onto my purse."

"Put the strap over your shoulder, swing the purse to your back, and wrap your arms around me, Sydney."

Sydney huffed at being told what to do. But when Jack gave the Harley some gas, both of her arms shot around his waist. Her hands flattened to his stomach, and as he headed down the driveway, he was acutely aware of her breasts pressed against his back. He grinned at having the gorgeous woman wrapped around him.

"What have you been doing all week?" she asked as they left the driveway.

"Not much."

"Brooding?"

"Kind of. Not exactly," he teased, using the answers she'd given him about her research.

"Have you avoided me because I'm such a motor mouth?"

"You haven't been a chatterbox for the past week. Why not?"

"I got the hint you didn't want a *nutty professor* for a friend."

Jack stopped for a red light, cupped his hand to her bare left thigh, and squeezed. "I apologize for giving you the impression I didn't want to be friends. Any man who has eyes would want you—for his friend." Despite his decision to be friends and nothing more, he had trouble keeping his hands off her. Purposely gripping both handlebars again, the light changed, and he sped toward St. Augustine's downtown area.

At the next stoplight, Sydney said, "I'd like to have you for a friend, too, and not just my neighbor."

"Same." Jack gave her knee a pat. Too soon, he said, "There's city hall."

In the historic district, city hall was on 75 King Street, a minute away from Flagler College, located at 74 King Street. The enormous and impressive old government building was beige with terracotta towers. He pulled into a parking lot and stopped. He was sorry to feel Sydney's slender arms slip from around his waist. He stood, bracing his feet on the ground so that she could safely dismount. As she wiggled off the seat, he heard a tear. He made a half turn and saw the fringe of her blouse tangled around the sissy bar at the end of the seat.

"Oh no." Sydney twisted to her left and looked at her side. The blouse's seam had ripped from the bottom nearly to her underarm. Still wearing her helmet, she plastered her hand to her ribs. "I can't go into city hall like this. Darn you and your dumb motorcycle, Jack."

"The girl in the Queen Anne house is the queen of the clothing malfunctions." Jack chuckled as he untangled the fringe. "Due to the *sissy* bar, no less." He removed his helmet and handed it to her. Next, he pulled his hooded green sweatshirt over his head, which left him in his black undershirt, and handed her the hoodie. "Take your helmet off and put this on."

"I can't," she said, handing his helmet back to him.

"Why not?"

"Because the rip in my blouse will show the world I'm not wearing a bra."

Jack's gaze dipped to her breasts. The tips beaded from the touch of his eyes. With another one of her feisty huffs, she thrust her purse in his lap and unstrapped her helmet. Jack plastered his left hand to the tear in her blouse as she took off the helmet and placed it over the

padded bar. He glanced from left to right as possessiveness washed over him. He was intensely aware of his
palm resting on the cushiony side of her naked breast. In
yanking the hoodie over her head and into place, she
brushed his hand away from her bare skin.

"Afraid somebody will think you started carrying a
purse, Jack?"

"No, why?" he asked, straddling the Harley.

"Because you're blushing."

"I am not." Jack draped the purse strap over her
shoulder and yanked her to him. He lifted her silky hair
out of the back of the sweatshirt, then cupped his hand to
her head and brought her lips close to his. Her breath had
a sweet scent, and he wanted to kiss her, but hadn't he
decided no kissing? Sydney laced an arm around his
shoulders, but shoved her purse between their bodies.
"You're the one blushing, friend and neighbor."

"Thanks for the ride, friend and neighbor," Sydney
said. "It was my first time."

"Your first time?" Jack asked.

Sydney's flush deepened. "You know, on a
motorcycle."

"Would it be your first time if we went to bed?"

Fifteen

Sydney gazed into his ocean-blue eyes, and her legs grew weak. Clad in a classic black, chest-hugging undershirt, beltless blue jeans, and black leather boots, Jack oozed virile masculinity. Why had she given this lady-killer the impression she was a virgin right after she'd indicated he was a heat-seeking torpedo? Cringing, she yanked herself out of his arms.

"Men don't make passes at girls who wear glasses," she said, studying the ground.

"Bull." Jack tipped up her chin with his finger, leaned forward, and put his lips to her ear. "I've heard being with a woman when it's her first time is almost like the first time for the guy all over again."

Sydney shivered as his warm breath touched her neck. "Thanks for the insight into the male point of view." She lifted her chin from his finger. "But, I never said I was a virgin."

"You didn't have to say it." Jack flashed a sexy grin and flattened his hands to his thighs. "I knew you were a virgin the day I first laid eyes on you."

Sydney gazed skyward. "I can't believe we're having

a conversation about my love life here in the city hall parking lot."

"The *lack* of your love life, but let's not make it a public record," he teased. "If the other guys you hang out with are like the professor, you might go to your grave a virgin."

In school, she'd been drawn to the type of man who was interested in studying. But not in the manner of making her want to go to bed with them. Then along comes Jack, so smart and irresistible. Yes, unruly and so exciting. "I suppose you'd be willing to help me change that?"

"How'd you get to be such a good kisser, Sydney?"

"What?" Was she a good kisser? None of her study partners had done more than peck her lips or cheek. A boring snooze-fest for sure. She'd come to assume she didn't inspire men to kiss her with passion or to be interested in taking things any further. Deciding to be a virgin on her wedding night, if that day ever happened, she'd told herself she liked boring men. "I'm a fast learner. I followed your lead."

"If you haven't been kissed a lot, I think it's because you intimidate most men."

"I do not." She was giddy to think she had some sex appeal. "Most men are not big bad wolves like you."

"Is that right, little green riding hood?" he asked with a frown. This man was exactly like the weather, hot one minute and cold the next. It occurred to Sydney he might be conflicted about something. Or someone. Maybe about her.

"Jack, I was teasing you. You're not a wolf. You're just very direct. Saying things before one thinks is a pitfall of being a chatterbox. I'm sorry if I upset you."

"Want me to wait for you while you go into city hall?"

"No, thanks," she said with a glance over her

shoulder at the big building. "From here, I'm going to the St. Augustine Research Institute, which is practically right next door. If I have time, I may wind up at the St. Johns County Library. I'll be a while."

"It's gonna rain. Call me, and I'll come pick you up wherever you are."

"I might have books. I couldn't hold onto them and to you. In the rain, *no less*."

"I'll bring my car."

Sydney reared back in surprise. "You have a car?"

"Sure. You would have seen it in the garage if you hadn't been preoccupied with Buster's doghouse and the basketball hoop."

"You risked my life on this motorcycle when you could have brought me in your car?"

Jack chuckled at her indignation. "You wouldn't have had a reason to hold onto me if we'd been in my Porsche, now would you?"

"Ooh!" She stamped her foot for emphasis. "Who says I wanted to hold onto you?"

"I thought a Harley ride might be *exciting*, since it was your first time."

"You didn't know it was my first time yet." The idea of going to bed with Jack hotly zipping through her mind and body, she asked, "Who says it wouldn't be your first time too?"

Jack laughed at that. "I will admit you'd be a whole new experience. So, do you want me to pick you up or not?"

"Not. I'm meeting Leslie later. He'll take me home."

"Bones." Jack rolled his eyes. "Will you have the barbecue dinner with me?"

"Maybe you should ask someone with experience."

"Maybe I should, but I'm asking you." Jack saw her lips purse and put a finger to them. "Don't give me that look. It makes me think you're about to try to push the bike and me over sideways. Will I see you around six?" Sydney parted her lips and bit down lightly on his finger. A muscle worked in the black beard stubble along Jack's strong jaw. She wrapped her hand around his thick wrist, released his finger, and lowered his hand to his thigh. "You have potential, Sydney."

"I'm not even going to ask what you mean by that. But I like old-school barbecues." She turned and tossed over her shoulder, "See you at six."

Jack kicked the Harley into a roar and lifted his chin. Raising a slashing black brow, his grin was cocky. Putting on his helmet, his boots left the ground, and he was gone.

Sydney hurried into the city hall building, her cheeks and naked breast still burning over the unexpected love life conversation and Jack's protective touch. Thoroughly distracted, she somehow managed to find the department and information she needed. Since she didn't have a printer at the Queen Anne house, she paid for several copies. Her mind continually wandered to Jack. When she looked at her watch, she realized it was time to meet Leslie. She skipped lunch and walked next door, anxious to dig into local history books she couldn't find online. The St. Augustine Historical Society over on Charlotte Street was on her list, too, but it would have to wait for another day.

~

"Hi, Sydney," Leslie said, waiting for her inside the library's lobby.

"Hi." Sydney's manners dictated a smile.

Leslie Bowen paled in comparison to Jack Malone. Literally. Pasty and plain instead of gorgeous and tan, skinny instead of muscular, Leslie was fawningly accommodating, while Jack was seductively aggressive. Leslie's chest was narrow, and his shirt baggy. Jack's undershirt had been tight across his broad chest and washboard stomach. Leslie walked, with his toes pointed outward, like a circus clown wearing oversized shoes. Jack moved with the cat-like grace of a panther.

Leslie's gums showed as he smiled. He smiled at her constantly, almost as if he were a simpleton, which of course he wasn't. Jack's smiles were smug with self-confidence and always disappeared too fast. Leslie, at thirty-two, was still working on his Ph.D. Once again, Dr. Malone was way ahead.

Leslie's company was painfully dull compared to Jack's. With Leslie, she stifled yawns of boredom. But with Jack, she'd shivered from waves of cravings she didn't quite understand. This afternoon, she needed dull in order to concentrate. Were Jack with her, he'd whisper in her ear or grin at her or touch her, and she'd be aware of nothing but him. Leslie followed her around so closely he bumped into her twice. After finding the books she needed, Sydney sat down at a small table in a far corner. Leslie sat across from her and picked up a book.

"Parapsychology?" he asked. "Like psychic phenomena, extrasensory perception, and the paranormal?"

"Exactly like that." Sydney leaned across the table and placed her hand on the top book in the stack. "Do you believe in ghosts, Leslie?"

"Do you?" he asked conspiratorially. Sydney nodded. He fumbled for her hand and grinned. "Then so do I."

Sydney pulled her hand from him. "Let's get busy. We have lots of research to do."

Sixteen

Jack hadn't guessed that Sydney's confirmed virginity would have been such a powerful kick start. But his decision to only be friends had evaporated into thin air. Settling into its place was an aching obsession to be her first lover. Could they be lovers and part as friends at the end of summer? When he had frowned at the idea of some other guy taking her virginity, Sydney had apologized, thinking he was upset by her referring to him as a wolf. What a sweetheart.

And she was mouthwateringly sensual. Even with his sweatshirt hiding her skin and curves, she exuded feminine allure. What would it be like to make love to Sydney, knowing no other man had been before him? Damn good. Not trusting where his hands might go should he touch her again, he had grabbed the handlebars of his bike. When she agreed to have dinner with him, his heart had raced. That *was* a first. He'd not shown it, but he'd felt it.

The rain had come and gone. At six-ten, Jack looked up from the grill and saw an older model silver sedan sputter to a stop in front of Sydney's house. As he watched Sydney swing graceful legs out of the front seat, he wondered if she was short on cash. Had she spent all her money on the rent she'd paid him? Was that why she had no transportation of her own?

Bones got out of the car carrying a gift bag. He walked around the back of the sedan and handed the bag to her. Sydney pulled what appeared to be an orange and purple plaid cloth satchel out of the bag. Not what Jack would have picked out for her. But at least Bones had given her a gift. Jack had mostly just given her grief. With her purse slung over her shoulder, she placed some books into the satchel and then hugged her skinny companion. Bones looked befuddled by her attention, and Jack chuckled.

But when the professor reached into the car and pulled out her pink fringe blouse, Jack's heart slammed into his ribs. What kind of research had Sydney been doing with him? Sydney lifted a hand toward a window in Jack's attic. Bones nodded, and then Sydney pointed to her second-floor window on the side of her house, which faced Jack's house.

"What are they up to?" Jack growled at Buster, who barked.

Sydney looked Jack's way, and he aimed the lighter fluid can in his hand at the grill. Squirting a pyramid of briquettes, he heard her call thanks and goodbye to Bones. Jack set the can down and lit the briquettes. When he looked up, Sydney was gone. But Bones lingered on the sidewalk, staring at him. Jack crossed his arms over his chest and glared back. Bones caved under the pressure and folded his lanky frame into the car. Without looking back, Bones slowly sputtered away down the brick-paved street.

Sydney burst out of her back door and sashayed toward Jack. "Hi."

"Hey," Jack replied, jealousy poking him.

"I know I'm a few minutes late," Sydney called, skirting the courtyard. "So I didn't take time to change." Barely an inch of her white shorts showed below the hem of his green sweatshirt. She reached his side and offered, "But, if you want your hoodie back right away, I'll go home and take it off."

"Keep it," he said coolly, his temperature rising.

"Okay, I'll wear it for now." Apparently noting his mood, she was going to play it sweet and innocent. He didn't like fickle females. He saw her glance past Buster's doghouse to the basketball hoop. "Did you work up an appetite shooting baskets today?"

"No." Jack shrugged, irritated his stomach had tied itself in a knot. Dammit, he'd warned himself not to care about anyone.

When she smiled, it reached her eyes. "I missed lunch. I'm starved."

Had Bones stared into those green eyes when taking off her blouse? "Want a beer?"

"I don't know if I'll like it, but I'll try it for the first time."

"Is that what you told him?" Jack asked as the image of Bones cupping her naked breasts taunted him. "Did I pique your curiosity with our conversation in the parking lot?"

She tilted her pretty head, appearing naive. "What are you talking about, Jack?"

"Why you're late." Jack turned and started toward the house. "I'll get us both a beer."

"No, wait." Sydney grabbed his arm and stopped him. "I said I was sorry outside the courthouse. Why are you so mad at me?"

Seeing his frown, Sydney let go of his arm. "Forget it, Sydney."

"No, I won't." Sydney shook her head. "You're as

unpredictable as you are handsome. One minute you're nice to me, and the next minute you're—" her voice broke, and she swallowed before continuing, "mean. Why is that, Jack?"

Jack placed his hands on his hips and glared at her. "Because one minute you're in my arms admitting you're a virgin, and the next you're in his arms with your blouse off. Are you starved because you worked up an appetite with him before having dinner with me?"

"You were right about our clashing personalities. Except now you're being emotional when analytical would be better." He clenched his jaw as they heard a car and turned toward the driveway as Patricia's silver Cadillac SUV slowed to a stop. "I see you took my advice and invited someone with experience to *cook* with you." Sydney glanced at the woman with brunette hair sheared off just below the ear. "She told me she was recently separated from her third husband. I guess she told you too."

"She told me the day she invited me to dinner. I wasn't interested then, and I didn't invite her here today, Sydney." As though to convince her, he picked up a beach wave curl of her hair and added, "I prefer long hair."

"I assumed too much, thinking I could show up ten minutes late and still barbecue with you." Sydney pulled her hair through his fingers as her shoulders drooped. Backing away, she said, "And you assumed too much thinking I was in Leslie's arms with my blouse off."

"You said you wanted him for his book and his body."

"I said maybe, and I was joking. Surely you knew that," Sydney said as Patricia opened her car door. "I took off my blouse at the library because by afternoon, it was hot, and their air conditioning wasn't working. Maybe you can give them the AC guy's number."

"Hot and bothered? Between rows of library books? "

"Hardly." Sydney trembled with obvious anger. "Never have I wanted to slap a man like I want to slap you. However, I won't embarrass you in front of your date the way you're humiliating me. But before I go, I'll admit the only time I've ever been in Leslie's arms was in front of my house a few minutes ago." She gestured toward the picket fence. "I doubt I'd overheat on the sidewalk where the whole world could watch. Although, I came close to it with you in the city hall parking lot."

Like a tidal wave, relief hit Jack full force. "Sydney, don't go."

Sydney waved to the realtor with the upturned nose. "Nice to see you, Patricia."

Resenting Patricia's intrusion, Jack said to Sydney, "I knew you were joking about wanting Bones

" He saw tears glisten in Sydney's green eyes before she pivoted away from him. "Wait," he barked as she jogged toward her house.

He hadn't counted on jealousy entering the picture. But without warning, it had exploded inside him when he had seen her blouse in Bones' hand. Jack had never felt possessive or protective about any woman until today. For the past two years, he'd not even felt alive. Sydney had changed that. He was back and then some. Wearing his sweatshirt, she had come skipping to him this evening with a big smile on her face. He'd blown it. She wouldn't want to be friends now. They were back to enemies. At least as far as she was concerned. And it was his fault.

"Hi, Jack," Patricia called and smiled.

Of all times for Patricia to bring him information on the issue of his houses being rezoned and recognized by the St. Augustine Historical Society. Why the hell did she have to come now? In the evening. Because she was calculating. With a last glance at Sydney, before she disappeared into her house, he clearly noted the stark difference in the two women.

Jack banged the lid onto the barbecue to snuff out the flames. He wished he could smother the inferno of emotions that Sydney ignited in him as easily as he had the hot coals. He refused Patricia's invitation to go out on the boat she was due to get in her divorce settlement. He dealt with her and bid her goodbye. She seemed irritated, but then so was he.

Seventeen

It was the last week of June when Sydney heard him call her name. With goosebumps prickling her skin, she sat up in bed. The voice had come from downstairs. It sounded like he was in the kitchen. She heard the voice again, flew down the staircase, and through the house. On the other side of the stained glass, in the back door, she recognized his silhouette outlined by the moonlight.

"Jack?"

"Yeah. Let me in."

Sydney opened the door. There he stood, all good looks and cocky grin. She told herself this man didn't invade her dreams and didn't assail her every waking thought. She was immune to his sex appeal and loathed the sight of him. And the ocean wasn't blue. Like his eyes.

"If you're here to ask if I liked the dozen roses you sent, the answer is yes," Sydney said, standing in the doorway. "If you came to find out if the dozen blouses you had delivered fit, the answer to that is also yes. Perfectly. If you're here about the batchel, well, who wouldn't love a leather satchel that doubles as a back-pack? However, it's late, and I'm tired. So, thank you, and goodnight."

"You're welcome, chatterbox." Jack brushed past her, kicked the door shut, and set a grocery bag down on the kitchen counter. "Were you asleep?"

Sydney flipped on a light. Her heart instantly raced. Jack had on a pair of low-riding gym shorts and nothing else. "Asleep? No, I'm always awake at," she squinted at the clock on the stove, "two in the morning." Turning back to Jack, her gaze riveted on the sexy masculine hair sprinkling that tan, muscular chest. Black hair circled his navel and trailed down his lower stomach before vanishing into his snug shorts. She shivered, not from cold, but from her fiery attraction to this man. "Why do you care if I was asleep or not? What are you doing here?"

Jack leaned against the counter, folded his arms, and crossed his ankles. "You have a lit candle in the window. I don't want my property burned down."

"Oh, my gosh! I forgot all about it. I'm sorry. I'll go blow it out."

"I'll wait."

Sydney dashed upstairs with a picture of Jack's gorgeous male body burning in her mind. She was completely immune...she totally loathed him. And the ocean wasn't wet. She blew out the candle and returned to the kitchen.

"Jack, why are you awake at this hour?"

"I was watching a movie, and when I turned off the flatscreen, I saw the candle," he muttered. "Want to have that beer with me while you tell me why you were trying to burn down the house?"

"Now?"

"Why not?"

"Fine. I'll try the beer, but I have no comment about the candle."

"We'll see."

Jack took two bottles of beer out of a carton of six, which he'd set on the counter. Sydney crooked her finger for him to follow. She turned the chandelier in the foyer to its dim setting and led the way into the living room. Jack dropped onto one end of the Chippendale sofa. Wearing his hoodie and pajama shorts, she curled up on the opposite end. He uncapped the bottles and handed one to Sydney. Narrowing his eyes, he sipped his beer and studied her. She combed her fingers through her hair, knowing it was in wild disarray. His eyes drifted to the sweatshirt.

"You figure possession is nine-tenths of the law?" Jack asked.

"I'm not possessed."

"I didn't think you were," Jack said. "I was referring to the hoodie."

"Oh," she laughed. "He likes it."

"Bones?"

"No," Sydney said too fast and studied the beer bottle in her hands. "I meant me. I like it." She placed the bottle to her lips and gulped. She swallowed twice and choked. "Yuk!"

Jack laughed. "Since this is your first time," he cocked a brow, "drinking beer, try it one sip at a time and tell me who *he* is."

"Jack, he is—" she sighed and shrugged. Ichabod wandered into the room and jumped onto Sydney's lap. Petting him, she remembered how soft Jack's hair was when she'd kissed him. "You'd never believe me."

"Try me."

Eighteen

She gulped her beer and coughed again. Despite Jack's warning to take a sip at a time, she figured if she drank fast, and enough, it would give her the fortification to confide in him. He waited, she drank, and when she finally glanced at the bottle, it was almost empty. One more swallow, just to be sure.

"Ugh." She made a face and shook her head.

"Who likes you in that sweatshirt besides me?"

"Philip."

"Philip?" Jack muttered.

"You were a good boy the last time he was here, Ichabod," Sydney praised her cat. The cat acted oblivious, but she hugged him anyway, almost as if seeking comfort.

Jack wished Sydney would crawl into his arms. And no matter what she said, he would not chase her away this time. When she set the bottle on the table, Ichabod launched himself into the Martha Washington chair. "Sydney, is Philip another professor at Flagler College?"

"I will tell you about him if you promise not to laugh or get mad at me."

"Cross my heart." He took a swallow of beer and said,

"But I might offer my opinion if I think you're mixed up with the wrong guy again."

"Who are you to say who the wrong guy is?"

"Your landlord," he said with a chuckle. "Bones isn't man enough for you."

"But you are." It wasn't a question, and he liked that.

"What's going on with you?" Jack leaned sideways, caught Sydney's elbow, and tugged her down the sofa to him. "Who's Philip?"

"A sailor." Sydney stared at their hands. "Who drops by."

Jack clenched his jaw. "Is he on his way here tonight?"

"I don't know. He said if I wanted to talk to him to put a candle in my window. I put it there tonight because I had some news for him. But he didn't come, and I fell asleep waiting."

"News?" Jack rubbed his forehead. "I don't understand. How would this sailor see a candle in your window unless he was already here?"

Sydney looked at Jack. "He's close by most of the time."

"Close by? Where?" Jack asked. "Just talk to me straight without the cloak-and-dagger routine." It bothered him more than he cared to admit to think some sailor wanted this green-eyed innocent as his girl in port. "Who is Philip to you?"

"A friend. His name is Philip Burke and he...and he is—"

Sydney leaped off the sofa. His sweatshirt, being way too big on her, hung down to the hem of the pajama shorts. Damn, she was one sexy package. He fought against the desire heating his lower body. She paced past the Martha Washington chair and took a deep breath. Chewing her lip, she wrung her hands and walked all the way into the foyer.

Forlorn was the word that came to Jack's mind as he looked at Sydney standing alone under the soft glow of the chandelier. She was so close and at the same time so far. And so very vulnerable. Protectiveness stirred. Sydney was a sweet baby girl, if ever there was one. If this sailor were to hurt her—

She turned to Jack and crooked her finger.

Jack got off the sofa and walked to her. "How good of a friend is he?"

Sydney stepped up to the staircase, folded her arms under her breasts, and lifted her eyes to the second floor. "As good as a ghost can be." Jack followed her gaze upstairs, where the bedrooms were. "He usually comes and goes from upstairs."

"Talk about the wrong guy," Jack said but didn't laugh. "You're taking what I said about going to your grave a virgin way too seriously." He saw confusion on her face. "As in a ghost for a lover?"

"Lovers? No." She shook her head. "Who said anything about being lovers?"

"Okay. I'm confused," Jack admitted. "Are we talking about the same ghost you told me about when you trampled the forget-me-nots or a different one?"

"The same one. Come with me. Please." She slipped her dainty hand into his and stepped onto the bottom stair. When he stayed where he was, she turned to him. "The first time I saw Philip in this house was in the kitchen and he said nothing. But the next time I saw him here on the stairs, he told me his name."

"Right." Jack rolled his eyes and blew out a frustrated sigh. "That beer went straight to your head, didn't it?"

"Absolutely, or I wouldn't be telling you any of this. I'll admit my head feels a little dizzy right now. But I know what I saw when I was stone-cold sober. I've seen and spoken with Philip a few times since the night he told me his name."

"I'm going home, and you can sleep it off." Jack let go of her hand, plucked her off the stair step, and set her feet on the floor. "Come walk me out, so you can lock your door."

"No, you come with me. Unless you're afraid."

Grabbing his hand again, Sydney started back up the stairs, and he went with her. She led him across the upstairs landing and down the hall to her bedroom. At the doorway, Jack stopped. She let go of him and walked in a stream of moonlight to the window.

"You send out mixed signals," Jack grumbled. "If you want me in your bed, just ask. Catch me in a generous mood, and I might even take you next door to my bed."

"Don't be sarcastic, Jack." Sydney glared at him. Like a surly teenager, he lounged against the doorjamb. "Come over here." At the snap in her voice, he leaned away from the door and strode to her. Cupping her hands to his shoulders, she turned him toward the window. Peering around him, she pointed. "See that attic window in your house?"

"What about it?"

"That's where Philip lives."

"Well, hell," Jack said, clamping his hands on his hips. "A damn freeloader. I'll have to charge him rent."

Sydney pulled her lips between her teeth as if to control her frustration, then said, "He would like nothing better than to have you ask him for rent." She moved around Jack's side and stood in front of him, her green eyes beseeching him to believe her.

"You can tell him to pay the same realty office you paid."

"Darn you, Jack Malone." Sydney smacked her hands over his biceps muscles and squeezed. "Be serious."

"You told me to be analytical the last time we had a disagreement. I'm being analytical." Gently, he touched his finger to her chest. "Why don't you try it?"

Sydney swallowed hard and lowered her hands. "If I'm being emotional, it's because Philip's been trying to reach somebody since the year 1776. Since the American Revolution."

"Can you hear yourself?" Jack asked with an incredulous expression. "For your information, no one could have lived in this house in 1776 because it's not that old."

"I know. I know." She bobbed her head. "Philip said the original houses on this road during the American Revolution were eventually lost to fires, hurricanes, or the Civil War. Knowing history as I do, I can easily imagine Union troops torching or otherwise destroying houses in 1861, when Florida seceded from the United States."

"Yeah."

"Anyway, Philip watched it all happen. He remembers the house at the opposite end of the street, along with the Queen Anne and Victorian houses we live in today, being the first to rise from the ruins.

Jack knew there was mockery in his voice when he asked, "Did he tell you both Union and Confederate troops stayed in those three houses, making them historically significant?"

"He did," Sydney replied with sincerity and a smile. "He recalls the joy in your house on April 9, 1865, when General Lee surrendered to General Grant in Appomattox Court House, Virginia turning to sorrow a few days later when Abraham Lincoln was shot in Ford's Theater and died the morning of April 15, 1865."

"Right." Jack wondered how she knew when his house and the other two were built. Sydney continued, "Philip told me he could hardly believe it when he realized I'd seen him through the dormer window in your attic. He says your mother suspected he existed. But, Jacqueline passed away before they were in tune enough for her to see or hear Philip."

"How did you know my mother's name was Jacqueline?"

"Philip told me."

"Or you found her name at city hall. Like you found out when the houses were built."

"No, I went to the city hall looking to verify what Philip had told me."

Keeping his promise not to laugh or get mad, instead, the familiar sadness rolled over Jack. "I guess Patricia Hudson could have told you my mother's name."

"Jack, I didn't mean to hurt you with a painful memory."

"No problem," Jack said as he strode toward the bedroom door. Sydney started after him, then yelped, apparently having caught her foot on the bedpost. Flopping down on the end of her bed, she rubbed her toe. "Are you okay?"

"I wasn't using my little toe much anyway. Can you let yourself out?"

Jack flipped on the light switch beside the doorjamb. A lamp on the chest of drawers softly illuminated Sydney's bedroom. The roses he'd sent her set on her nightstand. Jack figured his frown showed his confusion and disbelief over their conversation because Sydney dropped her gaze from his eyes to her toe.

"Sydney, why are you doing this?"

"Because he asked for my help."

"What does a dead man need help with?" Jack had been as good as dead until Sydney strolled into his life. Realizing the irony of his question, he clenched his jaw and raised a hand for her not to answer. "I'll see you around."

Sydney lifted her head, and her eyes glittered as a ragged sigh escaped her. "I wish you and I could have met some other time, under some other circumstances."

"Why? What difference would it make?"

"Maybe none. But I like you, and I'm sorry you're going to ignore me the rest of the summer because you think I'm crazy."

Jack frowned. "I didn't say I was going to ignore you."

"Sure you will," she said. "See ya, Jack."

He liked her too. Too damn much. "See ya."

Nineteen

Sydney managed to wait until she heard the back door slam before throwing herself face down on the bed. Ichabod joined her as she wailed into her pillow. It was a tear-drenched half hour later when she thought she heard someone speak her name. She sat up and wiped her eyes.

"My, but you do resemble my beloved Cammy in her forest green cape when you are wearing Jack's forest green sweatshirt."

"Philip?" Sydney turned her head toward the doorway. Even with the soft lamplight, crystal clear and seemingly as solid as anybody, he waited there. He wore, as always, his cap, navy coat, baggy britches, and buckle shoes.

"Did I not advise you Jack wouldn't believe you?" His voice, even after two and a half centuries of American influences, still held a British accent. "'Tis a bitter pill, isn't it?"

"Jack's a bitter pill. Forget him." Sydney sniffled, wishing she could do that. She had tried to and couldn't. "Where have you been, Philip?"

"At the cemetery where my mother and father rest. Of course, their spirits are not there. Were they, I should ask them of my sweet Cammy's resting place. When I returned to number One Magnolia Lane, I saw Jack making his way to this house. I arrived with him."

"One? Jack's address is *100* Magnolia *Road*." Sydney waved that away. "Why didn't you appear while Jack was here?"

"I was here then as I am now." Philip splayed his hands.

"My research indicates I may be seeing and hearing you through some kind of mental telepathy." Sydney rubbed her temples. "Maybe Jack sidetracked my concentration a little."

"Or perhaps Jack's disbelief in spirits is so strong he completely blocked your ability to be aware of my presence."

"Perhaps," Sydney murmured. "Jack won't interfere with us again because I've lost him as a friend."

"I know how it feels to lose someone."

"For you, that is an understatement." With a *whoosh*, Philip came toward her, and, despite their numerous visits, Sydney felt the goosebumps. Ichabod looked up at him, yawned, and went back to sleep. As Philip remained at the footboard of her bed, Sydney said, "I have information for you, Philip."

"Tell me, please."

"On my visits to city hall, the research institute, and the library, I found records which indicate that a descendent of yours, named Burke, owns a house on an island a few miles from here. The person's probably a great, great, I don't know how many greats…grandson."

Philip shook his head sadly. "Cammy and I had no children."

"Philip, during this past week, you admitted you've

forgotten things. For instance, you told me that you can't remember the name of your ship, but you're sure the captain's name was Bledsoe. You know Camilla's last name was Johnson, and you've recalled that she may have had to marry an elderly lord. But, you can't remember the lord's name or address." Sydney paused and asked as gently as possible, "Could you have forgotten you left Cammy pregnant?"

"I wouldn't have gone to sea knowing she was with child. But I will admit 'tis possible. Though my Cammy was a virtuous maiden, we lost control on the eve of my departure. A year apart loomed over us as heavily as an *eternity*." He lowered his head, and his shoulders sagged. "I advised her that if we eloped, we would become outcasts, never forgiven by flesh and blood and perhaps shunned by society. I pray I did not leave Cammy on her own and expecting my child." He lifted his blue eyes to Sydney's and straightened his stance. "I had a younger brother. Possibly the ever-so-many-greats grandson is his."

"There was no cell or landline phone number listed that I could find. So we won't know until I can locate the man and talk to him in person. I'll probably have to figure out transportation other than the city bus to do that. It's a cinch I can't ask Jack to take me."

"Will securing a ride be a…a…hassle?"

Sydney laughed for the first time in days. "Philip, that modern term sounds so funny coming from you."

Philip smiled. "Like the term sweatshirt, I have learned many new words and certainly forgotten some old ones. I heard Jack say hassle recently."

"What was Jack referring to when he said hassle?"

"The green-eyed nut case from California."

Sydney narrowed her eyes. "We'll show that uptight New Yorker."

Mockingbirds chirped outside the window the next morning as Sydney fastened the buttons of her scoop-necked, sleeveless blouse and glanced at her watch. It was ten, and she was anxious to get on the road. But how? Taxi fare was too expensive. She tapped her phone and went online to check out an Uber. The eighty-dollar fare to where she wanted to go was also more than she could afford. She punched a third number into her cell.

"Leslie?" She asked for a ride and offered to pay for the gas, but he explained his part-time professor clunker-car was in the shop. "Thanks anyway."

After placing a red and blue hair headband on her head, she called the city bus depot. The buses didn't travel nearly close enough to the place she needed to go. She'd suspected that. Guiding a red belt, which matched one of the dozen blouses from Jack, through the loops of her blue jeans, she tried to think of another way to get to her destination. She hadn't come up with one yet when she heard a knock on the front door. She opened it to a burly man holding a clipboard.

"Your scooter's here. Please sign for it," he requested.

"My what?" Sydney looked past him to the road. Parked there was a snow-white scooter. "That's not my scooter. There's been a mistake."

"If you're Sydney Crane, the scooter's yours. Signing for it only says you received it."

Sydney signed. She studied her copy of the receipt as the delivery man walked to the truck in which he'd apparently transported the scooter. Her receipt gave no clue as to who had ordered the scooter. She crossed the porch and walked to the now deserted road. Taped to the handlebars of the shiny new scooter was an envelope with her name on it. She opened the envelope and removed the card inside. It read, *Hey baby, I like you, too.*

Sydney's heart thumped and she said, "Jack."

Twenty

"Yeah."

The gorgeous girl whirled around as Jack and Buster stood at the corner of the wrought iron fence, where it met up with the white pickets.

Walking across her yard to him, Sydney said, "I can't accept this scooter."

"It's no big deal." He shrugged. "The scooter's paid for in full. So if you stay in St. Augustine and want to keep the scooter, it's yours. If you don't stay or don't like riding it, you can sell it and keep the money."

Reaching him and stopping on her side of the fence she asked, "Why would you do this for a green-eyed nutcase like me?"

Jack's eyes narrowed as he tried to remember if he'd said that phase in her presence. He knew he'd said it to Buster after he and Sydney had kissed for the first time. He looked down at Buster as though the dog had tattled on him. Buster appeared innocent and smiling, so looking back at Sydney, Jack smiled, too, and said, "We keep getting off on the wrong foot. Maybe that's because you're on your feet so much. The scooter will get you off your feet and blow the cobwebs out of your head."

"Very funny," Sydney said as she laughed.

"You're not as laid back as I originally thought. You're going after your doctorate. The scooter's my way of trying to help you get it."

"Thank you, Jack," she said. "You aren't as uptight as I originally thought." He raised an eyebrow, and she shifted the conversation back to the scooter. "This is great timing. I'll get my purse and give you a down payment. Do you prefer a check? PayPal? Cash?"

"None. This is a gift, just like that red blouse…which, by the way, looks great on you."

"Jack, I love this silk blouse, but a scooter—" she began, but he raised his hand as he'd done the night before. He thought her eyes were a little puffy and wondered if it was from crying, oversleeping, or both. With a shy grin, she said, "Thank you for the scooter and for the compliment."

"So, why is this scooter great timing?" Jack asked.

"I need to visit a relative of a friend."

"I would have taken you."

"Think you could teach me how to ride this thing? I've never done it before."

Jack couldn't suppress a grin. "I know." Sydney's cheeks flushed. "I'd be happy to teach you everything."

"What do I do first?"

"That's a loaded question."

She huffed, and he hopped the fence. He walked her across her yard and out the picket gate to the street. When she'd sat down on the white seat, Jack showed her how to turn the scooter on, give it gas, where the brake was, and how to signal. He pointed out the headlight switch and gas cap. She ran a finger over the wire basket attached to the handlebars.

"Something tells me the basket was an extra option." Sydney got off the scooter and admired it. "Right?"

"Right." Jack didn't admit that he didn't want Bones having any excuse to bring Sydney home. "You shouldn't have to walk everywhere. Besides books, I've seen you lugging a couple bags of groceries off the bus." Neither would Jack admit he'd tossed and turned all night thinking of a way to make up with her. "You can put stuff in the basket and zip home."

Evidently moved by his thoughtfulness, Sydney impulsively threw her arms around his neck and whispered, "I sure can."

Before the sexy woman could back away, Jack closed his arms around her. He lowered his head and touched his mouth to hers. Her lips were warm and supple. As he flattened his hands to her spine, her fingers gently laced through the hair at the back of his head. He shivered with hot desire. Rising on her tiptoes, she hugged him with an intensity that molded those perky breasts to his chest.

"Mmm, Sydney," he groaned hungrily, wanting her so badly.

Fire spread through Jack's veins as he tasted Sydney's lips with his tongue. A hushed moan escaped her, and then her tongue met his. He cupped one hand under the hair at the nape of her neck and kneaded the small of her back with his other hand. As she leaned into him, the hem of her short red blouse slipped from under his hand. Her skin was petal soft. He wanted to feel the bare flesh all over her body. His heart hammered at the thought.

"Jack," Sydney murmured, eyes half-closed.

Jack stepped out of the street onto the sidewalk, taking Sydney with him. She smiled at him as he leaned against the white picket fence. Slipping the toes of her red tennis shoes between his black leather boots, she tipped up her chin, inviting another kiss. He lowered his lips to hers and placed her arms around his neck. As she stood between his legs, his tongue dipped between her teeth and explored her mouth. His hands slid under her blouse, and his fingers splayed between her shoulder blades.

"No bra again."

"I rarely find a good reason to wear one."

With a glance up and down the quiet road, Jack's hands strayed from her back to her sides. His palms came to rest high on her ribs, and his fingers spread. When his thumbs brushed the sides of her breasts, he knew he was close to her nipples. The heat and blood had hardened his lower body. He didn't care as Sydney melted into him. The male anatomy in the crotch of his jeans pressed into her stomach. Breathlessly...feverishly, she wiggled against him.

"Sydney, let's take this inside. I think we're both overheating."

"I don't care if the whole world is watching."

She put her lips to his, but his hands slid down to her waist. His lips stayed on hers as his hands moved on top of her blouse, to the middle of her back, where they'd started. He lifted his head, smiled, and winked.

"Somebody *is* watching."

"Who?" she whispered and followed his nod. Bones' sedan sputtered down the street. Sydney quickly turned in Jack's arms. Since his hands had been at her mid-back, her sudden spin cupped them to her breasts. "Jack!" she squealed and elbowed his ribs.

"Sorry," he chuckled. "Stay right where you are."

"Why?" she asked.

Jack wrapped an arm around her waist and pulled her against the fly of his jeans. "That's why." He leaned over her shoulder, looked down her blouse, and muttered, "Sydney."

"What?" she asked and glanced down. Her nipples were as hard as Jack, and clearly visible against the silk. "You did that to me."

"You cover 'em up, or I will. Let's not give him any ideas."

"What ideas?" she asked as Bones' car neared and slowed.

"He doesn't need to be any more attracted to you than he already is."

"You said with his type I might go to my grave a virgin."

"Has his type ever caught you kissing another man?" Jack asked, his right hand moving from her waist toward her breast.

"No." Sydney placed her arms atop Jack's arm and covered her breasts. "This is called teamwork in hiding arousals, neighbor."

Jack groaned in her ear, "Teamwork is doing something with our arousals, friend." He paused and added, "I've gotta have you, baby girl."

With that unexpected truth stated, Jack remained silent as Sydney said hello to Bones. The man said something about getting his car out of the shop early just for her and offered to give her a ride. With Jack at her back, she told Bones that she didn't need the ride because of the scooter Jack had bought for her.

"I'm going to the site we're excavating around three o'clock," Bones said. "Did I tell you that it might be anywhere from two to three hundred years old?"

"Yes, and you said maybe I could go with you." Not thinking, Sydney lowered her arms from her breasts. "May I?"

"Sure." Bones' grin showed all of his teeth. "I could come back at twelve, take you to lunch, and then drive you to the site."

Jack frowned as he watched Bones' eyes go right for Sydney's breasts. Jack caught Sydney by the upper arm and turned her to him. He was staking his claim on her with every move he made and said, "I'll give you a ride."

"But, I have my scooter," Sydney quietly reminded him.

"It's going to rain this afternoon," Jack told her and looked between their bodies. Their arousals no longer showed. He let Sydney turn back to Bones, but draped an arm around her shoulders.

"Give me the address, and we'll meet you there," Sydney told Bones.

"I guess I could do that." Bones gave her the address with a glare at Jack.

"So long, Bowen," Jack growled, effectively dismissing him.

"See you this afternoon, Leslie."

Jack was glad he was the man holding Sydney. Had he caught Bones kissing her…had the pasty man's hands been under her blouse—

Sydney waved to Bones, and Jack watched his car pop and sputter down the road. Sydney turned to Jack, and he was rewarded with the smile he'd hoped to see after kissing her. Her green eyes sparkled with spirit, and her red lips beckoned his. She was devastatingly delicious.

"Let's go to my house," Jack said.

Sydney shook her head. "I have to get going if I'm to do my visiting and get back here before it rains."

"Syd-ney…" he drew out her name and looked skyward. "All right. You have to wear a helmet. Come on, let's get you one."

"Okay."

Twenty-One

Sydney's entire body tingled as Jack took her hand and trailed along behind him. Every nerve in her soul was alive as she followed the sexy, muscular man down the sidewalk and into his yard. She was expecting to head to his garage and get the helmet she'd worn when riding on the back of his Harley, but he headed down the brick walkway to his front porch. "Where are we going?"

"You'll see," he said. Entering his Victorian mansion, she was awed by the beauty of the foyer with the lovely dark wood and two-story ceiling. High above their heads was a lighted ceiling fan with slowly turning blades that resembled palm tree fronds. From a coat closet, Jack removed a box and held it out to her. But when she reached for it, he placed it behind his back. "The helmet hasn't been paid for. I'll need another kiss for a payment," Jack said with a charming grin.

"When you flash those ocean-blues at me, it's hard to say no," she flirted, so unlike herself. "Would an acceptable payment be a lollipop kiss?"

"Is it anything like the kiss you gave me to thank me for the scooter?"

"Pucker up and find out." Sydney flattened her hands to his chest, and he ever so slightly puckered his lips. She giggled. "Sucker."

"Well, hell." Jack chuckled in surprise. She pushed away from him and made a grab for the box. He'd seen that coming and held the helmet above her head. "What was that trick for?"

"For your trick of feeling me up outside." Belatedly embarrassed, she crossed her arms over her breasts, cocked her hip to one side, and informed him, "I'm not that kind of girl."

Jack cupped the back of her neck, pulled her close, and put his lips to her ear. "I know you're not that kind of girl. I wouldn't have been surprised if you'd slugged me in the gut."

"It's not too late."

"How about I let you feel me?"

The cocky grin on his lips sent tingling heat throughout her body, which dissolved her discomfort. She arched a brow and wrapped a hand around his sturdy wrist. "Are you that kind of guy?"

"I haven't been for two years," Jack replied. "But I could be again with you."

Sydney knew then Jack had been celibate since the death of his family. "I think you would be again without me."

"What does that mean?"

"Some things just take time."

Jack frowned and dropped his hand to his side. "For instance?"

"Becoming intimate after a tragedy."

"Don't start your cloak-and-dagger routine of talking in riddles. If you've got something to say, say it."

She took a breath. "I think you've been stuck in the grieving process."

"Ya think?"

Jack stood back, holding the box with one hand and jamming his other hand into his jeans pocket. She'd said the wrong thing again. Why couldn't she just shut up? "Jack, I'm a dumb chatterbox. I'm sorry. Maybe I'm wrong."

"No." His eyes bore into her. "I *was* stuck in the grieving process until you came along. Seeing you with Bones the other day popped me out of my grief like a damn crowbar. When I thought about that guy putting his hands on you..." He looked away. "I just—"

"Came unglued?" she asked with compassion.

"Yeah," he grumbled and looked back at her. "So," he folded his arms over his chest, "thanks for unsticking me."

"I guess the women here and in New York should thank me," Sydney said lightly. Clenching his jaw, Jack made no denial, and Sydney's heart sank. "It's going on eleven. I'm hoping to be back by two. I'd like to buy you a late lunch or early dinner to thank you for the scooter." He nodded. "If it rains, I'll take you up on your offer of a ride to the excavation site, if the offer still stands."

"It stands, rain or shine."

When she held out her hand for the helmet, she knew they'd made some progress. Instead of simply handing her the box with a scowl, as he would have done in the past, Jack took hold of her arm and tugged her to him. She wrapped her arms around his neck and rose on tiptoes. He kissed her, and she licked his lips like she would a lollipop. A low, masculine groan sounded in his throat, and he opened his mouth. Her tongue met his, and she nearly fainted when he licked her lips.

"Mmm," she moaned. Her nipples beaded against his

chest, and his pat to her fanny sent a zing between her legs. "Don't get unstuck with anybody else," she heard herself whisper and quickly giggled. "At least until I get back."

"Hurry back."

Jack gave her the box, and she opened a white helmet similar to his black one. He walked her back out to the scooter and waved goodbye. Riding the scooter was exhilarating. Taking San Marco Avenue, Sydney rode south through town. Via the Bridge of Lions, she crossed the Matanzas River to Anastasia Island. Listening to the directions on her cell, she went straight for a mile and then took a left turn. Road signs became few and far between, and the directions were a bit confusing. She made some turns on hunches.

Finally, she pulled into a gravel driveway holding an ancient but well-preserved Buick. She parked her scooter and went up to the door of a modest, country-style house. Before she could knock, the door opened as though the resident, or residents, had been expecting guests.

"Hello, are you a friend of the family?" an elderly woman asked.

"Sort of. I came hoping to see George Johnson Burke," Sydney replied.

"Then you weren't aware of his heart attack?"

"No, I wasn't."

"He passed. His funeral was yesterday."

Twenty-Two

Sydney needn't worry about him acting on being unstuck with anybody but her. Besides Patricia Hudson, other women in St. Augustine had tried to get his attention. In New York City, from the funerals to the day he flew to Florida, women had tried. Only Sydney had turned his head, snapped on the lights, and grabbed his interest with both hands.

Jack made a trip to see the zoning commissioner and returned to his house by noon. Within fifteen minutes, it started raining. Since she'd hoped to be back by two, at one-thirty, he ordered a pizza. It was delivered in a torrential downpour at two o'clock sharp. He'd never called Sydney, but had her cell number on the copy of her lease. He called her. No answer. At three, he contacted the police.

"Do you know of any accidents involving a white scooter?"

The answer was negative, and Jack felt relieved. But, by three-thirty, he was wondering why he hadn't insisted on taking her to the friend's house. Where could she be? By four, he was berating himself for giving Sydney the scooter. By four-thirty, he figured she was at the excavation site without him.

By five o'clock, the rain had lessened. He called Flagler Hospital asking about scooter accidents, happily to no avail. At five-forty-five, someone knocked on Jack's door. Sure it was Sydney, Jack raced through the house. He jerked the front door open and found the pasty professor on the porch.

"Hello," Bones said, raising a skeletal hand in greeting. When he shifted his weight from one foot to the other, the legs of his pleated slacks flopped back and forth. "I guess Sydney decided not to come to the excavation site because of the rain. I stopped by her house, but she's not there. Is she here?"

"What do you want her for?"

Bones' Adam's apple bobbed. "I came to tell her that the excavation site is a bust. We've already worked there for a couple of months. We'd agreed today was the last time we'd search. We found no bones or artifacts of any kind."

"Yeah, okay." Jack nodded impatiently. "I'll tell her."

Just then, Sydney putted down the street.

"It looks like I can tell her myself."

Jack took in Sydney's lowered head and her slumped shoulders and pushed past the lanky professor. Jack jogged down the walk, with Bones at his heels, and shoved open the wrought iron gate.

"Sydney, where the hell have you been?" Jack growled.

"Hi, honey," Bones chirped, a fawning smile on his face.

Sydney removed her helmet, looking exhausted and on the verge of tears. Her arms and legs were visibly shaking.

"Hi, Leslie," Sydney whispered with great effort. "Jack, I can't walk."

Jack scooped her off the scooter. Her right arm dangled uselessly, and her head lay against Jack's as he carried her and the helmet from the road to the sidewalk. Her eyes closed, and Bones followed them into the yard. Then, scurrying ahead, Bones opened the front door. Jack took Sydney inside and placed her on the cushiony leather couch in his den. She opened her eyes as he slipped a soft pillow under her head. The den was made cozy with heavy curtains and a plush carpet covering a large part of the hardwood floor. A flatscreen took up one corner, and Buster's huge dog bed sat near the couch. Jack and Bones stood looking down at her, and then Jack offered to get her some coffee.

"Yes, please. Thanks," Sydney whispered.

Jack left Bones standing there fidgeting and mumbling as to being worried about Sydney. When Jack returned with a mug of coffee, Bones still stood awkwardly. Sydney nudged herself into a sitting position, and Jack handed her the mug, then sat down across from her in a double wide recliner. He waved a hand for Bones to sit or go, whatever, as Sydney took a sip of her coffee. After she swallowed, she smiled at him.

"Decaf," Jack said with a wink. Then to Bones, he grumbled, "Either sit down or leave, Bowen."

Awkwardly, Bones ambled to a wing-back chair, sat primly on the edge, and asked Sydney, "So what happened today, honey?"

Sydney's pretty head tilted to one side, and she said, "I ran into a dead end, literally a dead end."

"Philip's descendent is dead?" Bones asked.

Sydney glanced at Jack, appearing to prepare for his reaction. "Yes."

Jack glared at Bones. "Don't tell me you're encouraging her with this ghost thing."

"I'm neutral," Bones mumbled, crossed his long legs, and pulled them under the chair.

"You said you believe in ghosts, Leslie," Sydney said tiredly.

Bones' Adam's apple bobbed as eyed Jack and then smiled at Sydney. "I want to."

Jack sat forward and braced his forearms on his knees. "Syd-ney—" he drew out her name as he did when he was frustrated with her.

"Jack," she interrupted him, her voice so faint with fatigue that Jack stopped himself short. "My research at the courthouse showed that a likely descendent of Philip Burke and Camilla Johnson owned a house on the Atlantic Ocean side of Anastasia Island."

"Are you telling me you rode that little scooter five miles one way?" Jack asked.

"And then some, because the house was a third of the way down the fourteen-mile-long island," Sydney admitted as Jack shook his head in disbelief. "I had to follow a lead. I found out that George Johnson Burke had lived there all his life. He died at the age of eighty-six and was buried yesterday."

"So, was George Johnson Burke a relative?" Bones questioned.

Sydney nodded. "His wife, Nellie, said yes. She showed me the Burke family history recorded in an old Bible. She and Mr. Burke had no children and her family is gone, so now Nellie is all by herself at eighty-two. Medical bills depleted their savings so her dream of moving into a retirement community won't happen. Losing those you love can sometimes cast a shadow over one's dreams." Sydney smiled gently at Jack, who didn't comment. "If Nellie uncovers any other Burke or Johnson family records, while going through her husband's belongings, she promised to share them with me."

"I tried to call you," Jack said. "But your phone went to voicemail."

"I was going to call you too. But by the time I got to the Burke house, my phone was dead, and Nellie doesn't own a cell phone, so there was no charger for me to borrow." Looking at Jack, she continued, "I didn't have your cell number memorized, so I couldn't use her land-line, and that's another story."

"What took you until almost six to get back?" Jack asked.

"Philip went with me to the Burke house, and after we were on our way back to St. Augustine, he wanted to go by the excavation site."

"Ghosts can appear in the daytime?" Bones asked.

"If you remember, our joint research at the library said they could appear at any time, Leslie," Sydney said.

"I forgot." Leslie sank back in the chair. "But, I do remember reading that ghosts could follow people from place to place."

"Anybody who's read *The Legend of Sleepy Hollow* knows that, Bowen," Jack said a bit sarcastically. Since Sydney had informed him the tale took place in New York, he had read the short story. "How do you think the headless horseman found old Ichabod? He followed him home one night. Although some people think the head-less horseman, who got rid of the schoolmaster, was really a local bully in disguise."

"Jack," Sydney snapped around a giggle and then gave him a *be quiet* look. Bones appeared leery not so much of ghosts, but of Jack.

"So...um..." Bones looked from him to Sydney. "I didn't see you at the excavation site, honey."

"Everyone was already gone when we got there. I'm

sorry I couldn't call you, either, Leslie," Sydney said. "But once we were there, Philip told me there were no bones or artifacts at the site." The men exchanged glances. "Philip has checked out every cemetery and possible lone grave in a hundred-mile radius." She felt a need to defend herself under Jack's appraising glare. "He's had plenty of time to do it."

Jack placed an elbow on the arm of the recliner and rested his temple against his fist. Bones sat up straight and showed all of his teeth and gums.

"Have you come across Bledsoe's name in any books?" Bones inquired. "He was the captain of Philip's ship, right?"

"Right. No, I haven't found him mentioned by name, but that doesn't mean he's a figment of my imagination," Sydney said with a glance at Jack. "My research says the majority of ship captains were well paid and the most welcome of guests at the sailors' rests, which flourished here in St. Augustine at the time Philip lived."

"What exactly is a sailor's rest?" Jack asked.

"It was what Philip's father turned the original house on this property into to make ends meet," Sydney explained and yawned.

"Like a bed and breakfast, which are popular in St. Augustine today?" Jack surmised.

"Yes, exactly." Sydney nodded at Jack. "Philip met Captain Bledsoe right here on your property, and that's how he got the job aboard the privateer ship."

Jack sat up straighter in the recliner and said, "Privateer ships were used by General George Washington against the British."

"Right," Sydney said. "If I keep digging, I'm hoping to find information on Bledsoe and his ship, which might shed light on Philip. I've contacted the historical society in regard to a Captain Bledsoe, but I've not heard back from them."

"So what did Philip have to say about all of this?" Bones asked.

"I thought no one would ever ask," she replied to Bones and looked back to Jack. "In 1776, Philip Burke took a year's commission on Captain Bledsoe's privateer ship. Doing so meant Philip had to leave the girl next door, his lifelong sweetheart, Camilla Johnson, behind."

"That's probably the one thing the guy did right," Jack grumbled. "Was she a nonstop chatterbox?"

Sydney rolled her eyes. "The reason Philip signed onto Captain Bledsoe's ship was to earn enough money to convince Camilla's father to give him her hand in marriage. Camilla, or Cammy as Philip calls her, promised to wait for him. He came back from sea a very rich man, but he never saw Camilla Johnson again."

"So she dumped him, he killed himself, and he's haunting you?" Jack asked.

"Or maybe he wants you to take Cammy's place, honey," Bones piped up.

Jack scowled. That was four times Bones had called her honey. "Sydney's not taking anyone's place...*honey*."

"Okay." Bones' Adam's apple worked in a nervous swallow, signaling he'd received Jack's message to stop calling her honey. To Sydney, Bones said, "But uh, the research states not only can hauntings last for centuries, ghosts can become attached to those people able to witness them."

"Both of you shh." Sydney held up a hand as Jack was known to do. "Philip does not want me to take Cammy's place. He's earthbound because of his unfulfilled promise to return to her. He knows he could move on, but he won't consider it. His soul can't rest until he knows where hers rests. Ghosts can have goals and dreams just like we do."

"Yes, yes, we read that too," Bones said carefully, with a sideways glance at Jack. "So what kept him from taking his fortune from sea straight to Cammy and her father?"

"Philip said someone shot him in the back and killed him the day he arrived in port." Looking at Jack, she said, "He says he left Cammy and tried to return to her where the little pier is on the other side of Magnolia Road."

"If I bought any of this which I don't," Jack narrowed his eyes at Sydney, then Bones, and plowing a hand through his hair, he continued, "I'd say somebody shot Burke for his money."

Bones chewed a fingernail, bobbed his head, and then asked, "Has Philip remembered the name of his ship yet?"

"No," Sydney said around another yawn and shook her head.

"Are you sure you need to know his ship's name?" Bones asked.

"Yes." Sydney nodded. Jack noticed her eyelids growing heavier as she said, "I'm going to track down any and all leads Philip gives me, hoping one will shed light on who murdered him."

"Going by scooter to Anastasia Island wouldn't be a quick ride," Jack said. "But still, it shouldn't have taken you almost seven hours to get there and back."

Finishing the last sip of coffee, Sydney set her mug aside and said, "The Johnson-Burke house wasn't easy to locate even with GPS. Not all the roads were clearly marked, and it took me more than an hour to find it. Nellie was so friendly and seemed so lonely that I stayed and we talked until I noticed it had started to rain. By then, I realized I'd missed lunch."

Jack interjected, "Because you're a chatterbox."

"Yes, and Nellie is too. At that point, I asked Nellie for her phonebook to try to find a landline number for you. But the rest of that story is the storm had cut off her phone service. By three-thirty, the rain had let up some, so I started back to town."

"You rode in the rain?" Jack scolded. "With a dead phone, so no GPS?"

"Kind of." Sydney flinched. "I got really lost."

"A dead guy, a dead end, and a dead phone." Leslie tittered and then quickly wiped the gum-revealing grin off his face. "I mean uh…couldn't Philip have told you how to get back?"

"Put it there, Bowen." Jack held out his hand, palm up, which Leslie cautiously tapped.

"Philip doesn't know all and see all without checking things out just like everybody else." Sydney huffed. "That's why he wanted to visit the excavation site." She swung her legs off the couch. "You two can disbelieve in ghosts all you want. I'm going home."

"No, stay where you are." Chuckling, Jack held up his hand to stop her and smothered the grin. "What happened next?"

Sitting up now, Sydney said, "I ran out of gas on a back road and had to push my scooter until I found a gas station."

"I'm sorry, Sydney," Jack said, picturing that. "I should have taken you there myself."

She shook her head. "It was no one's fault but my own."

Bones looked at him before saying, "I'd be happy to treat you both to dinner."

"No thanks," Jack said.

Twenty-Three

Even with the slight snarl, Sydney noticed there was less of an edge to Jack's voice than there had been minutes prior. She suspected Leslie's dinner invite including both of them meant he had conceded his pursuit of her to Jack. Two things the part-time professor didn't know: Leslie could never win her, and Jack wasn't pursuing her.

"Okay," Leslie replied to Jack.

"Sydney and I have had a couple of meal dates broken. We're making them up today." Jack looked at Sydney. "Right?"

"Right," Sydney agreed. Jack stood, and Leslie followed suit. Sydney fought back another yawn. "Maybe Leslie could join us."

"I don't think so," Leslie mumbled and shook his head.

"He's every bit as smart as you said he was, Syd," Jack remarked with a grin at Sydney and a slap on Leslie's slender back.

"Bye...Syd," Leslie said as Jack rolled his eyes. "Glad you're back safe and sound."

"Thank you. Bye, Leslie."

"I'll show you out," Jack told him, already on his way to the front door.

"I hope my car starts," Leslie said, following Jack out of the den. "I don't know anything about engines. I may have to stay for dinner after all."

"I know all about engines. There's not a *ghost* of a chance you'll have to stay."

Sydney stifled a laugh. She stretched out on the comfy couch and adjusted the pillow, planning to rest her eyes only until Jack returned. When she woke, it was fairly dark. Momentarily disoriented, she saw a flatscreen turned down low with its light revealing Jack lying in the recliner. Buster was asleep in his dog bed. Jack's chair was tilted back, and the footrest extended. He had changed out of his tee shirt and jeans into a pair of his low-riding gym shorts.

His blue eyes were closed, his hands stacked behind his head, and his legs slightly spread. Stretched out there, his broad chest rhythmically rising and falling, his magnetism held Sydney's gaze. Even in his sleep, he had the power to pull her to him.

"Jack," she whispered and placed her hand on his shoulder.

"Yeah?" Jack's voice was groggy, and his eyes stayed closed.

He took her hand and tugged her into the big recliner. Not opening his eyes, he made a half-turn, cuddling her in a web of muscle. The feeling was so thrilling Sydney's heart pounded wildly. She had to leave while she still could.

"Jack, I'd better go. What time do you suppose—"

His mouth closed over hers. Okay. She'd stay only long enough to kiss him once. With a will of its own, one of her arms twined around Jack while her other arm lay trapped between their bodies. His tongue teased her lips, and she flattened her hand to the rippling muscles in his bare back. His left arm slid under her, holding her to him. His right hand strayed under her blouse and settled on her ribs. As his tongue slipped into her mouth, his touch moved from her ribs to the side of her breast. He stroked her skin as he had earlier that day. His fingers splayed, and the pad of his thumb moved over her nipple in a tantalizing massage.

White hot heat raced to Sydney's most private parts. She felt wanton, and didn't care, as she arched her back to his touch. Jack groaned and cupped his palm over her breast, kneading her flesh. The sensation was spine-tingling, and she wanted more.

When Jack's mouth left hers, she whimpered a protest. He unbuttoned her blouse, and his lips closed over the tip of the breast he'd just caressed. A gasp of shock and pleasure escaped her as electricity crackled along an invisible cord from her breast to the vee between her legs. She buried her hands in Jack's hair as his tongue flicked her beaded nipple. He kissed his way to her other breast, and then his warm, wet mouth closed over the tip.

"Mmm." Sydney was experiencing desires never before tapped. She'd not been interested in having those passions explored until meeting Jack. When his lips traveled from her breast back to her mouth, Sydney gulped and wiggled anxiously against him. Jack calmly slipped a knee between her slender thighs, and Sydney spread her legs for him.

"Yeah, baby girl," Jack groaned and took her hand in his. "Remember what I said about you feeling me?"

"Yes," she whispered.

He pressed her palm to the hard length of his manhood. "Take your turn."

"Jack," Sydney murmured, her hand lightly gripping

him. She had a highly aroused man, a big man, on her hands, and she wasn't sure she could handle him. Truth, she didn't know *how* to handle him.

"Relax." Jack pulled his leg from between hers, rolled onto his back, and tugged her on top of him. "We're not gonna do it the first time in this chair." Her hair fell around her shoulders and his. His hands clamped to her waist, and he helped her to straddle him in a sitting position. "Okay?"

"You make me lose control," she admitted, feeling his male hardness pressed intimately to her womanhood. Her blouse was unbuttoned and barely covering her breasts.

"Sydney." Jack looked up at her and smoothed a lock of hair away from her cheek. "I thought you were a tease the first time you kissed me in the courtyard. But now I know you're innocent, and I have to remind myself to go slowly."

"I've gone really fast and far with you in just one day."

Jack grinned, opening her blouse. "Not nearly far enough."

Closing her blouse, she said, "Farther than I've ever gone in my whole life." She shifted her weight, moving her most secret spot away from his arousal and situating her bottom across his thighs. "Jack, if I were to get any more involved with you, I wouldn't get anything done this summer, except you,"

Jack chuckled. "What's wrong with that?"

"Oh, nothing, except that I wouldn't be preparing for my dissertation." Trying to calm herself, she rubbed her temples. The sight of his handsome face and naked chest was a powerful aphrodisiac. As her gaze roamed down his lower stomach, she closed her eyes. Sydney's desire for and fear of what was in his gym shorts warred within her. "If I get sidetracked with you and if I don't land the Flagler College job, I'd go back home with little to no research and no you so zip for my summer spent in St. Augustine."

Jack offered in a steady voice, "But if you do get the Flagler College job, we wouldn't have to go our separate ways at the end of summer."

"But chances are I won't." Sydney crawled off his lap, scooted to the edge of the recliner, and buttoned her blouse. "I don't want to write this summer off as a meaningless affair with my next-door neighbor."

"It wouldn't be meaningless if we stay friends." Jack grasped a lock of her hair and tugged, turning her toward him. "Stay and sleep with me tonight."

Sydney pulled her hair out of his grasp. "If I sleep with you once, I'll want to every night."

"That works." Jack cocked a brow. "Sydney, you're a very capable woman. Surely you can juggle me and your research." His grin was so suggestive and so hot. Sydney looked away from him. He touched his fingers to her chin and turned her to face him. "Can't you?"

"I wouldn't know where to start."

"I do. Let's pick up where we left off in my bed."

Sydney shoved his hand away in an effort to keep her wits about her. "In the first place, I'm not the type to sleep with you all summer and cheerfully wave goodbye to you in September. Which leads me directly to second place, I only intend to sleep with the man I plan to marry. And in the third place—"

Jack's expression was one of exasperation. "For crying out loud." He smacked the arms of the chair. "If I'd married every woman I ever slept with, I'd have—" He stopped and ran his hand over his mouth. "Never mind."

"Six dozen wives?" Jealously slapped Sydney so hard,

she hopped off the recliner, swiveled around, and glared at the magnificent man.

"No."

"Excuse me, a couple dozen wives." Sydney flung her arms as wide apart as possible and wiggled her fingers. "We're polar opposites. As you pointed out in the very beginning, you're analytical, and I'm emotional."

"Don't you know opposites attract?"

"I know you think I should wear a bra and because I don't, I'm a bad girl."

"You're not a bad girl, and we both know it," Jack said, which she took as a compliment. "But compromise is part of life, Sydney. For instance, I wished you would have had on a bra today in front of Bones. Alone with me, I'm glad you don't."

"I compromise only when it's worth it to me." Sydney doubled up her fists next to her temples and squealed in frustration, "Ooh!"

"Settle down before you explode."

"I'll explode if I want to." She glared at Jack. His masculinity was accentuated by his controlled composure in the midst of their disagreement. All she wanted to do was crawl back into his arms, kiss him, and make up with him. But she knew where that would lead. She had to stay mad to stay out of his bed. "We get along only when we aren't talking."

"Let's not talk." Jack's stomach growled as the eleven o'clock news came on the flatscreen. He put the footrest down and stood. "I haven't eaten all day, and you haven't either. I ordered pizza for us. Let's heat it up and eat. We'll both feel better."

"No." Sydney knew something else would heat up if she stayed. "I'm tired. I'll just go home to bed."

"Oh, come on. Let's eat."

Sydney was starving so she followed him. In the

kitchen, she sat at the table while he heated the pizza in the microwave. He didn't act as though he felt self-conscious about what they'd done in the den, so she told herself not to feel awkward either. But, images of their bodies…kissing, nibbling, entwining, feeling, needing, and wanting—

"Want a beer, wine, water, or more decaf?"

Sydney gave herself a mental shake. "I'll take wine."

Jack poured her wine, let Buster out, and then polished off a beer and five pieces of pizza. Sydney was comfortably full and sleepy by the time she washed down the last bite of her third piece of pizza with her final swallow of wine. She scooted back her chair, picked up their plates, and took them to the sink.

"What's your third reason for not sleeping with me, Sydney?"

Sydney walked toward him and said, "You don't want to know."

"Yes, I do."

Jack let Buster back in and grabbed the wine bottle. He took her hand and led her back to the den. Sydney knew she should walk out the front door even as they sat down in the cozy two-person recliner. The recliner where they'd gone so fast and so far. Picking up the remote, Jack switched the flatscreen to music only, keeping the volume low and leaving a soft glow in the room.

"It's midnight. Even though Ichabod has plenty of food, I should go check on him."

"Not before you tell me the third reason. I don't have anything contagious."

"I didn't think you did. Besides, that's not it."

Not touching her, Jack said, "Then what is it?"

Sydney pulled her lips between her teeth and stared at the flatscreen. "Is that Jason Aldean, Tim McGraw,

Blake Shelton, or Kenny Chesney singing? I don't know the country singers as well as you do."

"Garth Brooks. Don't try to change the subject. Answer me." Snuggled against him and out of topics with which to sidetrack him, she whispered in his ear. Jack sighed and repeated, "Because Philip might be watching."

"I said you didn't want to know."

Jack dropped his head to the back of the chair and extended the footrest. He stacked his hands behind his head and closed his eyes. Sydney's eyes traveled down his bare chest, over his low-riding shorts, to his long muscular legs. Back to where they'd started. The memory of him lying almost fully on top of her made her want to hug him. And she wanted him to hug her...to kiss her lips...her neck...her breasts.

"Come here, Doc." Jack yawned and wrapped his arms around her. Closing his eyes, he said, "I'm too tired to walk you home. Stay and go home in the morning."

"You're practically naked and as tempting as a freshly baked cake," she admitted. Blue eyes still closed, his sexy smile said he enjoyed her compliment. Lightning shot up Sydney's spine at the truth of her own words. "I guess I could snooze for a while on your sofa."

"We're in the recliner, so besides that nothing will happen because of the three dumb reasons you gave me. But that deal is good only for tonight, Don't think you can hide behind it the next time you spend the night with me."

"There won't be a next—" Sydney was cut off by Jack's hand clamping over her mouth. She pried his fingers away, and he groaned as if in pain. "What about my scooter?"

"I put it in your garage."

"Thank you," Sydney whispered as Jack tightened his

muscular arms around her, molding her to his bare chest. He closed her eyelids with gentle fingers. Sydney snuggled against him, finally giving in, as she'd yearned to do all along. "You're so sweet."

"Yeah." After a moment, he said, "You might not think so if you could read my mind."

Twenty-Four

"Hey, sleepyhead, wake up."

Jack opened his eyes and found Sydney perched on the edge of the recliner cushion. Her hair was damp, and she smelled like shampoo and soap. She'd exchanged her blouse and jeans for one of his long-sleeved, pale blue denim shirts. He'd never seen a sexier woman. She waved a piece of crisp bacon under his nose, and he grasped her hand. He bit off half the piece, and she ate the other half. She licked her fingers and started to get up, but he caught her wrist.

"Got some more of that?" he asked.

"Breakfast is being served in your kitchen."

Jack put the footrest down and sat up. "Ouch, my back. Next time, we sleep in my bed."

Sitting beside him, Sydney raised her left hand and said. "I'll take a diamond engagement ring. Size five and a half."

"Compromise, Sydney. You give, and you get," he told her. "I'll marry you when you start wearing a bra. Do you have one on under my shirt?"

"Yes."

With familiarity, he cupped his hand over her soft breast. "You little liar."

She giggled and stood up. "Don't hold your breath waiting for me to wear a bra, but thanks for letting me borrow a shirt. I figured since you rooted through my garage putting my scooter away, I could root through your drawers for something to wear."

"Listen, baby, anytime you want to root through my drawers, you're welcome to." He put a wicked grin on his lips and stretched. She flounced away toward the kitchen, and he followed her. When they neared the table, he flipped up the tail of the shirt. "Damn."

"Jack!" She turned and smacked his hand.

"Hell, I was hoping you hadn't found my boxers."

"You sit, eat, and keep your hands to yourself."

After he was seated, she served him breakfast and coffee. She sat with him, and they enjoyed a hearty portion of bacon, eggs, and flirting. He could hardly take his eyes off her. The sleeves of the oversized shirt hung off her shoulders, and the front was buttoned only to the tops of her breasts. The cuffs were rolled up to her wrists, and the hem reached halfway down her thighs. He was just thinking about coaxing her upstairs when she jumped up from the table.

"Oh no!" Sydney gasped, looking at her house.

Jack saw two older ladies walking down her cobblestone path. "Who are they?"

"The ladies from the St. Augustine Historical Society."

"What are they doing at your house?" Jack asked.

"Maybe they've found some of the information I requested."

"They've got rotten timing."

"I have to get dressed." Sydney dashed out of the kitchen. As Jack sauntered down the hallway behind her, he watched her panicked ascent up the stairs. He took the stairs two at a time and saw her dashing past his black cherry king bed, dresser, chest of drawers, and night-stands into the master bathroom. "I know I left the red blouse you gave me here in the bathroom, but I can't find it."

"Uh, Buster, give it to her, pal."

Sydney hopped out of the bathroom, yanking up her blue jeans. She stopped with the waistband of her jeans at the hem of the denim shirt. Dangling from Buster's mouth was her red silk blouse.

"It's dripping with dog spit."

Jack splayed his hands and chuckled. "Buster likes you."

"Now what?" Sydney cried and flailed her arms. The long shirtsleeves unrolled with her frantic movements. Her jeans slipped to her knees, she grabbed them and tugged them over the boxer shorts. The cuffs of the shirt-sleeves covered her hands as she tried to zip the fly of her white jeans. "Jack, help me."

"Jack, I can't walk. Jack, I'll take a diamond engage-ment ring. Jack, keep your hands to yourself. Jack, help me," he taunted, folding his arms over his chest.

Sydney let out a soft but nearly hysterical cry. The jeans zipper ate the fly of the boxers, and her hair fell over her eyes as she struggled to correct the problem. Buster chewed on her blouse, and tears stung Sydney's eyes.

Jack yanked down her jeans, and the boxers went with them. The long tails of the denim shirt kept her naked parts private. Jack ripped the red belt out of her jeans and buckled it around her waist, transforming the shirt into a dress. Without a word, Sydney combed her long hair with her fingers and rolled up the shirt sleeves. Sydney tugged on her red sneakers, and Jack grabbed her hand. Behind him, she hurried down the stairs. Reaching the front door, he opened it. Barely stopping, she kissed his cheek. He swatted her fanny as she stepped onto the porch.

"Thank you, Jack."

"Don't bend over," he said. "And don't forget to ask them about my houses."

"We never made a deal about that," Sydney reminded him as she jogged backward across his front yard. "I don't need protection from Philip, and you refused to barter your services in exchange for information."

Jack watched Sydney twirl away and call to the ladies on her porch as she came to the wrought iron fence. Amazingly she crawled over it without revealing her bare butt. Then, before she turned back to the ladies, she blew him a kiss.

For the remainder of the week, Jack only saw Sydney as she came and went on her scooter. He wished he'd never bought it for her. Then maybe she'd have asked him for a ride.

Jack hadn't suspected he'd miss a chatterbox, but he did. Yet, pride wouldn't let him go to her. She'd said they had no deals and that he'd taken her too fast and too far. And though he wasn't offering her an engagement ring, his ego had been bruised a little by her rejection the night she'd spent with him. To get his mind off her, he passed some time during the day playing shirts and skins basketball with some friends on the outdoor courts at the country club. His team was skins, and his tan deepened...along with his interest in his elusive next-door neighbor.

And the nights...the sultry summer nights seemed to last forever. He was lonely for his friend as he sat in the den watching the flatscreen and her house. He didn't have to be alone. Women called him every day or two, wanting to go out or to come over. But, all he felt was disappointment at hearing their voices instead of Sydney's.

Early on July 3, his cell rang while he was still in bed.

"Yeah?" he grumbled. It was Angus Dolan, manager of the New York City office. Everything was fine, and he wondered if Jack was flying up for the company dinner and fireworks. "I haven't decided yet." A call beeped in, and he saw Sydney's number. "I'll call you back, Angus," Jack answered Sydney's call. "What's up, Doc?"

"I'm outside on your porch and need your help."

"Key's under the mat." God, he was glad she was here, but he could play it as disinterested as she was. She'd never know he'd left the key there in case she'd needed something. "I'm upstairs." And with that, he rolled over in bed and closed his eyes.

Twenty-Five

Skipping up the stairs, Sydney stopped at the door to Jack's bedroom and swallowed. Hard. He was in the middle of his bed, on his stomach, eyes shut. There was a day's growth of black stubble along his jaw, and she glimpsed patches of the black hair under his arms. When he gripped his pillow, his biceps muscles flexed. Oh, but he looked outrageously sexy, with his upper body bare and the sheet lying below the small of his back. He was all male, utterly sexy, and completely mesmerizing.

She'd missed this exciting man more than she cared to admit. But she'd embarrassed herself by giving him such free reign of her body and, thus, had kept a low profile. She'd noticed him leaving his house every day and figured since he was unstuck, he'd found another woman or women to occupy him. She only had herself to blame for that. Finally, she had gotten up her nerve and figured out a way to come see him without damaging her pride.

"I knocked. I guess you didn't hear me. I'm sorry to bother you so early in the morning, but my scooter won't start." Her heart was racing. "I woke you up. Want me to leave?"

"I was already awake. I want you to tell me what you've been doing for the past week and where you're going so early today."

Jack rolled to his back, and the sheet twisted around him. He stretched and the sheet rode dangerously low. Sydney's eyes traveled from his chest to the black hair surrounding his indented navel. In a line from his navel down his flat stomach, the masculine trail of black hair vanished under the sheet. Sydney drove her gaze back up his muscular body and collided with his knowing blue eyes.

She lowered her lashes to say, "In answer to your first question, I've been busy. When I answer questions like the second one, you get mad at me."

"Maybe if you answered me in bed, I wouldn't get mad," Jack suggested and crooked his finger. "We seem to do better when we're lying down."

Clutching tight to the batchel in her hand, Sydney walked to him and perched at the foot of his bed. "I've been checking out leads given to me by the historical society."

"What leads?"

"Leads to Philip Burke and Captain Bledsoe. You remember the captain who took Philip on for a year?"

"When I'm on vacation, I don't remember things well this early in the morning. Crawl under the sheet, and we'll try this again in a couple of hours."

"With any luck, in a couple of hours, I'll be knee-deep in Captain Bledsoe's personal journal and ship manifest. I found out who has them."

"Who?"

"An antique dealer in Jacksonville."

Jack glared at her. "Did you think you were going to ride your scooter forty miles north to Jacksonville?"

"Yes, I was. That's why I was getting an early start."

"Maybe you don't remember things so well this early in the morning either. Have you forgotten what happened when you rode to Anastasia Island?" Jack asked. Sydney shrugged. "Did you ever hear from the woman you met there?"

"Nellie. No, not yet, but I believe I will."

"And now you're going to chase down an antique dealer?"

"If you'll take me, I'll give you gas money."

"I'm thinking of flying to New York City today."

"Oh," Sydney said. Obviously, he hadn't missed her at all. He was flying out of state without giving her a thought. "My request for a ride was really short notice." Sydney stood and backed away from his bed toward the door. "I'll ask Leslie to take me."

"Suit yourself."

"Oh, I almost forgot, I—" Bumping into the dresser, she wished she was crawling into bed with Jack instead of leaving him. Was he naked under the sheet? "I bought you something." She took a fancy gift bag out of her leather batchel and tossed it onto the bed. "Bye."

"Wait." Jack sat up and grabbed the bag. Sydney chewed on her lower lip as he plucked a pair of boxer shorts, which matched his eyes, out of the bag. "Designer silk shorts?"

"You gave me silk when my cotton blouse tore on your motorcycle." One pair had been a stretch, no way she could afford a dozen to match Jack's generosity. "So I'm replacing your cotton shorts I tore on my jeans zipper with silk."

"You're so sweet."

"You might not think so if you could read my mind," she flirted, shocking herself.

"Thank you, Sydney."

"Weren't you going to tell me goodbye before you flew off to New York?" She shrugged. "I mean, I'd be happy to feed Buster for you."

"I was going to ask you to come with me."

"Really?" Sydney's heart thumped so loudly she covered it with her hand so Jack wouldn't hear. When he held out his hand, she went to him, and he pulled her to sit beside him. "What about Jacksonville?"

"We have to fly out of Jacksonville anyway."

"Will I be able to get a ticket to JFK or LaGuardia at the last minute?"

"LaGuardia. It's smaller and closer to Manhattan. I'll get you on the flight."

"I'll pay you back," she offered, hoping he didn't ask when.

"No, I invited you."

"If I go with you, will you take me to see your Wall Street office and the brownstone where you live in Manhattan?"

"The brownstone is leased out now. But I'll take you to my new apartment." Jack cocked a brow. "If you're a *good* girl and wear a bra."

Excitement shot through Sydney. She dropped the batchel as he tugged her into bed. His lips touched hers in an exhilarating but all too short kiss. Then he rolled away from her toward the opposite side of the mattress. Sydney sat up and quickly covered her eyes.

"Are you naked?" she asked.

"Look and see," Jack challenged, but she shook her head. "You'll need to pack a bag. When I fly to New York, I stay a night or two."

"Okay." Uncovering her eyes but keeping them on the floor, she headed for the door.

"I'll take you to a little joint in Jacksonville for lunch before we head to the airport."

"Perfect." She hoped *little joint* meant inexpensive. "I'll treat."

"No, you won't, but this is gonna be fun."

"Yes." Sydney heard Jack turn on the shower and, stopping near the door, called, "What do you suppose could be wrong with my brand new scooter?" She smothered a giggle. After having run out of gas on Anastasia Island, she knew exactly what was wrong. But this time, her scooter had no gas because she'd siphoned it out. Jack's reply was muffled by the shower. "What did you say?"

Louder, he said, "It's missing a sparkplug."

"A sparkplug?" That wasn't what she'd expected to hear. "How do you know?"

"I took it. Go home and pack your bag or strip and hop in the shower with me."

Twenty-Six

When Jack emerged from the shower, Sydney was gone. He called Angus back to let him know he and a friend were flying up for the dinner and fireworks. He arranged for their flight and let Buster outside. After that he called David, one of the friends he often played basketball with at the Y or country club, and asked him to stop by to let Buster out and feed him. By the time Jack was ready to go, Sydney was rolling a carry-on bag down his brick walk.

And she looked fantastic.

Not only beautiful, Sydney was sophisticated. She had transformed her ponytail into three swirled knots atop her head, with wisps of hair curling around her face and neck. Her emerald eyes were shadowed in forest green, a favorite shade of his, deepening their color as thickened black lashes made her eyes alluringly mysterious. Her soft cheeks were a shade pinker than usual, and he could almost taste the full, sweet lips shimmering in crimson.

Wearing a white jacket, the white skirt she wore with it was short and snug enough to send of jolt of heat through

Jack's lower body. Completing her outfit was one of the blouses he'd given her, a black silk one. She carried a small white purse that matched open-toed white stilettos.

"Wow, you look great," Jack complimented, wearing a long-sleeved, white button-down shirt with tan khakis, a black belt, and black loafers without socks.

"Thanks. So do you, Doc," Sydney said, stopping at the steps to the porch. "Are you going to invite me in?"

He chuckled. "Yeah, sure." Walking across the porch and down the steps, he took her bag. She smelled as delicious as she looked. As they made their way through the house, he picked up a navy sports jacket and assured Buster his good buddy, David, would be checking on him. Crossing the back yard to the garage, Jack asked, "Got somebody to feed your cat?"

"As you may remember, cats can spend a night or two alone without being checked on."

Jack knew she was referring to the night she'd spent with him in his recliner. "Some animals need more attention." He grinned, letting her know he didn't necessarily mean Buster.

Sydney blushed but at the same time raised her chin. "No bag?"

"I might have a change of clothes in New York."

Sydney rolled her eyes. "Of course you would."

"Wait here, and I'll get my car." Jack clicked a remote, and the garage door opened. Tossing his jacket onto the passenger's seat, he backed out of the garage and stopped alongside Sydney. Hopping out, he grabbed her bag and walked her around the car.

"Your car is beautiful," Sydney whispered seemingly in awe as her head turned from the front end to the back. "This will be my first ride in a Porsche."

"Now, why does that not surprise me?"

"I can't imagine." She laughed. "I love the color of your car."

"It's called Irish Green. I think of it as the color of money."

"Expensive?"

"You don't want to know," Jack responded, using a recent response of Sydney's. "Slide in and buckle up, baby."

"What model is this car?"

"A 911 GT3."

She plucked his jacket off the passenger's seat, and the black leather, with its yellow stitching, scrunched as she sat. Jack closed her door and stowed her bag in the front end of the car called the *frunk*. Since the engine of this model car was in the rear, and there were no back seats, there was enough room in the frunk for a couple of soft bags.

When Jack got in beside her, she had already looked up the Porsche on her cell. She gaped at him and whispered. "Four hundred thousand dollars?"

"Give or take a couple bucks."

Jack looked at her long legs, and she tugged on her skirt, but it remained mid-thigh. When he raised his eyes to hers, he smiled and held out his hand. She took his hand, and he kissed her fingers. When he let go, she ran her fingers through his hair.

"You haven't had a haircut since we met. Maybe you're not such an uptight New Yorker after all."

"Maybe." Jack cupped his hand to the nape of her neck, pulled her close, and whispered against her lips, "But you're still a green-eyed nutcase, or we wouldn't be going to Jacksonville to check out a ghost."

He kissed her lips before she could protest. Then he sat back and chuckled. Sydney huffed but with a smile.

He backed down the drive and onto the road in front of their houses.

"The ladies from the historical society don't think I'm a nutcase," she informed him as they left Magnolia Road. "They were really helpful to me."

"What did the historical society ladies say?" he asked, heading through town toward the interstate onramp.

"Mention of Captain Bledsoe was found in their archives on the subject of sailors' rests. The reason being he was one of the richest captains, if not *the* richest, to stay in St. Augustine."

"In the location of my house, right?" Jack asked a little sarcastically.

"Yes," Sydney answered seriously. "The historical society also found an article from an antique magazine which said Captain Bledsoe's journal was bought by the Jacksonville antique dealer, we're going to see, on Park Street. I called him, and he was gone on a fishing trip. But Mrs. Jenkins, his wife, said he still has the journal and," she paused for effect, "the ship's manifest."

"Did the historical society know the name of Bledsoe's ship?" he asked, surprised at his own curiosity.

"The ladies didn't know. But Philip said yesterday he thinks it was *Sea* something," Sydney answered as Jack shifted the seven-speed sleek sports car and drove onto I-95 North. For a few minutes, they rode in an easy silence under cloudless blue skies and past thick green trees along the Interstate. "I know you don't believe I talk to a ghost, but I think you'll change your mind if I can verify what Philip told me through Captain Bledsoe's journal."

Jack glanced at her. "Verify what, for example?"

"That the location of your house was the former sailor's rest where Philip lived and Captain Bledsoe stayed."

Jack grinned. "Seems like my house was open to you for bed and breakfast recently, wasn't it?"

"Yes. But I had to cook my own breakfast and yours," she teased him back.

"You did." He chuckled, shifted gears again, and took her hand. She gave him a squeeze, and he said, "I warned you I don't cook much."

Sydney nodded and laughed. "I guess a girl can't have everything."

"Guess we'll see."

Twenty-Seven

Forty-five minutes later, in Jacksonville, they stopped on Park Street in front of an elegant antique shop. Sydney could hardly contain her excitement. As she and Jack entered the shop, a bell over the door tinkled merrily, but Sydney's heart sank. The store was nearly devoid of antiques, books, furniture, knickknacks, or other collectibles. A portly man with a gray beard and a big smile greeted them. Shaking hands, Sydney introduced herself and then Jack, who also shook hands with him.

"Nice to meet you both," the antique dealer said. "Ms. Crane, I've been expecting you. Another week, and you'd have missed me. I'm retiring, closing my shop and moving to Arizona with my wife."

"Thank goodness, I'm not too late again," Sydney said more to herself than to the men as she recalled finding out that George Johnson Burke had died. She got right to the point. "Mr. Jenkins, do you still have Captain Bledsoe's ship manifest and personal journal?"

The antique dealer nodded and led them into his private office, where she and Jack took seats in, appropriately enough, captains' chairs. On a wooden desk, the dealer laid the captain's leather-bound manifest and journal before them.

"American maritime documents like Captain Bledsoe's manifest are the detailed invoices of a vessel's cargo," Mr. Jenkins explained politely, probably not sure how much they understood. "For instance, a typical ship's cargo in Bledsoe's time might register nine hundred bales of cotton. On a privateer ship, during the American Revolution, a haul of munitions and arms from plundering British ships might also be recorded as bales of cotton."

"A friend of mine, named Philip, said that privateers were called the militia of the sea," Sydney said as Mr. Jenkins nodded in agreement. "When it was rumored the Continental Congress was on the verge of legalizing these ships and their sailors to officially prey on the British Royal Navy, Philip signed onto Bledsoe's ship."

"What?" Mr. Jenkins asked, catching her reference to Philip.

"You mean Philip told you about sailors like those?" Jack said, covering for her.

"That works," Sydney replied, using one of Jack's phrases with an appreciative smile. "Sure enough, in March of 1776, privateers were legalized. On Bledsoe's ship, the sailors received a government commission in addition to a share of the spoils. Philip said they raided the enemy and then vanished like *ghosts*," she added with a glance at Jack.

Mr. Jenkins nodded again and opened the manifest. "The American privateers did far more damage to the British than the United States Navy. Captain Bledsoe's handwriting can be a bit difficult to decipher at times, but from all accounts, the captain and his men were skilled seamen, and rich ones at that."

"Well deserved," Jack said. "They were a major weapon in the battle for independence."

"Yes, indeed they were," Mr. Jenkins said. The tinkling bell signaled the arrival of a customer. Placing his hand on the other bound book, he said. "This is Captain Bledsoe's journal. It tells of life on the ship and of its sailors." With a nod, the shop owner excused himself.

Sydney pulled her glasses out of her purse and put them on. She carefully opened the journal as Jack studied the manifest. She read for several minutes and then nudged Jack.

"I found Philip Burke's name," Sydney whispered excitedly. "Captain Bledsoe writes that he took Philip on as a favor to the people who'd been so kind to him in the sailor's rest at #1 Magnolia Lane. That's the address Philip attaches to your house." She peered over the top of her glasses at Jack, and he smiled. "The captain said Philip wanted to prove himself worthy to marry Camilla Johnson, the young lady who lived next door at #2 Magnolia Lane. That's exactly what I told you, that Philip told me!"

"I remember." Jack crooked his finger, drawing her closer to him and the manifest. "Here's what I found. Captain Bledsoe captained only one ship. And its name was," he pointed to the page, "*Sea Phantom*."

"Oh, my gosh." Sydney's skin was alive with goosebumps as she clasped her hands under her chin. "Phantom was the rest of the ship's name that Philip couldn't remember." *Whoosh*. She glanced up from the manifest and saw him. She tugged her glasses down her nose and looked at Jack. "Jack, your mind's opening up at least just a little."

"I don't know about that."

"Yes, it is, or I couldn't see Philip standing behind you, looking over your shoulder at the manifest." Jack frowned and opened his mouth to speak, but she laid a hand on his arm and stared past him. "Was your ship called *Sea Phantom*, Philip?"

Tears collected in Sydney's eyes. "Philip says yes, it was *Sea Phantom*."

"I know you believe in all this, and I can't explain how you know so much when you arrived in St. Augustine, totally in the dark, but—"

"I can't explain why I can see Philip either."

"So maybe I've gone from disbeliever to objective bystander."

Sydney brought her gaze from over Jack's head to his eyes. "Philip is encouraging me to buy the manifest and journal. He's sure there will be clues to his death related by Captain Bledsoe in it."

"Is he giving you the money?" Jack asked with a tease rather than sarcasm in his voice.

"Philip says I can have the silver coins he brought back from his year's commission." Sydney looked at Philip again, and when Jack swiveled around to look behind him, she felt somewhat validated. And surprisingly, Philip didn't disappear. "But, there's a catch."

"That figures."

"Shh." Sydney put her finger to her lips. "What, Philip?"

She listened. "Camilla predicted his death the day he left St. Augustine. So when the *Sea Phantom* docked, Philip left his money with the captain. If something happened to him, Bledsoe was to give the money to Camilla. If she refused it, the captain was to bury the coins until she came to her senses."

"So, did she take the coins, or were they buried?"

"Philip, can you answer Jack's question?" Sydney paused for the answer, looked at Jack, and shrugged. "Philip has no memory of the weeks immediately following his death. He doesn't know if she took the coins, and he can't remember where he and the captain decided the money should be buried if she refused it."

"If Bledsoe was dishonest, the coins are long gone."

Sydney shook her head as Philip shook his. "Philip thinks he was an honest man and that the location could be buried in the captain's journal or manifest."

The antique dealer returned at that point and asked, "Have the captain's journal and manifest been of any help, Miss Crane?"

"Yes, sir," Sydney answered. "Are they for sale?"

"They can be yours for twenty-hundred each."

That moved the articles out of her reach. With a glance over Jack's shoulder and a shake of her head at Philip, Sydney closed Captain Bledsoe's journal with resignation. She spoke to the dealer in a soft but determined voice.

"I'll come back if we find..." Sydney began, "...when I have the money."

"You only have a week," Mr. Jenkins reminded her.

"If she's not interested in buying today, I could use the journal and manifest to help establish the histories of my Florida properties," Jack told the antique dealer. "The St. Augustine zoning commission has granted me permission to turn a couple of residential properties into a museum and an office."

"Oh, Jack, that's wonderful news," Sydney exclaimed.

"I'll give you two thousand for both, cash," Jack offered.

Twenty~Eight

Ten minutes and twenty-five hundred dollars later, Sydney nipped at Jack's heels as he carted the old leather-bound books in a box under his arm, away from the antique shop.

"May I read your books?" she asked sweetly as they walked to the car. "After all, you'd never have found them without me. Of course, they rightfully should belong to you since the houses are yours. And I'm really happy for you, so may I read them? Please?" She flirted playfully and batted her eyes at him. "Pretty please with sugar on top?"

"Slow down, chatterbox," Jack said with a chuckle. "Bledsoe may mention the location of the coins in his journal. If they're buried on my property, do you think a ghost can give them away to you?" Jack stopped at the Porsche and took out his car keys. "Were you going to steal them from me?" When her shoulders sagged, he felt guilty for teasing her.

"I hadn't thought of it like that," she whispered and looked him in the eye. "I'd have used the coins to buy the books. If you find them, why don't you use the money to restore your houses to their original selves?"

Jack laughed and handed her the box. "As far as the coins go, it's," he wrapped his arms around her and the box and kissed her lips, "finders keepers, baby."

"Losers weepers?" Sydney asked and gazed over his shoulder. "Philip says he'll try hard to remember where the coins were buried in case Cammy refused to accept them."

Jack rolled his eyes skyward. "Philip can't fly, can he?"

"I don't know." Sydney paused and added, "He's gone now."

"Let's have lunch and head to the airport."

"You don't think we'll miss our flight, do you?"

"I know we won't. We're flying in a private, eight-passenger Cessna."

Sydney's eyes widened, and her mouth fell open. "A private plane will be a first."

"Jet," Jack corrected with a chuckle and let her into the car. He drove to St. Johns River Park in downtown Jacksonville. Putting on his jacket, he walked her into a restaurant, looking out at a spectacular fountain.

"This is a beautiful setting for lunch," Sydney said over her crystal goblet, fine china, and linen tablecloth. A waiter clad in a crisp black shirt and trousers approached, and as Sydney took the menu he offered, she commented, "That's the prettiest fountain I've ever seen. Does it have a name?"

"Friendship Fountain," the waiter replied.

Sydney looked at Jack, who winked and took the menu handed to him. Sydney's smile alone was worth every cent of bringing her to the most expensive restaurant in Jacksonville. She opened the menu, saying she was so excited about the manifest, journal, and jetting to

New York City she couldn't concentrate on the menu choices. Jack made a couple of suggestions and ordered. After a delicious lunch of Caesar salads, fresh baked bread, and lobster tails, the waiter returned with the check. Sydney fished her credit card out of her purse, and as she handed it to the waiter, Jack snared it. He shook his head and gave his credit card to the waiter. They departed the restaurant and headed to the airport.

"Are you going to return my card?" Sydney asked.

"Maybe when we get back to St. Augustine. This trip is on me."

"Thank you, Jack," Sydney said softly.

At the Jacksonville International Airport, Jack left his Porsche in a parking garage near the private plane entrance. He tipped an airline employee to take Sydney's bag, tucked the box of books under one arm, and grasped Sydney's hand with his other hand. She was all eyes as he walked her through a V.I.P. waiting room and out to the tarmac.

"Hey there, Jack." The pilot sitting in the cockpit of a white jet saluted Jack as he and Sydney stepped into the plane. "Touched down a little while ago. We're refueled, and I'll request clearance to take off whenever you're ready."

"Sounds good," Jack said, shaking hands with him. "Monty is my favorite pilot, "Jack said, turning to Sydney. "Monty, this is my friend, Sydney, and we're ready to go."

The airline employee stowed Sydney's bag and departed. Jack and Monty caught up with each other for a couple of minutes as Sydney gazed into the interior of the jet. Up front, there were four white leather seats facing each other. Behind those seats, a white couch set on the right side, opposite a large flatscreen and two more white leather seats. As Jack hung back and spoke to the Monty, Sydney took a seat on the white sofa. Beyond the sofa was a wet bar.

"Obviously, there's no stewardess, but the wet bar and galley are stocked with snacks, soft drinks, liquor, and wine," Jack said, walking toward her. "What would you like?"

"Surprise me."

As the pilot closed the plane door, Jack placed the box with the books beside her and went to the wet bar. As the engines revved, he thought Sydney looked a little over-whelmed by it all. He filled a couple of crystal tumblers and returned to the sofa. Taking off his jacket, he sat down next to her.

"Bourbon and cola?" He handed her a glass. As they taxied down the runway, he said, "To fireworks in the city."

"To fireworks in the city."

They clinked glasses and drank. Sydney coughed, and Jack chuckled. "Buckle up, baby," he said to her as he had in the Porsche and buckled his seatbelt as she did the same.

"Your company must be doing very well," Sydney murmured.

"Yeah," was all he said as the jet picked up speed.

"No wonder we're polar opposites," Sydney said. "We're from two different worlds."

"East Coast versus West Coast," Jack replied casually.

Sydney made no further comment, but that wasn't what she'd meant by polar opposites. Should she level with Jack? If not, might he feel her silence on the subject was the same as a lie? It wasn't fair to pass herself off as someone who was accustomed to his lifestyle, living in a home like the Queen Anne house, or a person who could easily afford to buy men's silk shorts. Or riding in a car worth more than a house...or flying in a private jet.

Sydney clasped her hands in her lap and cringed. It had taken her since high school graduation to save up five thousand dollars. Jack had pulled half that out of his money clip, like pocket change, when he'd paid for the journal and manifest.

However, she reasoned, she fully expected they'd go their separate ways at the end of the summer. In that case, she could leave without embarrassing herself in regard to her modest roots. Hugging herself, she wished she could hug Jack. But not trusting herself to ever let him go, she didn't touch him.

"We're airborne now, you can relax," Jack said.

Letting him think the take-off was the reason for her apprehension, Sydney nodded. Jack handed her the box from the antique store, and with a tremble in her voice, she turned to him and asked quietly, "Do you want the journal or the manifest?"

He asked for the journal, and for the next hour, they spoke only when passing along bits and pieces of information. Jack decided aloud that Captain Bledsoe enjoyed the local gossip as he knew everything about everybody in St. Augustine per the musings in his journal.

When they were over Virginia, according to the pilot, Jack said, "The captain refers to Camilla as Philip's noble maiden. For the last few pages, he has written about a guy named Striker. He says in 1772, Striker began calling himself the *Lord of St. Augustine*. Sounds like Striker was loyal to the King George III of England." Referring to the journal again, he continued, "The captain detested Striker, saying he cheated people out of property, chased women a third of his age, and had henchmen eliminate anybody who got in his way. Wonder what, if anything, Striker had to do with Camilla after Philip went to sea."

Sydney leaned lightly against Jack in order to see Bledsoe's handwriting in the journal. "Striker must be the so-called lord whom Cammy feared she would be forced to marry should something go wrong with her plan to marry Philip."

"If Camilla's family was wealthy, Striker probably wanted her for the dowry her father would have offered," Jack suggested in a grumble.

"If Cammy's father wasn't wealthy, he may have been selling her to Striker."

"That's true. Some people will do anything for money."

Sydney flinched. Jack had thought she was going to steal the coins from him. He'd surely suspect she was a gold-digger when he found out she was from a middle-class family. Her father was an electrician and owned a small construction company. Her mother was his secretary, and Sydney's two older brothers worked for him.

Jack was way out of her league. Simply stated, she wasn't good enough for him. As that sinking feeling churned in the pit of her stomach, she leaned away from Jack and tried to read. But he held the journal at an angle to make that impossible. Trying to lighten her own mood, she teased, "Jack Malone, let me see that journal, or I'll punch you."

"I'm shakin' in my shoes, baby." He grinned and tugged her back to where she'd been. "Promise you'll do bed and breakfast with me tonight and in the morning, and I'll let you see the journal."

"That's blackmail." Desire shot through Sydney as she pictured herself snuggled in bed with Jack as they'd been in his recliner. She definitely would…probably should… maybe could try not to let that happen. "I have to use the ladies room." She pulled away and said, "Think about giving me the journal when I get back."

Jack lassoed her with his arms and locked his fingers at her upper arm. "Give me an answer now about bed and breakfast, or I'll make you sit here and wet your panties."

"Who said I have panties on?" If she couldn't keep from flirting with this man, however would she keep from going to bed with him? "But I am a *noble maiden*."

Jack groaned. "Don't I know it."

When Sydney raised a brow, he let her go

Twenty-Nine

A s Jack sat alone, he imagined Sydney in bed with another man. Though the man was faceless, he had proposed and married her. On their wedding night, as the husband leaned over her in bed, Sydney placed her left hand on the back of his head. On her finger was a diamond ring. Sydney had gone to her imaginary husband a noble maiden, as she'd planned. Her marriage bed sheets were white, her gauzy negligee was white, and Jack saw red. A red blood stain, proof of her virginity, on the white sheet.

Then he saw white, Sydney's short, white skirt. Her rounded fanny was so sexy he'd like nothing better than to clamp his hands to her hips and pull her onto his lap for a kiss. But he kept his hands to himself, like she'd told him to do. When she was seated beside him, he handed her the journal she'd asked for without pressing her for an answer about bed and breakfast.

Offering nothing but a smile, Sydney put her nose in the journal. She was still a noble maiden. What right did he have to alter that? Why should she change her values to please him? He'd recently lectured her on compromise.

But how much compromise was too much? Jack was a million miles away until she grabbed his arm.

"Jack," she gasped. "According to Captain Bledsoe, Striker went to jail for murder."

"Does the captain say who Striker murdered?"

Sydney opened her mouth to answer him when Monty spoke to them over the intercom. "Thanks for requesting me on this flight, Jack. Shawn was at LaGuardia and livid over finding out you gave the job to me."

"You're welcome, Monty," Jack said, hoping he'd leave it at that.

"Who's Shawn?" Sydney asked Jack. "Why is he so mad?"

"Shawn's another pilot."

"Yeah," Monty continued, "she was ranting and raving."

"Oh," Sydney murmured. "Shawn has a name which can go either way. Like mine. Do you fly her often?"

Jack chuckled at the way she'd phrased that. "Not lately." Sydney showed no reaction. Maybe he wouldn't have minded a jealous pout. "Did Striker murder the person with a gun?"

Sydney looked at the journal and answered, "Yes. Captain Bledsoe claims Striker shot one of his sailors in cold blood. As of this page, Bledsoe hasn't said who the sailor was, only that Striker was arrested."

"Let me see." Jack carefully tugged the ancient journal halfway between them. "The Old Jail Museum on San Marco Avenue in St. Augustine might have historical records to verify some or all of this. I've heard the jail also has ghost tours."

"I have my own ghost for tours," Sydney reminded him. They scanned the next few pages together, and then she read the captain's words aloud, "The sadness at

#1and #2 Magnolia Lane is overwhelming. As I set sail today, I can rejoice only in knowing Malcolm Striker will stand trial for the murder of young *Philip Burke*." Sydney looked at Jack in wonder. "Maybe he did kill Philip!"

"There ya go." Jack sounded noncommittal, but how the hell did Sydney know all of this random history unless a ghost told her?

Sydney squared her shoulders. "My first stop when we get back to St. Augustine will be the Old Jail Museum. I'm not going to tell Philip anything until I have solid facts."

"Does that mean you don't see him on the plane?"

"He said he was staying near Cammy in St. Augustine." She smiled as though she appreciated the lack of sarcasm in his voice. "I want to forget about Philip while we're in New York. I'll deal with him when we get back to Florida. Would that be a good compromise?"

"Yeah, good deal." Jack wrapped an arm around her and kissed her.

After the plane touched down at LaGuardia Airport, Sydney descended the steps as Jack grabbed her bag. Jack called out thanks and goodbye to Monty. A black limousine waited for them near the runway, and a uniformed driver opened a door for them.

"A limo?" Sydney whispered. "Wow."

"Easiest way into the Financial District," Jack said, grasping her hand.

The limousine whisked them toward Manhattan. Along the thirty-five-minute ride, Sydney said she was excited to see New York City for the first time. Jack smiled and opened the sunroof so that she could view the tops of skyscrapers. Then she swiveled in her seat as he pointed out the East River, Central Park, and Museum of Modern Art. On Wall Street, she was astounded by the honking taxis, yelling cabbies, and general traffic jam.

"How do you ever find a parking space?"

"It's tough."

"This is life in a faster lane than I'm used to coming from the midst of orange groves," Sydney said.

"Orange groves sound nice. Maybe I'll fly you out there if you decide to go home."

"Oh no, you'd find Redlands boring," she told him a little too fast.

Jack looked away, figuring he wasn't the type of man she wanted to take home to meet her parents. Bones was the kind of guy they were no doubt accustomed to meeting. Jack, however, would have been proud to introduce Sydney to his parents. He wished that were possible. Since it wasn't, he couldn't wait to show her off to the people in the Wall Street firm.

"In case you noticed the gap in the skyline of buildings in uptown Manhattan, that's due to the bedrock not being sturdy enough to support the structural integrity of skyscrapers," Jack said, bringing his thoughts back to the city. "We're on Wall Street now, which is only eight blocks long." Sydney nodded, asked questions, and soon he pointed out the New York Stock Exchange at 11 Wall Street and 18 Broad Street. "This headquarters is actually two connected buildings accounting for the two addresses. The Exchange is a national historic landmark."

"Is that a statue of a child in front of the building?"

"That's Fearless Girl," he replied. "She was moved from Broad Street in front of the Charging Bull statue to the Wall Street location on International Women's Day in 2017. She stands for equal rights and a safe and fair work environment for women."

"I like her." Sydney smiled. "I can't wait to visit your Wall Street office."

"Here on the east side of Lower Manhattan, as you can see, the skyscrapers are back." As the limo slowed down, he said, "My office is in a medium-tall building."

"There's a beautiful building." Sydney pointed. "It reminds me of pictures I've seen of the Arc de Triomphe in Paris." She said as the limo double-parked in front of the building.

"My building. Neo-classical Roman architecture," Jack replied. "We're here."

He enjoyed the impressed surprise on her face. Stepping onto the curb in front of one of the two buildings he owned in New York City, the other being the brownstone, Jack helped Sydney out of the car and grabbed her bag. The brass front door of this building, established after the great stock market crash of 1929, was opened by a doorman who greeted Jack warmly but formally. Jack left her bag with him. The lobby had three elevators; one was for large pieces of furniture as well as tenants on the twenty floors between the ground floor and penthouse. The ceiling was two stories tall and had been tastefully decorated by his mother. Above three gold-framed portraits of the firm's founders was a huge gold plaque that read *Malone Building*.

"Your relatives," Sydney said, stopping near the oil portraits with nameplates.

"My dad, Granddad, and great grandfather Malone."

Sydney paused to look at each one. Jack gave her a tug. The moment they walked into the expansive suite of offices on the first floor, the manager of the firm spotted them.

"Hi, Jack," Angus called.

Jack proudly introduced Sydney to the prematurely gray-haired man wearing glasses and a three-piece suit.

As Angus shook Sydney's hand, Jack saw her through the intrigued gaze of his friend and senior employee.

Sydney was not just the girl next door. She was an educated, sophisticated woman. She was beautiful and effortlessly sexy, commanding attention without trying. Leslie Bowen was tame competition compared to what Jack would face had he met Sydney in Manhattan. As he walked her in the direction of his office several of the brokers, who worked in the open area of the bullpen, noticed her. These employees were a long way from having earned a private office. But a couple of them who had been with the firm since Jack had taken over came charging, yes charging, like bulls. They greeted him, their eyes on the woman beside him.

Possessiveness washed over Jack. The enjoyment of introducing Sydney to his friends and colleagues fought with the unexpected urge to keep her to himself. Jack noted blatant lust on men's faces as they stared at Sydney. Even the female brokers seemed charmed by her.

Placing his hand on the small of Sydney's back, he steered her away from the group of people. Heading down a wide hallway, they passed the private offices of the established brokers and were stopped several times. Jack sensed the envy of his colleagues. One man released Sydney's hand only when her arm had stretched as far as it could.

As they continued down the hall, Jack envisioned himself in place of the faceless, imaginary groom who had walked Sydney down an aisle of a church. Marriage is what it would take to keep a woman like Sydney to himself. His parents had had a great marriage. He would settle for nothing less. To him, a great marriage meant a loving wife and kids. Jack stopped, stunned by his train of thought.

"Is this your office?" Sydney asked.

Jack gave himself a shake. "Yeah."

"Beautiful."

"Yes, you are. The most beautiful woman in any room."

From the gleaming black walnut furniture to the plush color-of-money carpets over hardwood floors, from the window treatments of the tall windows to the leather couches and chairs, this was the Wall Street office clients expected of the firm's owner. Jack sat down in an executive-style leather swivel chair behind his desk. When he crooked a finger at Sydney, she glided to him, and he pulled her onto his lap.

Without a word, he slid his hand to the nape of her slender neck and kissed her sweet lips. The things this woman could make him think and feel were monumental. In her own way, she was a first for him. Whenever he saw her, he wanted her in his arms. And when she was there, he wanted to take her beyond into limitless skies.

"I think you should be licensed," she whispered.

"I am." He wrapped his arms around her and laced his fingers at her hips. "With the Securities and Exchange Commission."

Sydney slipped one arm around his neck and grasped the lapel of his jacket with her other hand. "I mean licensed as lethal because your appeal is dangerous. Didn't you notice the way those women out there ogled you?"

"Ogled?" Jack chuckled. "All I saw were the men lusting after you the minute we walked in the door."

"The women couldn't keep their hands off you," Sydney said. "Brushing against you when they welcomed you or touching your arm while asking a question." She placed a hand on his arm and squeezed for emphasis. "I'll bet you run a tight ship around here because you have the female secretaries and brokers eating out of the palm of your hand."

"Know where the palm of my hand is itching to be?" he asked. She arched a brow, silently telling him she knew. "I wanna take you to my city home, Sydney. Come on."

With a pat on her hip, he let her off his lap. Indicating a private bath, he escorted her past the room with his workout equipment and a walk-in closet. Through a back door of the office, they entered a private hallway and elevator. There, Jack picked up her bag, delivered by the doorman. Using a key instead of pushing a button, when the elevator opened, it was to his living room in the penthouse. Being on the twenty-second floor and filled with floor-to-ceiling windows, it offered a panoramic view of the Financial District and overlooked the East River.

"This is beyond words, Jack," Sydney said in obvious awe as she looked right and left.

Leading her further into the room furnished with traditional-style sofas and chairs, he casually walked her through it to a formal dining room that could seat twelve, an airy kitchen full of stainless steel and granite, a mahogany wood-paneled library, and three bedrooms. Sydney commented, using the words *palatial* and *magnificent*. In the third bedroom, he set down her overnight bag.

Decorated similarly, to the St. Augustine house and the Upper East Side brownstone, the penthouse held expensive artwork and leather furniture with plush carpets over hardwood floors. Before taking her into his master bedroom, it occurred to him Sydney had commented less and less during the tour.

"This building originally belonged to my great grandfather Malone, who bought it for a song, as they say, after the 1929 stock market crash. It was passed down through the family to my dad, who gifted it to Alexander and me when I got my master's degree and Alex got his bachelor's degree," Jack explained. "With the agreement I'd keep an eye on my little brother, we moved out of our apartments in the brownstone and into this penthouse. I found Buster abandoned in Central Park and Alex referred to us as the three amigos."

"Buster is, as they say, a lucky dog." Sydney smiled with empathy, not mentioning his brother. Jack took her hand and walked her into his bedroom. "How can you consider leaving all of this and living in St. Augustine?" she asked. "Everything in New York City seems so much more, I don't know, important than anywhere else I've ever been."

He turned to her and said, "People are important."

"Yes." Sydney wound her arms around his waist and flattened her hands to his back. "People are more important than anything. I'd miss my parents if they were gone. But you know what they told me once?" Jack leaned back and shook his head. "That when they're gone, they hope I'll remember them with love but not give up my dreams."

"Who said New York City is my dream?" Wondering why she would say that, he pulled out of her arms. "You were the one who said I could furnish one of the Magnolia Road homes as a branch office."

Sydney brought her hands to his chest, her green eyes capturing him. "I don't think you should let their deaths cost you the enjoyment of this inheritance. You owe it to the people you loved so much not to change."

Why had she been so quick to shoot down the idea of him flying her out to California? Why didn't she want him next door in St. Augustine? "Who else do you love, Sydney?"

Thirty

"**B**esides my parents, Mike and Kathy, I love my four brothers who go by their nicknames; J.D., Will, T.J., and Chuck, two sets of grandparents, aunts, uncles, and too many cousins to count."

Jack chuckled. "You're the lucky dog." He walked away from her to a plate glass window. Sydney followed him and pretended to be interested in the traffic down on the street and the boats out on the river. "I don't have anybody like that to love."

You have me, and I love you, Jack.

What? She loved this man? Yes! She had fallen head over heels in love with him. And yet, Jack had all but just said he didn't love her. To keep from expressing her thoughts aloud, she pressed her lips tightly together.

Standing at the huge window overlooking New York City, the small window in Jack's house with a view of the forlorn pier flashed in her mind. What she'd seen in that attic was a fleeting ghost of a man. Were the emotions Jack evoked in her fleeting or solid? Maybe thinking she loved him was nothing more than jet lag. She chided herself. Seeing Philip Burke for the first time hadn't been jet lag. And neither was this all-consuming love she'd just admitted to herself that she felt for Jack Malone.

He'd not mentioned his brother for a while. Was Jack thinking of Alexander now and the escape route he'd taken from pain? She might not be good enough for Jack to love, but he should know someone loved him. If she couldn't say it, she could hint, and she could show it.

"Besides my family," Sydney began, mentally treading on eggshells, "I love my friends. You're my friend, Jack."

"Just because I'm your friend doesn't give me the right to change you, Sydney," he said without looking at her.

"It's too late, Jack." Taking hold of his arm, she turned him to face her. "You've already changed me."

"Yeah, by taking you too fast and too far." Jack shook his head. Shoving his hands in his pockets, he said, "I haven't changed you physically. Forget what I said about compromise, I don't want you to feel pressured. That's why I left your bag in a guest room. You say no to bed and breakfast, and I'll back off."

"I know you would." She slid her hand down his arm and took his big, strong hand in hers. She swallowed the lump in her throat. "I'm not feeling pressured to compromise, I'm feeling scared to death of what I'll miss with you if I don't compromise." She didn't mean just the physical aspects. But she didn't want to *scare* him off by admitting she had fallen fast and far for him. "I don't want you to back off."

His ocean blue eyes narrowed as he studied her. "Then you'll cheerfully wave goodbye to me at the end of the summer."

Sydney saw him tense. She didn't want to lie to him, but she realized she couldn't turn him loose now, no matter what. At least not cheerfully. Her heart would break. "Stockbrokers are risk takers, aren't they?"

"Did Philip and Camilla risk becoming lovers?"

"Yes."

"We see how that worked out."

His cell rang, and Jack motioned her to follow him as he answered the call. He led her back to the guest bedroom. She saw her bag and walked past it to the window. Sydney realized Jack had confirmed his plan for them to go their separate ways at the summer's end. Had he just tried to give himself an out by offering to back off and by bringing her to the guest bedroom?

Polar opposites again. She'd gone from admonishing herself to tell him no to asking him not to back off. Such inner turmoil and confusion swirled. Sydney placed her fingertips to her temples. She wanted this man, body and soul. She'd take the risk and deal with the consequences...later.

"That was Angus, he made dinner reservations for us," Jack said.

Turning to him, Sydney smiled, determined to stay upbeat for Jack's sake. "Sounds wonderful."

Standing just inside the bedroom, he said, "Yeah."

"How should I dress?"

"For a dinner cruise and dance around the Statue of Liberty."

"How exciting!" Sydney clasped her hands under her chin.

"Exciting," Jack repeated, maybe remembering when she'd called him exciting. "I'm going to shower. You have a private bath. I'll meet you in the living room."

He left her standing at the window.

~

Sydney unpacked and showered. After doing her hair and makeup, she selected an outfit and met Jack in the living room. Standing near a wet bar, he looked spectacular. Sipping a drink, he wore a white dress shirt with a navy and green paisley tie. His navy slacks were sinfully snug, and on his feet, he wore shiny black loafers. As she neared him, one thought took precedence, coming back to the penthouse with him. Stopping next to him, his masculine scent thrilled her. He smelled absolutely delectable.

"You are so handsome," Sydney whispered.

"Thank you, color of money." Jack smiled.

Sydney wore her hair in long waves with a one-piece, green silk jumpsuit. Billowing long sleeves cuffed her wrists and were in sharp contrast to the silk clinging to her body. An almost invisible zipper, which started at hip level, fastened the front of the outfit, stopping at a daringly low, vee neck. She hoped the fragrance she had misted on her skin would appeal to him as much as his did to her. If he kissed her, she feared—no, she hoped— they'd never make it out of his penthouse.

Grabbing a navy jacket, he winked and held out his arm. "Let's go."

The doorman had a car waiting, and it whisked them to Pier 36. There, they boarded a three-deck vessel where they met up with Angus, his wife, and four other couples. Shortly after seven o'clock, over shrimp cocktails and champagne, Angus made a toast mentioning the Malone Building. Seeing those words in writing and now hearing them spoken caused the memory of asking Jack if he'd gone belly up in the brokerage business to smack Sydney with embarrassment. After clinking her glass to

Jack's and others and taking a sip, she lowered her head and rubbed her left temple.

"What's up, Doc?" Jack asked, slipping his arm around her shoulders.

With his friends nearby, there was only so much privacy. Sydney turned her head to him and asked softly, "Why didn't you level with me about all of this?"

"I thought I gave you a couple of hints," he said with a charming grin tugging at his lips. "Besides the Porsche, the jet was a tip-off."

"It was part of a cloak-and-dagger routine, which you don't let me get away with," she reminded him. Didn't the same apply to her in regard to her modest background? "Why didn't you just come straight out and tell me you were a multimillionaire?"

"You didn't ask. But isn't that why you wanted to see my New York office and brownstone? You suspected?"

"No." Sydney shook her head. "Did you offer to fly me home at the end of summer to find out if I'm a middle-class gold-digger?"

"I know you aren't a gold-digger." His smile was sincere. "Middle-class or not, you're rich with family. Why didn't you tell me you had four brothers who might kick my ass for lusting after their baby sister?"

"Your first hint was when I said I knew guys as big and tough as you. Your second tip-off was telling you I knew other guys who played basketball. And I'm the baby sister to only two of them. I'm a big sister to the other two." She paused then and asked in amazement, "Are you lusting after me?"

Jack's eyes and grin smoldered, and his voice was husky as he said, "Yes, I am, chatterbox. Wanna skip the Statue of Liberty and swim the East River?"

"Yes," she said, desire simmering within her. "Let's go."

Jack chuckled. "Afraid we're stuck on this boat for a three-hour tour, Gilligan."

"Aye, aye, Skipper," she said with a laugh. "I watched reruns of Gilligan's Island with my grandparents."

～

They sailed past Lady Liberty, and eight o'clock sharp found them in an elegant dining room. Sitting at a large, round table, filets, lobsters, salmon, and prime rib were served as wine, beer, and cocktails flowed. Desserts were rolled to the table on a fancy cart. Sydney chose chocolate cake, and Jack picked cherry cheesecake. At nine, music sounded above them, and they climbed the stairs to the top deck. As a live band performed, Jack leaned against a railing and pulled her to him. But he didn't kiss her.

When the band played a slow dance, she whispered, "Dance with me, Jack."

Jack led her to the dance floor. Sydney was only vaguely aware of the fabulous city lights glittering in the background as the handsome man took her in his strong embrace. Starting out with one hand on his shoulder and the other holding his hand, mid-song, she closed her eyes and twined her arms around his neck. The next dance was a fast one, and Jack grasped her hand, twirling her in a circle and then pulling her back to him. All too soon, it was ten o'clock, and they docked where they'd begun at Pier 36. They bid Jack's friends and coworkers an upcoming Happy Fourth of July and goodnight.

Thirty-One

On the way back to the penthouse, Jack asked the limo driver to take a different route. Pointing to a brownstone on the Upper East Side, he gave Sydney an outside view of the place where he'd grown up. From there, they headed back to the Malone Building. In record time, he walked the beautiful woman through the empty lobby and into the private elevator. As they zoomed to the sky, Jack wrapped Sydney's tempting body in his arms, all the while telling himself to back off.

"You don't own that beautiful brownstone we saw too." She laughed. "Do you?"

"Yes."

The elevator stopped, and Sydney stood still, seemingly awestruck. Jack chuckled as he stepped out of the elevator and into the living room. Sydney didn't move. He slapped his hand to the elevator door to keep it from closing.

"Come on," he urged and held out his other hand to her.

"The house I grew up in could fit into this elevator," Sydney whispered.

"So?"

"So—I just thought you ought to know."

Jack tugged her out of the elevator and into the living room. If there was urgency in his step, he knew it was due to his need to be alone with Sydney. Whether they went to bed or not, she'd offered to compromise her standards. He wondered if she might care about him beyond the summer. But for now, tonight loomed, and he wanted to make love to her.

"Want something to drink?" he asked, and she nodded. Good, it might help her relax. She seemed nervous. He understood. She was a noble maiden who found herself on the probable brink of surrendering her virginity to a man promising her absolutely nothing. In accompanying him across the room, when she caught the heel of her stiletto on the carpet, he scooped her up and carried her from the living room to the kitchen. Setting her on the granite counter beside the stainless steel refrigerator, he said, "Your choices include my specialties— beer, wine, bourbon and cola, or decaf."

"Hmm," Sydney said in thought as he flattened his hands to the granite on either side of her hips. "You choose for me."

Looking her in the eye, Jack grinned. "Seems to me that beer loosens your tongue, wine loosens your inhibitions, and decaf puts you to sleep in my arms. Have all three."

"No." Sydney giggled.

"Wanna try bourbon and cola without the cola?"

Jack stepped back and took off his jacket. He tossed it onto the counter and ran a hand through his hair. Sydney reached forward and grasped his tie. Tugging him closer, she loosened it. Jack untied it the rest of the way and gave it a toss onto his jacket. She unbuttoned the first two buttons on his shirt, and he pulled the tails out of his slacks. He took off one of her stilettos, then the other. He set them on the floor and opened the fridge.

"Let's go for the wine," Jack decided and gave her a rakish grin as he pulled out a bottle of Chardonnay.

"Let's."

At the whoosh of the refrigerator door, he noticed Sydney tense. He lifted her off the counter and handed her the chilled bottle. Taking two wine glasses out of a cupboard, he led her into the living room. After they sat down on a long couch, he placed the glasses and wine on an end table and took her in his arms.

"What's wrong, Sydney? You're shaking."

"I thought I heard Philip in the kitchen. But I think it was just the closing of the refrigerator door."

Jack let go of her and lit a candle in a glass jar. He poured their wine and handed her a glass. "When you said Philip was number three on your list of why we couldn't make love in St. Augustine, it occurred to me to bring you to New York. You said you wanted to forget about him while we're here. But if that's changed—"

"It hasn't," Sydney interrupted, and they touched glasses. "I know Philip's not here, so why am I still shaking?"

"You're nervous about going to bed with me."

In the sweetest of whispers, she asked, "Are you nervous?"

"No." He eased back and smiled. "But I'm looking forward to it."

Jack drank his wine slowly and watched Sydney take several gulps. He made her slow down, and when her glass was empty, he set it on the end table. Wrapping her in his arms again, he stared into her eyes before closing his and then touching his mouth to hers. Gauging her response, he noted her lips parting and her tongue playing with his as she wrapped her arms around his neck and snuggled closer. He pulled her onto his lap and grinned into their kiss.

Apparently feeling his smile, she said against his lips, "Our deal was if you showed me your office and apartment, I'd wear a bra. I've had one on all day."

"I like that you're not a deal breaker." Leaning back, he smoothed a lock of silky hair away from her cheek. I'm a deal keeper too."

Sydney wiggled off his lap, stood, and held out her hand. Jack took hold, and with her slight tug, he was off the sofa. Holding tight to her hand, he wrapped an arm around her waist and molded her body to his. Running a hand down the small of her back to her fanny, when he squeezed, she stood on tiptoes, deepening their kiss.

Ending the kiss and keeping her hand in his, Jack grabbed the candle and trailed Sydney behind him to his master bedroom. There, he placed the candle on a nightstand. The light flickered on that side of the room as moonlight spilled in from the windows on the other side. He stepped out of his shoes beside the king-size bed. Kissing a fragrant spot behind her ear, he took hold of her zipper and lowered it. Opening the front of her outfit, he smiled at seeing her delicate, white lace bra.

"Up or down, you're good with zippers," she said, reminding him of when he'd zipped up her shorts in his kitchen.

"Let's take your back pockets off."

"I don't have back—" she caught his tease and giggled. Nervously.

Blood pounded in Jack's veins. With his mouth on hers, he stroked her lips with his tongue. Sliding his hands into the front of her jumpsuit, he laid the sides open and eased them off her shoulders. The green silk fluttered to her waist, and she slipped her arms out of the sleeves. Jack reached around her, unfastened her bra, and let it drop to the floor.

"You're sensational, Sydney."

With her breasts fully exposed, he took their weight in his hands and massaged the tips with his thumbs. The hot blood racing into his lower body hardened him. Sydney moved her hands up between his forearms and, starting where she left off, unbuttoned his shirt. Jack shed his shirt and placed his hands on her waist. With a tug, her outfit fluttered down her shapely legs and puddled on the floor around her bare feet. He took her hands and brought them to his belt. She unbuckled it and unzipped his slacks. He let them follow her outfit to the floor and stepped out of his pants. They faced each other, her in white lace panties and him in the blue silk shorts she'd given him.

Sydney's lashes lowered. Long waves of silky blond hair framed her gorgeous face and touched the pink tips of her breasts. Splaying pretty hands over her indented belly button, she hooked her panties with her thumbs. Without looking up at him, she tugged her underwear down. Desire flamed in Jack's loins as he gazed between her legs. She stepped out of her panties, and as her hands would have covered what Jack was burning to touch, he stopped her.

"Please don't hurt me, Jack."

"I won't." Jack's masculinity rocketed to the moon as male protectiveness kicked in, heightening his craving for this delicate virgin. Hurting her in any way was the furthest thing from his mind. Placing his hands to her face, he tilted her head up, and when her eyes met his, he said, "You tell me to stop, and I will."

Sydney circled a finger over the black hair surrounding his navel, and Jack shivered as she traced the path down his stomach to the waistband of his shorts. As she skimmed her finger back up his stomach, Jack lowered his boxers.

"I've never seen a naked man," she said, a quiver in her voice a moment before Jack's erection sprang free. His shorts dropped to the floor, and her gaze followed them. From the glistening, dark pink tip to the base of his manhood, the source of his heat was long and thick. Studying him, she said, "It's way too big. It's not going to fit—you know, inside me."

Jack wondered how she could say all the things that made him feel like twice the man he'd ever felt with any other woman. Was he falling in love with Sydney? Yes. Could he stop himself? No. He had fallen hard, and there was no turning back.

"Let's make it fit." He flipped the comforter and top sheet back on his bed. "Come on."

Sydney's magnificent body graced his fresh, white cotton sheets. With a brave smile, she crooked her finger, and he was the sailor drawn to the siren's shore. As he stretched out beside her, she placed a dainty hand on the back of his head, and he felt her trembling. When her lips touched his ear, he heard the echoing tremor in her soft voice.

"Tell me what you want, Jack. I'm so afraid I won't be able to please you."

Jack groaned in disbelief. "You've got to be kidding."

This woman was every man's fantasy. He kissed her lips and rained kisses down her graceful neck. Tasting the swell of her breast quickened the beat of his heart. Closing his lips over the beaded pucker of one breast kicked his need for her into high gear. She arched her back, and he kissed her other nipple, tenderly sucking it further into his mouth. His lips took the same journey her zipper had made, and he teased her belly button with his tongue. Parting her knees, he touched his lips to her inside thigh. She moaned, and he nibbled up her leg.

"Jack, where are you going?"

"Crazy."

He loved this woman, body, heart, and soul. He wanted her first time to be as exciting, as sensual, and as memorable as he could possibly make it. Jack's gentle kiss found her velvety center. Sydney gasped and momentarily stiffened. Then, giving in to the pleasure, her legs widened, and she shivered from head to toe. Jack held her as she clutched the sheets and moaned his name. With a kiss to her tummy, he rolled away and reached into his nightstand.

"Did I do something wrong?"

"Baby girl, you're perfect," Jack said then stretched out on his back with a condom in his hand. "Wanna put this on for me?"

"I'll try."

Giving her some instruction, she placed the protection at the damp tip of him. Glancing at him for approval, he smiled, and she covered him with the condom. Then he covered her by rolling on top of her. A dreamy sigh escaped her as she wrapped her arms around his neck and spread her legs.

"Mmm, Sydney," Jack whispered at her sexy, eager response.

With his hips between her silken thighs, he opened her with gentle fingers. As much as he needed to quickly fill her with aching heat, more importantly, he wanted to please her so totally she'd never want any man but him. He wanted…he needed to make Sydney his.

Bracing himself above her, blood pounded hot and hard. The fire coiling in his loins threatened to burn out of control if he didn't find relief. With a groan, he began his exploration. Her body quickly reminded him that she was a noble maiden, yet to be won. She was a tight squeeze but with patience he hadn't known he possessed, Jack buried his manhood to the hilt.

"Oww," Sydney's soft voice broke on a sob as she gripped him.

"I'm sorry," Jack whispered. Hardly believing this sensational beauty was giving him such a gift, he kissed away a single tear on her cheek. It was a priceless present that she could give only once in a lifetime, and she'd given it to him. "Want me to stop?"

"I want you to love me, Jack."

"Wrap your legs around my waist."

Sydney did so, roping his neck in an urgent embrace and pulling him to her. Brazen and wanton. That's the way she'd describe herself at having this handsome, intelligent man between her legs. Desirable and victorious. That's how this sophisticated, muscular male made her feel when he slipped his tongue into her mouth while his manhood was deep inside her.

Her body sizzled like a firecracker. Hard and fast, Jack built the electricity hotter and hotter until Sydney exploded with a white hot climax. Her bliss coincided with his ecstasy, and as he throbbed within her, Jack breathed heavily against her neck through clenched teeth. Sydney squeezed him, internally enjoying each pulse of his body. Every inner caress rippled new waves of rapture throughout her being.

"You're so good, Sydney," Jack whispered huskily as he lay on top of her. "If I hadn't had to work so hard to get inside you, I'd have sworn you'd had a lover before me."

Sydney stretched like a sated cat under him. "You

would have thought anybody was good after going without for two years."

Jack was quiet. Concerned over his silence, she scolded herself for her tendency to chatterbox the wrong thing at the wrong time. Sydney didn't let go of him when he started to roll off of her. He chuckled, rolled again, and tugged her on top of him. The summer was racing by too quickly. Though this was a meaningless affair to Jack, it meant everything to her. When she visualized waving goodbye to Jack, an unexpected sob escaped her as she lay on top of him.

"Regrets at what you gave me?" Jack asked.

"No. I need you to make love to me all night long."

And so he did.

Thirty-Two

"Hurry up, slow poke," Jack called at the penthouse elevator the next night. "Or you're gonna miss seeing the Fourth of July fireworks from the roof."

Laughing, Sydney dashed away from the fridge and out of the kitchen with two glasses of champagne. They had stayed in bed that morning, working up an appetite, and then strolled through Manhattan to a Chinese restaurant for lunch. Since Jack's firm in the Malone Building was closed in honor of the Fourth, they had made love on the couch in his office. Via limousine to a steakhouse near the brownstone he owned, they'd enjoyed a delicious seven-course dinner.

It was a sultry July night in New York City, so returning to the penthouse, they had changed out of their date clothes, had a glass of champagne, and showered together. Jack had tugged on a navy tee shirt and cargo shorts while Sydney pulled a red sundress on over her head. Surprising him with another glass of champagne to celebrate the fireworks, she met up with him in the living room.

They entered the elevator, and after pushing the button to the rooftop, Jack stepped behind her. Holding their glasses of champagne, Sydney giggled when Jack pressed her back to his muscular chest and cupped his hands to her breasts.

"No, I don't have a bra on," she offered before he asked. "You said you're glad I don't wear one when we're alone."

"You're exactly right," Jack began, and as she wiggled her fanny against him, he groaned. "Except, we won't be alone on the roof."

When the elevator doors opened to lively music, twinkling lights, and a flock of people on the rooftop, with a familiar pat on her butt, Jack let her go and took his champagne glass. He explained that tenants who leased apartments or offices in the Malone Building also had access to the rooftop. She vaguely wondered what twenty floors of leased space in Manhattan brought in a month and couldn't even fathom such a figure.

As they mingled, Sydney didn't miss the women who stared at or were bold enough to flirt with Jack right in front of her. He paid only polite attention to them and kept his arm around her or his hand in hers. At first, Sydney felt uncomfortably jealous, as she had the previous day with his female brokers and secretaries. But slowly, she began to appreciate that when he kissed her goodbye at summer's end, he wouldn't be alone. And that was a good thing. By the time fireworks burst across the sky, Sydney had formulated a tentative plan.

"Spectacular," she breathed, looking at the brilliant colors exploding and blending with the stars and moon. They toasted, and she asked, "Where are these fireworks being set off?"

Leaning against the brick wall around the edge of the building and also looking skyward, Jack replied, "They're launched from barges that are positioned in Midtown Manhattan along the East River." As people oohed and awwed, came and went on the rooftop, most of them paused to say hello. Jack said in her ear, "I swear the next guy who shakes my hand and *ogles* you will take a fast trip to the sidewalk. This'll be his twilight's last gleaming."

"You wouldn't throw somebody off this roof during a perilous fight, would you?"

"Hell, with all the bombs bursting in the air, no one would notice somebody flying over the ramparts."

"You're as gallant as you are glaring." Sydney laughed, but to be on the safe side, the next guy who stopped to speak to Jack only saw the back of her head. When the man left, Jack held her close, kissed her lips, and gave her hip a squeeze.

Red, white, and blue erupted in a spectacular fireworks finale, waving the American flag with its thirteen stars from 1776 across the night sky. Sydney recalled that the Treaty of Paris, which brought the American Revolution to a close after eight years of battle, had been signed in Paris, France, on September 3, 1783. It occurred to her that Philip Burke's tragic death in 1777 had stolen from him the opportunity to celebrate America's independence.

But she sensed this trip to New York City had signaled Jack's independence from tragic death and suffering. He had won a two-year battle. His scowls were gone. The loneliness in his eyes had vanished. His anger had dissipated. He was making love and back among the living. With every bone in her body and beat of her heart, Sydney knew Jack would thrive. By September 1of this year, she would fly back to Redlands, and Jack Malone would be free.

"Land of the free," Sydney whispered with a choke in her voice.

"Home of the brave," Jack added and hugged her. "Come on, *fearless girl*, let's go make our own fireworks."

"I thought you'd never ask."

Thirty-Three

Thirty-Three

The next afternoon, Jack set Sydney's bag by the elevator door. He was anxious to get back to St. Augustine. He could hardly wait to resume the slower pace on Magnolia Road with Sydney in his arms and bed every night. He couldn't remember ever being so happy. He was looking forward to the future again instead of resenting it.

As he walked to the kitchen, it occurred to him that Sydney had been dragging her feet all day about going home, and he couldn't figure out why. As usual, when they were out of bed, they tended to be on different wavelengths. He'd been toying with the idea of asking her to move in with him. She walked into the kitchen wearing her hair in a bouncing ponytail and a sassy blue sundress as sexy as the red one he'd stripped off of her after the fireworks.

He loved this woman and figured now was as good a time as any to ask her to live with him. "Sydney—"

"Jack," she interrupted, purse in her hand and gaze on the floor, "when we get back to Florida, I'm going to have to concentrate on my research. I'll give you any information about your houses that I find, but I may just text it rather than pester you in person."

"What are you talking about?" Jack asked, taking her jab to the heart.

"I chatter too much, and I'm sure you have better things to do than listen to me drone on about Philip and Cammy, especially considering how you feel about ghosts."

"When you asked if forgetting Philip while we were in New York was a good compromise, I agreed." Jack stared at the top of her head as she picked a piece of invisible lint off the short skirt of her sundress. "But I didn't know you meant he would be your sole interest when we got back to Florida."

"Actually, I'm not sure I can deal with Philip should I fail to find out what went wrong back in 1776." Studying the front of the refrigerator now, she said, "So, I think I should move out of the Queen Anne House."

Jack flattened a hand to the granite counter to brace himself. The agony of losing someone you loved slammed into him all over again. "Are you giving me notice?" Instead of answering, Sydney turned away from him. He thought she might have swiped a tear off her cheek. He caught her arm, turned her to face him, and repeated. "Are you giving me notice?"

Finally meeting his gaze, she raised her chin and answered, "Yes."

Jack didn't speak to Sydney on the way to the airport. Not only would she have said no to moving in with him, she didn't even want to live next door to him. She was slipping through his fingers, and the pain he'd thought to bury came to life with a vengeance. After boarding the plane, he was angry and confused as he sat at the opposite end of the sofa from her.

After the jet was in the air, he asked, "What's the real

reason you want to move out of the Queen Anne house?" She gave him more of the same double-talk about ghosts, research, and being a chatterbox. When he held up his hand, she quit speaking. He watched her put on her glasses and stick her pretty nose in Captain Bledsoe's journal. Over Georgia, Jack decided on a different approach. "Sydney, why did you jump from wanting to sleep only with the man you intended to marry to having a two-night stand with me?"

"Passion pushed principals to the back burner," she replied without looking at him.

"So you can turn passion on and off like a light switch?" He watched her shrug without looking at him. "I've never been with a woman who refused to see me again."

Keeping her eyes on the journal, she said, "A first time for everything."

"You've been a first for me in more ways than one," he admitted. "I know you aren't the kind of girl to have a meaningless fling."

Immersed in the journal, Sydney mumbled, "How could you know what kind of girl I am since you were my *first* time?"

"Look at me." Jack put his hand on the journal, and Sydney brought her eyes to his. "By the fact that you were a noble maiden when we flew to New York."

"Maybe I don't want to be any less noble than I am now, you know, if and when I do get married." She brushed his hand aside and lowered her gaze to the journal once again.

Tell me what you want, Jack. I'm so afraid I won't be able to please you. I want you to love me, Jack. I need you to make love to me all night long.

Jack took the journal from her and laid it aside. "I knew you wanted to give yourself to the guy you marry.

I'm sorry for taking the gift which you could give only once." He inwardly flinched as she glared at him over the top of her glasses.

"Being sorry you took me to bed isn't very flattering. Hopefully, the silver lining is that the next time I make love, I'll be better than I apparently was with you."

For Jack, making love with Sydney had been unsurpassable…a million times better than with anyone else. He'd hoped to have a lifetime of days and nights of making love with her. "I told you how good I thought you were. I didn't mean to insult you just now."

"Forget it."

"Forget it?" He couldn't. Though he'd had longer relationships, none had been serious. Was Sydney serious about someone else? Jack ran a hand over his forehead, which pounded like a drum. "Is there a guy waiting for you in California?"

"I hope so," Sydney said with the smile he found so sexy while it dug a wickedly sharp knife in his gut. "I'd really love to have a couple of children someday."

The blade twisted in Jack's stomach. He recalled the faceless man he'd pictured marrying her. Now he saw him fathering Sydney's children. "I mean is there one particular guy you were seeing before you came to St. Augustine?"

"Not really."

"What's 'not really' mean?"

"It means there was no one I'd wear a bra for."

"Okay." Jack had said he'd marry her when she wore a bra. Even though she'd done so, she certainly didn't want to marry him. He remained calm despite the tension he felt. "So this sudden decision to move out isn't because you cheated on somebody in California. Have I done something you didn't like? In or out of bed?"

Sydney blushed and reached for the manifest. "No."

"I had a really...nice time," he complimented carefully.

"Me too. But it can't happen again."

"I just don't understand why not," he admitted.

"I can't explain it any more clearly," she snapped.

Talk about cloak-and-dagger. None of this abrupt turn of events made sense to him. The truth was cloaked, and that knife in his gut was the worst kind of dagger. Though Jack was certain she hated him, he had nothing more to lose by telling her how much he loved her.

"Sydney, I—"

"Jack, you said you wouldn't pressure me, but that's what you're doing. I don't want to hear anything except your promise to back off now that I'm asking you to."

"Look, Sydney, we went for days avoiding each other at the beginning of the summer. You shouldn't have to move for the sake of a few more weeks. If seeing me is a problem for you, we can avoid each other again."

"That would be too difficult for both of us." She shook her head and patted his hand without looking at him. "I'll have to move."

Jack rolled his hand over and grasped hers. She pulled on her hand, and when he didn't release it, she met his gaze. He searched her green eyes for a trace of caring. He saw none.

"If you think I plan to interfere with your research, I won't. Do all the work you want during the day." Thinking a tease might get her to smile, he said, "Do me at night."

"And perhaps end up a single mom with an illegitimate baby?"

"No. I'd marry you."

"I'd never marry you under those circumstances." She shook her head to confirm that. "I'm sure the women in

St. Augustine, like in Manhattan, will be lined up at your door to do you day or night. Don't you think?"

"Hell yeah." He let go of her hand. He wasn't going to beg. "I'll back off."

"Thanks, because I can't juggle you and my research."

Thirty-Four

Sydney's heart splintered into a million tiny pieces. What had she been thinking when formulating this horrible plan? She was thinking of Jack and not herself. That's what. How in the world would she ever get over her love for this man? She wouldn't.

So, she had freed him but locked herself in a lifelong prison of sorrow and regret.

Jack was angry now, but he'd appreciate the favor later. Knowing he'd send her packing at the end of summer, Sydney had decided to do her packing ahead of time. She didn't want Jack to guess how much she loved him and pity her when she was gone. He'd had enough heartache because of his parents and brother. She realized she had no interest left in her dissertation work and remembered Jack saying he had felt this way about his career. Apparently, the loss of someone you loved had that effect.

"Ironic that we're flying south, in the same direction as this relationship is headed," Jack said as they sat in somewhat close proximity on the sofa, but miles apart in every other way. "I always thought success was achieving one's goals and happiness was the result. I achieved a goal with you, and I was happy. But since you're not, and I want you to succeed, we'll go our separate ways."

"Okay." No! Sydney silently screamed. He frowned and looked away. She didn't want to live a day without Jack. And to imagine him seeing someone else, someone of his own class hopefully, was a spear in her heart. But isn't that exactly what she wanted him for him? Yes. She had to get a grip on herself and let go of him gracefully. "That will be for the best."

Jack glared at her. "Sydney, I have one more question. If you can care about what went wrong with Philip and Camilla, why don't you care about what went wrong between us?"

"You were the one who pointed out Cammy and Philip's affair didn't work out." Nothing could change the fact that Sydney was from a blue-collar family and Jack had a blueblood legacy. Her throat ached as if on fire as she dropped a hint as to the real reason why she was breaking off with him, "Sometimes one person is not worthy of another."

Sydney could tell Jack was furious by the sparks in his narrowed eyes and the flexing of his clenched jaw. She wondered why he should be angry at the put-down she'd dealt herself.

"I guess that explanation is clear enough, Sydney."

So, he'd interpreted the hint. He obviously agreed she was unworthy. Had his family been alive, he'd never have introduced her to them. "Let this go. Please. Let me go."

Jack snarled, "Done, dammit."

∽

Back in the Queen Anne house, Sydney cried for a solid week. The following week, she called Patricia Hudson and asked her to look for something else for her to rent. Sydney didn't see or hear from Jack. Three weeks to the day after she'd last spoken to Jack, Leslie Bowen knocked at the door. She sent him away.

"Have I ever mentioned this was Cammy's bedroom?"

"Philip?" Sydney whispered the morning on the last day of July as she lay in bed with a box of tissues and Ichabod. So deep in her misery she hadn't even heard Philip's *whoosh*. She opened puffy eyes and saw him near the open window facing Jack's house. "July is almost over. Where have you been?"

"With Jack." The young man drifted toward her. "My God, what did you do to him in New York?"

"I fell in love with him, Philip," she blurted out, so glad to admit it to someone.

"Tell him, Sydney."

"You tell him," she said, pushing herself up to a sitting position.

"You know he can't see me or hear me," Philip replied. "You are repeating my history with Cammy. Just when you and Jack have consummated your love, you've separated. Perhaps, had I not gone to sea so soon after making love to Camilla, I'd not have lost her."

Sydney dabbed her eyes with a tissue and blew her nose. "How do you know that Jack and I made love? I thought you stayed here."

"I did stay here. But Jack looks the way I felt when I had to leave Cammy the next morning for Captain Bledsoe's ship. If you're not careful, you'll lose Jack forever as I did Cammy."

"There's a big difference." Sydney shook her head.

"You loved Cammy. Jack doesn't love me." She shrugged. "I even wore a bra for him."

"You wore a what?"

Sydney started to gesture and then said, "Never mind. He wasn't serious when he said he'd marry me if I wore one. He made no commitment to me as you did to Cammy."

"I know Jack loves you."

Sydney's heart fluttered as she studied Philip. "Have you heard him say he loves me?" She twisted the tissue in her hands. "Philip, if you've heard him say so, that would make all the difference." Or would it? They'd still be from opposite worlds. "Never mind that either. One day, Jack would be embarrassed of me and my family."

"No, I haven't heard him say he loves you." Philip grimaced. "But his actions are speaking far more loudly. He hasn't shaved and hardly eats. He won't answer his phone and barely talks to Buster. Jack sits in front of the thing you call a flatscreen all day and drinks himself to sleep in the recliner every night. This is exactly how he reacted after his parents and brother died, and you know how deeply he loved them."

"Yes." Sydney pulled her knees to her chest. "But Jack's not pining away because he loves me, he's brooding because I bruised his male ego."

"Why did you bruise him? Hasn't he been hurt enough?"

Wrapping her arms around her knees, wishing she could hug Jack, Sydney considered Philip's comments. "I believe it would hurt Jack more to reject me at the end of the summer than for me to tell him goodbye now. He'd have to admit he couldn't fall for a girl like me. You should understand this, Philip. You told me you felt unworthy of Cammy."

"Nay! Nay, I said I went to sea to prove to her father I *was* worthy of Cammy. I would never have washed my hands of her as you have Jack."

"I'm usually not a quitter." Sydney turned her head toward the window and looked longingly at Jack's house. Slowly she turned back to Philip. "I miss him so much."

"Has Jack said you were unworthy, Sydney?"

"He had the chance to say that I was worthy, but he didn't." Sydney splayed her hands. "He's a brilliant man. He knows it could never work between us. He'd be the first to tell you that he and I are opposites, most importantly regarding financial backgrounds."

"Jack doesn't give a fig about that." Philip's voice was firm, "You're kindred spirits."

Sydney jumped as she heard Jack's back door slam. Hopping out of bed, she rushed past Philip to the window, starving for a glimpse of Jack. She saw anger in his step as he strode toward the garage. Black sunglasses and a dark growth of beard were on his handsome face. He wore a black tee shirt, blue jeans, and black boots. He vanished into the garage and, a moment later, roared out of it on his motorcycle.

"Follow him," Philip urged.

"No, he might see me. What would I say?"

"You would say you love him. Tell him and let Jack decide for himself what to do, instead of you deciding for him."

"I told you he would pity me."

"You are assuming too much."

Walking away from the window, she said, "I've put off going to the Old Jail Museum long enough. I'm going to ride my scooter to San Marco Avenue today. Meet me back here tonight because I want to tell you my findings and say goodbye."

If a ghost could look stricken, Philip did. "Goodbye?"

"I paid three months' rent when I moved in here. Patricia says Jack won't refund any of it, and I can't afford to move without it. It's killing me to stay, so I'm flying home tomorrow."

It ghosted across Philip. *How Google's?*

I paid fifteen dollars each when I move...in here, Patricia says Jack would round any of it, and she can't afford to move without it for Philip had to stop "T" perhaps late tomorrow.

Thirty-Five

J ust after midnight on August 1, as Sydney paced the floor of her living room, Ichabod watched her from the Martha Washington chair. Where had Jack gone the previous afternoon? Had he come home while she was at the museum? Was he seeing someone else already? She heard the familiar *whoosh* and saw him in the foyer. "Philip, where did Jack go yesterday?" She tensed, fully expecting to hear Philip say a woman's name.

Philip moved to the sofa and sat down. Ichabod jumped out of the chair and onto the sofa next to him. As Ichabod groomed himself, Philip petted the cat, then looked at Sydney.

"Jack asked the person he talked to today not to mention his visit. That person asked the same of Jack. So, I don't think I can divulge any information."

"He went to see Patricia Hudson," Sydney reasoned aloud. "He wants to know why I haven't moved out yet."

"Since he's withholding your money and the thing you call a credit card, I suspect he knows exactly why."

"He went to see Leslie Bowen. Of course." Sydney's

fingers went to her temples. "Since I'm still here, he asked Leslie to take me off his hands."

Philip laughed. "How you remind me of Cammy. She was an impulsive chatterbox who jumped to the wrong conclusions just like you do."

Sydney said quietly, "Cammy's impulsive prediction that things wouldn't work out for the two of you came true. I know without love on both sides, things could never work out for Jack and me."

"Even when there is love on both sides, sometimes things don't work out," he replied with a pained expression. "Please tell me your findings at the jail museum. Then I have a favor to ask you before I go back home to see about Jack."

"I wish I could go see him with you." When Philip opened his mouth to speak, she held up her hand as Jack had often done to her. "But, I can't. So, let's talk about you." Sydney finally took a seat in the Martha Washington chair. On their last visit, it had been all about her and Jack. This time, it needed to be about Philip and Cammy. "Jack kept the manifest and journal, or I would read to you now what he and I read on the plane."

"I can guess why he kept those books."

"Yes. He paid for them."

"Nay. He wants you to come ask him for them. For your credit card. For a refund."

Sydney shook her head and related Captain Bledsoe's story of sadness in the Burke and Johnson households resulting from Philip's death. Philip pointed out the sadness was back. Then he listened to Bledsoe's writings without any reaction.

"In conclusion, the jail museum records confirmed that the man found guilty of the shooting death of one Philip Burke and hanged from the neck until dead—" she took a breath, "was Malcolm Striker."

Philip flew off the sofa. His form blurred as he whirled himself into a maelstrom of fury in her living room. Ichabod beelined up the staircase. Sydney gripped the edge of the chair-arms a little scared, a lot sad, and totally lonely. When Philip calmed, she could see him clearly again.

"I should have known it was Striker who murdered me."

"How could you? He shot you in the back."

Now it was Philip who paced. "Cammy so feared marrying him that I gave her a brooch as my solemn oath to return to her. The brooch. I'd forgotten about that brooch. "

"You fulfilled your promise to Cammy. You returned."

"I didn't return to her arms and kiss her lips." Philip paced in *whooshes*. "Did she conceive my child? Did she marry Striker? Why can't I remember what happened during the months following my death? Why couldn't I find Cammy while she was alive? If she eventually crossed over to the other side, why didn't her spirit come for mine? Where is she buried?"

As her heart went out to Philip, Sydney said, "I think following your death you were stuck in a state of shock and grief similar to how Jack was stuck. If Cammy moved away, that would explain why you couldn't find her. After she died, maybe her grief trapped her in some kind of limbo."

"You think she's somewhere around here stuck in limbo? Is that possible?"

"How should I know?" Sydney shrugged helplessly. "You're the ghost, Philip."

"You're the one doing all the research."

"My research leads me to believe anything concerning ghosts is all conjecture anyway. I wish I had the answers to your questions, but I don't. I'm so sorry."

"You've supplied me with more answers than I've had since 1776. Thank you." Philip *whooshed* toward the stairs, preparing to leave as usual through Cammy's former bedroom. "I know one thing. If Cammy was married to Striker when I died, she would have refused the coins Captain Bledsoe was supposed to offer her."

Sydney turned her head to look at him. "Maybe not, if she were unhappily married. She may have taken the money and run away to make a new life for herself."

"But, if she ran from Striker, would she not have returned home after he hanged?"

Sydney sighed. "It's a mystery I can't seem to solve. Have you remembered where you told Captain Bledsoe to bury the coins in case Cammy refused them?"

"Nay, and I cannot remember where Striker lived. But I believe if you could find the coins, Jack might believe you're telling the truth about me. And you would be rich."

"Even if Jack believed me, he wouldn't love me. And the location of the buried coins would determine to whom they belong. In any case, certainly not me."

"I suppose you're right about the ownership of the coins. They are no longer mine to bestow as a gift." Philip stood at the bottom of the staircase and shook his head. "'Tis odd that someone as rich as Cammy once was could love someone as poor as I was the day I went to sea. People have changed greatly. Apparently, Jack is an example. He is cold and heartless."

"That's not true!" Sydney said, shooting to her feet. "Jack is not cold and heartless. You just said he loved his parents."

"Jack is a rich snob if he judges you by what's in your goldsmith house."

"My what?"

"Your...umm...bank account."

"Either you've turned against Jack, or you're baiting me."

"You have dark circles under your eyes, and your hands shake as if you have not eaten in days. Is Jack worth your pain?"

Sydney didn't answer. She bowed her head, heard a *whoosh*, and felt pressure on her shoulder. She saw Philip's hand there. It was the first time he'd touched her. "Yes, he's worth the pain." The pressure increased as Philip hugged her, and tears slipped down her cheeks.

"Sydney, he went to Flagler College today."

"Of course he did," she said. Philip moved back, and Sydney placed a hand over her broken heart. "He bought them off. He has my credit card, and he won't give me a refund. He's making sure I won't get the job, so I'll have no income and have to go home." Sorrow fell over her like a heavy tarp. "Thank goodness, I changed my plane ticket after going to the museum jail. I'll be flying out tomorrow."

"Jack initially intended to scare you off. It appears he's finally succeeded."

Sydney was shaky from not having eaten in two days. "Philip, whatever happens, don't turn against him. Jack has done me a favor by taking the teaching job out of my grasp. I'd not have been able to concentrate on my work, and that wouldn't have been fair to the Flagler College students." She paced to the window and stared at the estate next door. "All I think of is Jack Malone every waking moment. I dream about him every night." She paused and then admitted in a whisper, "I love Jack so much that each day without him...I die a little. If I don't go back to California tomorrow, I'm truly afraid I won't live to see my family again."

"How the tables have turned," Philip whispered. "If I had a cell phone and if I could lift it, I would call Jack and let him hear you saying how much you love him." He shook his head in defeat. "Now, for my favor. Please, do not leave until we have found Cammy."

Before she could protest, Philip *whooshed* and vanished.

Thirty-Six

The first week of August, it rained. Jack was sick of the gloomy, long days. Of course, it was all in one's point of view. It was dreary sitting alone in the den, staring at the flatscreen. But it would have been cozy lying in the recliner with Sydney curled at his side. He'd thought about returning to New York, but somehow, he couldn't leave while she was still in Florida.

She hadn't texted him about his houses like she'd said she would. Maybe she'd learned nothing new. He guzzled the last of his beer, then turned off the TV and a dim lamp. He sat in the dark of midnight, brooding. Five minutes later, he heard something other than raindrops splattering the windows. It was a whoosh-like noise.

"Buster?" he called. Buster barked from the dog basket, then trotted to him. Jack petted his head. The whoosh sounded again. Jack sat forward in the chair and put the footrest down. *Whoosh*. In the pitch black, he got up and walked to the window. "What the hell? he grumbled, putting his hands to his hips. "Who'd want to steal your doghouse, Buster?"

Jack watched a hooded person pushing on the

doghouse. Finally, atop the slippery mud, the doghouse slid to the right. Was the guy going to push it out all the way out to the road? When the doghouse was a good three feet from where it had sat for the past four years, the rain-drenched person knelt on the ground and stuck a small garden spade into the ground.

Jack thought about calling the police, but didn't feel the need. He could chase off whoever this nutcase was. Spade-full after spade-full of dirt was removed from the ground which had been under the doghouse. Rain filled the hole as fast as the person could dig.

Seriously. What the hell?

The person leaned over, reached into the muddy water, and then dug some more. Jack had had enough. He'd been in a foul mood since returning from New York. The guy outside had picked the wrong time to cross him. Removing Buster's collar so the electric fence wouldn't shock him, Jack made his way out of the house and across the backyard. Silently, he came up behind the person hunched over the hole.

"Lose something, pal?" Jack asked at the guy's back. The person froze, then stood and bolted across the backyard. "Hey!" Jack yelled in surprise. "Get him, Buster!"

Buster raced forward but didn't knock the man down as Jack had expected. Furious, Jack sprinted after them, catching up in his front yard. Only after he'd grabbed the guy's arm, did Jack consider he might have a knife or a gun. The guy slipped on the wet grass, stumbled, and took Jack down with him. He struggled to crawl out of Jack's grasp, but instead, Jack flipped him onto his back. Jack reared back his arm, clenched his fist, and saw the face.

"Darn you, Jack!"

"Sydney?" Jack stood, grabbed her hands, and yanked her to her feet.

"I waited forever for you to turn off your lights," she said, squaring off with him. "I was sure the rain would cover any noise I made trying to move the doghouse."

"You told Buster his doghouse was nice, but you like it enough to steal it?"

"Steal it? No." Sydney backed away from him. "Come with me."

"Go to your doghouse and get out of the rain, Buster," Jack said, and followed Sydney to the back door of the Queen Anne house.

Sydney led him into her kitchen and tore off a couple of paper towels from a rack. Giving him one to wipe the rain off his face, she did the same. As she tugged off his hoodie, he hid his surprise at seeing her wearing it. He said nothing as she placed it over a kitchen chair.

"I've still got your long-sleeved denim shirt I borrowed," she reminded him. "Would you like to put it on?"

"No." Seeing this gorgeous girl was a gut-wrenching mixture of pleasure and pain. "Just tell me why I'm here, and then I'll go."

"Okay." Sydney walked to the kitchen table and picked up her cell phone.

Leaning against the counter, Jack watched her. Her wet pink pajama tank top clung to her perky breasts and flat tummy. The matching pink bottoms were boxer shorts style. To keep his hands off her, he shoved them into his front jeans pockets.

Wanting to be the only man in her life, he had tried so hard to please her on the trip to New York. But now, he was the one man she didn't want anything to do with. Why? What had he done wrong? How had he disappointed her? She turned to him, holding her cell phone to her heart, her head lowered. She hadn't made eye contact since they'd come into her house.

Searching for answers, Jack said, "I guess when somebody hasn't made love in a while, they lose their touch."

This woman who had so completely thrilled him in bed, making it feel like his first time all over again, finally looked at him. Her cheeks were pale, and her nose as pink as her pajamas. He wondered if she'd had a cold. Had he been sulking while she'd been ill?

"When somebody's never made love before, they have no touch at all." She lifted a shoulder in a shrug. "I warned you I didn't think I could please you."

"You pleased me, Sydney," Jack said as she remained beside the kitchen table. "I thought we had a good time in New York."

"A good time is not enough when things aren't equal."

"What's not equal?"

"Everything. Nothing." Clutching her cell phone as she took a few steps closer, she asked, "Would you like a beer or a glass of wine?"

"Just get on with this. I want to go home."

"I was in your back yard, hoping to surprise you."

He cocked a brow. "You did." She nudged a lock of wet hair away from her cheek just as he was about to do so. "Surprise me, how?"

"Philip remembered where the coins were buried," she said. Jack covered his eyes with both hands. When he rubbed his face and sighed, she asked, "Are you okay?"

"I thought you weren't a gold-digger. Okay. So where are the coins?"

"You scared me before I could find them. But listen to this. Philip will back me up." Sydney tapped her cell and held it between them. After fifteen seconds, she asked, "See? You heard?"

"See...heard...what?" Jack had to get away from Sydney before he made a fool of himself. Were he to stay much longer, he'd fall on his knees and beg her to take him back. "Is that it? Because if it is—"

"I recorded Philip's voice."

"All you recorded was air."

"Maybe I pushed the wrong buttons. Let's try it…"

"No, you pushed all the right buttons," Jack growled.

"Philip agreed to let me record him. I'm not a crazy nutcase." Sydney pushed cell phone buttons, but nothing happened. She looked at him with such pleading in her eyes Jack almost reached out to her. Sydney waved a hand in the air and told him, "Philip said something to the effect of, *Jack, my friend, this is Philip Burke. If Cammy refused the coins, I have finally remembered asking Captain Bledsoe to bury them in my…in your back yard. They should be in a small iron box approximately in the space under Buster's doghouse.*"

Jack put his hands on his hips. "Instead of trying to convince me a ghost exists, why don't you try dealing with the man before you?"

"I tried to deal with you." She took a step back. "It can't work." In frustration, she hurled her cell phone across the kitchen.

"Sydney, stop being so emotional," Jack barked, grabbing her wrist. "Settle down."

"Telling a woman to settle down is the best way to rile her up!"

She pushed at his chest with her free hand and he clamped a hand around her delicate wrist. She balled up both small fists. He jerked her against his chest and glared down at her.

"You're damn lucky you didn't make those fists outside before I knew who you were." Jack grumbled, "I'd have nailed you."

Jack looked at his large hands around her dainty wrists. In recent weeks, he had cuddled her like a baby and treated her like a woman. He wanted to do both now, but he released her. Sydney's knees collapsed, she fell at his feet and sobbed on the kitchen floor.

"You're too analytical for me, Jack. Go home."

Jack reached down and lifted Sydney to her feet. "I'm sorry I changed you in New York, Sydney," he said, holding her against his chest. "Because the gorgeous woman who made love to me there disappeared, and the nutcase who fights with me flew home in her place."

"Go!" she cried and shoved out of his arms.

Three nights later, Jack sat at his kitchen table, recalling how Sydney had collapsed in tears in her kitchen. It had replayed over and over before his eyes and was ripping him apart. He would have stayed as long as she needed him. Forever. But she'd told him to go.

"Damn," Jack sighed. He stared at the turkey sandwich. Even though it was hours past dinnertime, and he'd not eaten since a bowl of cereal that morning, he had no appetite. He tossed the sandwich in the dog bowl. Buster titled his head, his soulful eyes communicating he understood things weren't right. "Maybe if we texted Sydney a video of you not eating a turkey sandwich, she'd come see about you." Jack pressed the video button and motioned for the dog to eat. Buster stayed where he was and whimpered.

"Jackson."

Jack swung his head around and saw her. In a soft glow, she stood at the far end of the kitchen. All of his life, she'd said this was her favorite room. Two years ago, it had become his favorite too. Her black hair was in a chin-length bob like always. Her dress was the one she'd worn the night he'd graduated with his Ph.D. As lovely as ever, she smiled.

"Believe her." The voice was a whisper. "Help her, and she will help you."

"Help who? Sydney?"

"Yes."

She vanished. He sat. Stunned to the core.

Thirty-Seven

Ten pm found Sydney trying to focus on reading a book as she sat on the Chippendale sofa. She jumped, startled by the pounding at her back door. She and Jack were the only ones who used her back door. Barefoot and wearing a short green nightgown, she bailed off the sofa and ran through the house to the kitchen.

"Jack?" she asked, just to make sure.

"Yeah, open up."

She unlocked the door, and he stormed into the kitchen. Carrying a camping lantern, he smacked it and something else onto her kitchen table. Jack's muscular body blocked what he'd set down next to the lantern. She trembled as he turned to her, his eyes knifing into her like daggers.

"You've finally gotten to me," he accused taking off leather gloves and tossing them onto the counter. "I'm as crazy as you are." Placing gentle hands loosely around her neck, his thumbs caressed her skin. "I knew there'd come a day when I had to strangle you. I'll just plead temporary insanity."

"What's wrong?" Sydney wrapped her hands around his iron wrists. As usual, late at night, he was clad in gym shorts and nothing else. Her body pulsed with the craving that always lay on the surface with Jack and only with him. "Tell me why you want to strangle me."

Jack's hands slid down her neck to her shoulders. With a sigh, he pulled her into his embrace and rested his chin on her head. Her empty arms, which had ached to hold him, wound around his waist, and she hugged him tightly. She closed her eyes and flattened her cheek to his bare skin. She splayed her fingers on his back and savored the feel of his muscular body. This was the man whom she had loved to the very best of her ability in New York City. As he pulled out of her arms, she resisted the urge to cling to him.

"Listen to this," he said. He played a short video that showed Buster and his dog bowl in Jack's kitchen. "Tell me word for word what you just heard."

"Jackson. Believe her. Help her, and she will help you. Help who? Sydney? Yes." Sydney shook her head. "I recognize your voice, but who were you talking to?"

"My mother."

Sydney, who had never before in her life fainted, now did so.

~

"Sydney?" His voice sounded far away. "Wake up. Come on, talk to me."

She put her hands to her stomach and touched the smooth satin of her short green nightgown. She'd been dreaming about him again. "Jack," she sighed. Her dreams were becoming so real, she had awakened at his command.

"Hi."

Sydney gasped and opened her eyes. Jack was standing over her as she lay on her bed. She wasn't dreaming. He was here. She sat up and grabbed his hand. Pulling him to sit beside her, she flung her arms around his neck. A tidal wave of emotions flooded her. She was at once comforted and protected and, at the same time, terrified and nervous. Apprehension reined as she realized he wasn't hugging her back. But, this time, she didn't resist the urge to cling to him. She hugged him ever tighter.

"Hi," she said.

"Are you okay?"

"Yes." Sydney nodded.

"When's the last time you ate?"

"I don't know." She closed her eyes and rested her head against Jack's. She placed one hand on the soft hair at the nape of his neck and flattened her other hand over the muscles in his bare back. "Did you see your mother? Or did you just hear her?"

"Both. If you look at the video closely, you can see her glow appear and disappear in the background."

"What a priceless gift." Sydney was so happy for Jack and, at the same time, sad when he pulled out of her arms. From the nightstand, he picked up a box and placed it in her lap. The box was iron, about half the size of a shoe box, and heavy as it lay on her thighs. "What's this?"

"Open it," Jack said.

Sydney opened the lid. It creaked and released a musty scent. She stared into the box, and her throat grew dry. She lifted her eyes to Jack's and wasn't sure what she saw in their ocean blue depths. She reached into the box and lifted out one of many silver coins.

"Philip's fortune," she whispered. "His share of the

bounty from British warships Captain Bledsoe and the *Sea Phantom* crew seized and looted in 1776."

"There are twenty-two coins, and each one is a Continental Dollar," Jack told her. "I'm sure Bledsoe was only too thrilled to take them back from the British and return a fair portion to General Washington, thereby supporting our fight for independence."

"Yes, and these coins were meant to be Philip's independence from poverty and the freedom to marry Cammy." Sydney handed the coin to Jack. "Where did you find the box?"

"A couple of feet below the hole you dug."

Sydney smiled at the handsome man, loving him so much. She placed the box in his lap, and as he dropped the coin back into the iron box, she whispered, "Finders, keepers, Jack."

"Losers, weepers."

"Right." So, they both agreed Philip's treasure belonged to Jack. She didn't give a fig about that. The only treasure she wanted was Jack. Keeping a smile on her face to hide her sorrow, Sydney asked, "What happens next, Jack?"

"I could answer that in ten different ways," Jack replied. "Let me experiment with two." When she nodded, he asked, "Crazy?"

"I like crazy," she whispered and blushed.

"We need to put the coins into a safety deposit box at the bank. How about after the bank, we go to the Johnson-Burke house?"

"And talk to Nellie. Good idea," Sydney agreed. "We've found out just about all we can on Philip. I think we should concentrate on Cammy."

"We, as in you and Philip?"

"We, as in you and m—" Sydney's voice broke, and she strengthened it. "Me."

When she smiled at him, Jack placed the box on the nightstand and pulled her into his arms. "Yeah, you and me." When she hugged him back, he tightened his embrace. "Let's go to Anastasia Island tomorrow."

"Yes, let's."

"If you're sure you're okay, I'll go home now and come back in the morning."

Sydney cupped a hand to his bearded face. "Please don't leave."

"As in, spend the night?"

"Why not?" Stroking his cheek with her thumb, she flirted, "The damage is done."

"The damage being me breaking and entering you in Manhattan?" he asked. "Do you think of me as a thief? Having stolen your virginity?"

"No." She shook her head and swallowed. She thought of him as the man she loved. "You may have thought I was trying to steal the coins the night you found me in your back yard. But, you stole nothing from me. I gave myself to you."

"I'm glad to hear you say that. You need to hear me when I say I know you only wanted to find the coins to convince me you weren't crazy."

"Your mom helped us with that." She vaguely wondered why his mother had done so.

"Sydney," Jack sighed. "I don't know how I could have kept seeing you and left you a virgin. But sleeping with you changed things for the worse. I regret that more than you know."

Sydney's only regret was losing Jack. Then, as a timid idea formed, courage claimed victory. "Speaking of change, continuing to see you won't change the way I feel about you. So, if I couldn't possibly lo—like you any more than I do right now, what's the harm?" Her heart would break. That was the harm. So be it. Forget the future. She was grasping at straws for a way to be with Jack in the present. "Since my landlord won't refund my money, I may as well stay until my lease runs out. Are you game?"

"My mother obviously wants you to stay so we can help each other," Jack said. "So yes, I'm game. I've even got an idea how to make it interesting."

"Interesting?" Sydney asked as Jack smiled. She'd missed his smiles more than food and water. "We're in tune on hearing things tonight, so let's hear your idea."

Thirty-Eight

"Since I couldn't possibly care about you any more than I do tonight, I'll make you a bet," Jack said. Sydney tilted her head, the curiosity on her face and in her body language urging him on. "If you make me fall in love with you by the end of August, you win the bet. If you fall in love with me, I win the bet. We'll be our own judges, and the prize for the winner is the coins."

"Game on," she whispered.

When Sydney closed her green eyes, hugged him, and nodded, Jack thanked God for this second chance to win her love. He pulled her onto his lap and held her to his heart, pouring his love into her without saying the words. He had no intention of losing the contest and watching her fly away come September.

"Game on, baby girl."

"And maybe by helping each other, like your mom wants, we can help Philip fulfill his promise to be reunited with Cammy."

"I hope that happens."

Sydney leaned back and he watched her eyes grow wide. "You believe in ghosts."

"Yeah, well," he chuckled as happiness spread throughout his soul. "I believe in you."

"I believe in you too. Perhaps by the end of the month, one of us will love the other as much as Philip loves Cammy. "I know you're right about one thing." She glanced around at their intimate surroundings and said, "We do get along in bed."

"Yeah, we do," Jack agreed. He hoisted her off his lap, plopped her back into bed, and lay down on top of her. "We get along very well in bed. Philip isn't here, is he?"

"No, he says he gives us our privacy. Only he says privacy with a short *i* like they do in England. He also told me he figured out we'd been intimate in New York."

"I'm sorry I asked."

Sydney giggled and roped her arms around his neck. Jack lowered his head, closed his eyes, and kissed her lips. When his hardened manhood pressed into her soft tummy, she lassoed his waist with her legs. A groan sounded deep in his throat as she squeezed his hips between her slender thighs. He raised his head, braced himself on his elbows, and smiled down at her.

"It's August seventh," she said. "I have twenty-four days to win this contest."

"Great. I'll take the nights. Starting tonight."

"Fine. I'll give you this head start," Sydney said. "September first will be the day of reckoning. I'll know on which coast I'll be teaching, and we'll settle up."

Jack asked, "Remind me what happens if you're offered both jobs or neither job."

"Both means I'll stay here. Neither means I'll go home."

"I never dreamed I'd base my decision of New York

versus Florida on a bookworm neighbor who drives me out of my mind."

"I'm not sure exactly how to interpret that. But driving a motorcycle hood out of his mind isn't so hard now that his mind has opened up."

"I've got something hard for you," Jack whispered huskily. He nibbled behind her ear and added, "Are you gonna open up and let me in?"

"Mmm...yes."

As Sydney ran her hands down his back and over his rear end, Jack knew that she'd already won the contest. He loved her so much he'd have made her any promise, gone anywhere, and done anything to win her love. For this magnificent woman to agree to a contest where she'd be trying to make him fall in love with her was too good to be true. He prayed it wouldn't occur to her that he didn't need to win the coins. If she knew he was already in love with her, she'd surely collect her winnings and wave goodbye.

He trailed a hand down the short, silky nightgown and pulled it up her hip. When his fingers touched her underwear, he asked, "Will you let me take off your panties?"

"Yes, but..." Sydney's soft lips brushed his ear, and he closed his eyes. She sprinkled kisses down his neck and across his shoulder. Her lips trailed back up his neck, and she purred in his ear, "You can't take off my panties while you're between my legs."

Jack knew there were a million guys on the planet who would give their right arm to take his place at this moment. To have this sensational beauty whisper those words in his ear as she tightened her legs around his waist unleashed his wildest passions. Jack raised his head and smiled down at her. Her green eyes glistened, and her lips parted for his next kiss. He kissed her and rolled off her to the bed. As he lay at her side, he slipped his fingers into the waistband of her panties.

"Dammit," he growled.

"What's wrong?"

"I don't have a condom with me, do you?"

"No." Sydney giggled, rolled to him, and slid a leg between his. "And even if I did, it's nighttime. I'm not going to help you win on your time. Now…" She gave him an innocent grin and said, "If it were daytime and I had a condom, I'd give it to you."

"We can't do it without a condom. Can we?"

"Well now…" She circled his navel with her index finger and said, "I had the impression you never failed to use them."

"That's because I never wanted to *have* to marry somebody as a result of having sex without a condom."

"So, how would you feel if I got pregnant tonight?"

He grinned and answered from the heart. "I wouldn't mind having a baby with you."

Sydney pulled herself closer to him. "You're just saying that because you've gone without since we got back from New York." She paused and asked, "Haven't you?"

"Hell, yes, I have." He reared back and said, "You better have gone without too."

"You know I have." She trailed her fingers up his chest and wound her arms around his neck, molding her soft breasts to his bare skin. "As for condoms and me, I want you to create your block of recognized historical landmarks before you create anything else."

"I want you to have your chance to teach before you get pregnant. But, right now, the fuse is lit, and I'm about to…"

"Overheat?"

"Yes." With a will of iron, Jack rolled away from her.

He grabbed her hand and hauled her out of the bed. "Let's go."

"Where?" Sydney asked as he pulled her behind him to the bedroom door.

"My house because I have condoms," he said as they crossed the upstairs landing.

"No!" Sydney wailed playfully. "You have to forfeit trying to win for tonight. It's not my fault you want to submerge into my territory without a wrapper for your torpedo."

"My torpedo?" Jack laughed as they descended the stairs.

"Yes, your torpedo. You know what I mean." Sydney made a quick turn on the bottom step and pulled her hand from Jack.

"Oh no, you don't," Jack said, and before she could make a getaway back up the stairs, he grasped her hips, swiveled her to face him, and tossed her over his shoulder.

Thirty-Nine

As he sauntered down the parquet hallway, her long hair brushed the back of his legs, and she teased, "This is unfair! It's kidnapping." As they entered the kitchen, the thought entered her mind that Patricia the realtor, Shawn the pilot, and every female in Jack's New York office would beg, borrow, or steal to be carried over his shoulder to his bed. Seeing the white fur ball at the cat dish, she said, "I'll be right back, Ichabod."

"She'll see you tomorrow, cat." There was victory in Jack's deep voice as he carted her outside. "When we're at my house during the day, but don't have any wrappers for your tunnel, just toss me over your shoulder and haul me back here, Doc."

"Oh, right!" Sydney laughed breathlessly as the big, muscular man effortlessly toted her across the courtyard. "It wouldn't do me any good even if I could kidnap you because I don't have any wrappers." She paused and then asked, "My tunnel?"

"You know what I mean."

"Yes, I do!" She smacked his slightly rounded, masculine backside. As they passed the bench he'd yet to paint, she hoped he didn't notice.

"Sydney! When are you going to paint my half of that bench?"

She shot back, "When are you going to buy paint and wrappers?"

"Don't tell me you're too embarrassed to buy condoms."

"Yes! No!" She heard a bark. "Hi, Buster." From upside down, she waved at him as Jack climbed his back door steps. She saw the kitchen floor pass under her eyes and said, "Maybe I think *you* should buy the condoms."

"Maybe *you* should go on the pill. That way, I can torpedo your little tunnel without a condom between us."

"Mmm, Jack," she moaned as his words sent vibrations shooting up her center. "Find the nearest place to lie down, quick! I have to have you right now. It's not the right time of the month for me to get pregnant.

"Now you tell me." He chuckled. "Talk about unfair."

"All's fair in love and war, baby."

Jack strode into the den and put her feet on the floor. He tugged her nightgown over her head, and she yanked down his shorts. He stepped out of his shorts, pulled down her panties, and tossed them over his shoulder. Sydney burned with anticipation as she lay down in the wide recliner for two. Spreading her legs for Jack, he nestled his hips between her thighs. She arched to him as he opened her with gentle fingers. Touching his lips to hers, masculinity caressed femininity. As he buried his hardness inside her, his tongue slipped into her mouth. Sydney's tongue met his, and she wrapped her legs around him as his hips moved with long, urgent strokes. Deep inside her and then almost pulling out, he picked up speed. Sydney felt her ecstasy build, and she moaned his name as bliss burst in sweet shiverings. In as far as he could go, Jack's low, masculine groan sounded in her ear as he pulsed in hard throbs deep inside her.

When their breathing slowed, and with their bodies still one, Jack said, "The condoms are in the pocket of your suitcase."

Squeezing him with internal muscles, Sydney purred, "So you got me over here, on your territory, under false pretenses."

"All's fair in love and war, baby." He chuckled and told her, "There're only a couple left. We'll need to get some more."

"Okay," she whispered. He didn't know it, of course, but she'd already lost the contest. "Love me, Jack."

He took her to his bed and did so.

"Wake up, sleepyhead."

Sydney opened one eye. She didn't see Jack and guessed she'd been dreaming of him again. She saw the curtains at the window of his bedroom flutter with a morning breeze perfumed by the ocean. Lying on her stomach, Sydney closed her eye and hugged Jack's pillow. It smelled like the man she loved. She sighed and smiled. When his hand flattened on her bare bottom, she giggled.

"You *are* here. Do I have to wake up?"

"If you want breakfast."

When he moved his hand, she rolled over, stretched, and smiled at the handsome man sitting beside her. She sat up, modestly tucking the sheet in around her naked breasts.

"Breakfast in bed from the guy who doesn't cook?" Sydney asked, playfully suspicious. "When it's daytime, it's my turn to work on winning the bet, not yours. This is all-out warfare."

Jack grinned with innocence. "This land once housed a sailor's rest with breakfast, did it not? I'm just keeping with tradition."

He wore snug boxers, which accentuated the sexy bulge between his legs. Excitement soared within her at the idea of eating breakfast in bed with him. Jack set the tray on her lap, leaned against the headboard, and swung his legs on top of the sheet. Sydney took the cup of coffee he handed her. She sipped, fixed just the way she liked it.

He knew it too. The smoldering fire in his eyes and the cocky grin on his lips sent tingles to every corner of her body. She wanted to make love to him again and again. But for now, she ate the toast he'd buttered for her, sure that there was no better tasting toast in the entire world. She drank the coffee and then took a sideways peek at him.

As he drained a glass of milk, she saw the vulnerable little boy inside the powerful, large man. Knowing he didn't cook made this simple breakfast precious. Somehow, she suspected he'd made such breakfasts for his mother. If only she could win this contest, she'd love to help him fill the void of family in his life.

"Thank you for breakfast in bed," Sydney whispered, placing the empty tray on the nightstand. "I'd like to take a shower. Want to join me?"

Jack cocked a slashing, black brow. "Okay. But, if we take one now, we're going to take another one tonight... on my time. Because I don't plan to lose the bet."

"We'll see," Sydney said, purposely coy.

At precisely the same instant, they jumped out of opposite sides of the bed. As Sydney raced by the window, she saw a woman getting out of an ancient but well-preserved Buick parked in front of the Queen Anne house.

"Oh no!" Sydney gasped. "It's Nellie, the wife of George Johnson Burke, and she's carrying a cardboard box." Sydney wrung her hands and cried, "This is worse than the day the ladies from the historical society showed up unannounced. You!" She pointed at Jack. "You got me into this mess by carting me over here in my nightgown. Now what do I do?"

"At least she's coming to us. Now we don't have to go to Anastasia Island." Chuckling and shaking his head, Jack tugged Sydney into his walk-in closet. He grabbed a polo shirt. As she yanked it over her head, Buster trotted to them with her nightgown in his mouth.

"Buster!" she wailed. "You and your dog drool!"

Jack handed her a pair of his drawstring gym shorts, smothered a laugh, and said, "I'll be over when she's gone and race you to your shower before we go to the bank."

Sydney watched him crawl back into bed, roll onto his stomach, and hug her pillow. It was all she could do to leave him.

Forty

An hour later, from his front porch, Jack watched Sydney walk Nellie out to her car. Even his shirt and shorts, both baggy on her, could not conceal the sensuous blonde's appeal. Though he'd made love to her three times during the night and early morning, he ached for more. Sydney and Nellie spoke for a moment and hugged goodbye. As soon as the car pulled away from the curb, Sydney looked at Jack's house.

Wearing jeans, but barefoot and bare-chested, he leaned forward with his hands curled over the wooden porch railing. At precisely the same instant Sydney yanked open the picket fence gate, he vaulted over the railing. Giggling, she raced down the cobblestone path leading to the Queen Anne house. He leaped over the wrought iron fence separating their front yards and sprinted toward her. Sydney reached her porch steps as his feet met the cobblestones.

Laughing wildly, she skipped up the steps, but he caught her halfway across the porch. Lifting her off her feet, he twirled her around, setting her back at the edge of the porch. Entering the house ahead of her, she squealed and scrambled after him. When he shut the front door, she raced past him and tore up the staircase. He took the stairs two at a time, and she barely beat him into the master bath. Still giggling, Sydney leaned against the wall and gasped for breath. Popping open his fly, Jack stripped off his jeans and stepped into the shower first.

"Why aren't you winded?" she asked, holding her side.

He chuckled, turning on the water. "Because I've played basketball all my life."

"I know how to play basketball."

With that stated, Sydney tugged his polo shirt over her head. Standing under the hot spray of water, Jack never took his eyes off her. She pulled the drawstring of the shorts into a knot. Desire burned within him as he watched her frantically picking at the knot. Maybe she was as hungry for him as he was her. Jack leaned his head under the water and smoothed his wet hair back. Sydney finally untied the knot, and he let his gaze drop along with the shorts. He saw her shiver as he slowly brought his eyes back up her body to meet her green ones.

"It's about time you made good on your shower offer," he told the naked woman.

With a grin, he brought her under the spray. Pinning her slippery body to the tile wall, he covered her mouth with his. Thinking he was the one in control, he realized he wasn't when she kissed her way down his chest. He shielded her from the water as she slid down the wall and cupped her hands to his hips. Desire coiled in Jack's stomach as her tongue teased his navel. He craved each kiss she gave him and wondered how much lower she'd venture. As he watched, she nibbled her way down the trail of dark hair under his belly button. Anticipation engulfed him as she closed her hands around the hard length of his manhood.

As he hoped, she kissed that which he'd buried deep inside her so many times in Manhattan and St. Augustine. Despite the water spraying him, Jack was on fire. He could not get enough of this woman. She was beautiful, intelligent, and sexy. She was sensitive and caring with a sassy sense of humor. She was driving him out of his mind with happiness.

The water beat on his back as she trailed kisses up his chest. When she was standing, he positioned her so that the water wouldn't hit her in the face. Covering her lips with his and her breasts with his hands, she moaned as he massaged her beaded nipples with the pads of his thumbs. He stepped between her feet, and she spread her legs.

"Mmm," she whispered as his body molded to hers with the water peppering them.

Sydney wound her arms around his neck, and he picked her up. Instinctively, she wrapped her legs around his waist. He'd taught her well, as she helped him slide his hard inches into her gripping warmth. She kissed him, her tongue dipping into his mouth. It took only a few slippery up-and-down slides before he throbbed as her orgasm squeezed him.

An hour later, on the way out of the bedroom, Sydney smacked Jack's butt and flirted, "I'd say I scored some bonus points toward the contest in the shower."

"Yeah," Jack said with a knowing grin. "I'd say you're temporarily in the lead."

A thrill zinged through Sydney to know she had satisfied this sophisticated, experienced man. She was now wearing a crop top with a matching flared miniskirt that had attached panties. Descending the stairs in front of Jack and trailing her fingers along the banister, she peered over her shoulder. He looked outrageously sexy as he casually fastened the top button of his jeans. With great effort, she kept herself from stopping him, undoing his fly, flattening her hands to his washboard stomach, and nudging him back upstairs to her bed. She'd let him borrow his long-sleeved denim shirt with the promise he'd give it back to her.

"Whoops!" she squealed, missing a step as she watched him roll the sleeves of the shirt up his forearms.

Jack caught her elbow, steadied her, and said, "You can stop daydreaming because we aren't doing it again in the daylight unless you come up with your own protection."

"You do drive a *hard* bargain." Blushing, she yanked her arm from him.

"Yeah, I do."

"Dreaming is all you might be doing tonight, mister."

"I doubt it, lady." His husky laugh rang of confidence.

As they came to the bottom of the stairs, Jack buckled his belt. Sydney's fingers itched to unbuckle it. Maybe she had scored points in the contest, but he was so far in the lead she'd never catch him. Jack smiled and sauntered into the living room ahead of her.

They rode the Harley to the bank and placed the coins in a safety deposit box with both of them having independent access to it. After grabbing burgers and fries for lunch they headed back to the Queen Anne house. Sydney plopped down on the sofa and Jack took a seat beside her. She handed him the cardboard box and put on her reading glasses. Ichabod joined them and jumped onto the Martha Washington chair for his catnap.

"What all did Nellie bring you, Syd?"

"Well, Jackson," she grinned and so did he, "there's a diary, also a different family Bible, and some ancient newspaper clippings from the *East Florida Gazette~Herald* in the box," she said. "What we should start with?"

Jack reached into the box and pulled out the small, leather book which was on top. As he flipped to the first of many yellowed pages, Sydney told him that it was Cammy's diary. She chose the family Bible, and they read.

"Sydney." Jack sat forward, staring at the diary.

"What?" She was carefully sifting, due to the age of the ancient newspaper articles, through the clippings, but stopped and looked over the top of her glasses at him. "Tell me."

"You're not going to believe this."

"What is it?"

"Camilla just explained why she married Malcolm Striker."

Forty-One

S ydney crawled across the sofa to Jack. Perched on her knees she draped an arm around his broad shoulders. He wrapped an arm around her waist, tugged her close, and patted her hip.

"Why did she marry him, Jack?"

"Are we alone?" Jack asked.

"I haven't heard the whoosh, and I don't see Philip. Go ahead."

"Yeah, the whoosh," Jack said with a nod. He distinctly remembered that sound from the night he'd found Sydney digging in his backyard. "Camilla was pregnant," he said, looking at the woman to whom he'd made love without protection.

"Are you sure?" Sydney asked, and Jack nodded. She directed her gaze to the Bible. "I found marriages, births, and deaths noted in the family Bible, but no evidence that Cammy ever had a baby. There's a Johnson family tree in the Bible, but it stops with Cammy."

"Camilla says in her diary she and Philip conceived a child on the eve of his departure to sea."

"Philip knew it was possible, but he hoped that

wasn't the case for her sake. He had a younger brother and thought he might be the Johnson-Burke ancestor." Sydney shook her head with compassion. "In 1776, being an unwed mother would have been a terrible scandal. Her parents were probably too embarrassed to note the birth in their Bible."

"They were so embarrassed, they forced her to marry Striker." Jack read from the diary, "'*Again this morning I beseeched Mama and Papa to send me away until my child is born. Still angry with me, they refused. Thus, on this rainy afternoon, I married a man twenty years older than my father. His name is Malcolm Striker. He calls himself a lord, but he is a monster. He has a mouth full of rotten teeth and foul breath. I wonder if my folks would have allowed the marriage had they known the real reason he married me.*'" Jack sensed the tension in Sydney as she sat beside him. He held the diary away from her and read ahead silently.

"What was the real reason?" Sydney asked, taking hold of a corner of the diary.

Jack smiled. "Are you hungry?"

"No," she laughed. "We just had burgers and fries." Sydney took the diary from him and read aloud, "'*Malcolm Striker informed me directly after the nuptials that I am far beneath him socially. He says a rich man such as himself is of a much higher class than my father who owns a tavern. But Papa doesn't own just one, he owns half a dozen and serves meals. At least he did before the British burned them for his loyalty to General George Washington.*'"

Jack saw Sydney grimace. After returning from New York and doing some heavy brooding, it had occurred to Jack that his money might be intimidating Sydney. If he were to come straight out and tell her not to let it affect her feelings for him, she'd deny that it did. Or worse yet, accuse him of thinking she was a gold-digger again. He'd thought the best thing to do was ignore the issue. Now, he decided to hint that his money shouldn't keep them apart.

"My mother must really like you since she wants us to help each other."

"Have I mentioned that my dad is an electrician with a small construction crew consisting of J.D. and Will? My mom is the secretary." Sydney said without looking at him. "I was the first one in the family to go to college." She added with a smile, "Now, my two younger brothers are working their way through the same school I attended."

"Sounds like they're all hard workers. On my mother's side, my great-grandfather labored at the Brooklyn Navy Yard, originally called the New York Navy Yard, repairing and maintaining ships." Jack saw Sydney's head snap sideways and recognized surprise in her eyes. Jack continued as casually as she had, "His son, my grandpa, was working his way through college at the shipyard when he met my grandmother, who was a nurse at the nearby Brooklyn Naval Hospital. My mother also became a nurse. She and my dad literally bumped into each other on Wall Street one day. He spilled his iced coffee on her scrubs and offered to make it up to her by taking her to dinner."

"Aww, I love that story." Sydney's smile hinted at a crack in the chain around her heart. "Your mother's history involved ships—like Philip's history. Maybe that's why they were starting to connect."

"Maybe so."

Pushing her glasses up her cute nose, Sydney said, "I was researching Wall Street recently," she arched a pretty brow, "and I read that an actual wall was built by Dutch settlers in 1653 to repel any British attacks. Later, the wall was left intact because it kept barnyard animals apart from the bankers."

"The Brooklyn Navy Yard and the Wall Street building didn't keep my parents apart. Both sets of grandparents were thrilled when my dad and mom announced their engagement."

Sydney tilted her head and smiled. "So your dad's side of the family approved?"

"For a wedding gift, my grandfather gave my parents the deed to the Malone Building on Wall Street. My grandfather and Dad worked twelve-and-fourteen-hour-days for years, and then just weeks before Grandpa died, Dad took him to see the brownstone he and mom bought on the Upper East Side. My parents' similar goals turned into making dreams come true."

Tears glistening in her eyes, Sydney said, "You must be so proud of your parents."

"Nobody had a better marriage than they did."

"Or had a better son," she added and then lowered her lashes as if the words had just slipped out. She cleared her throat and clasped her hands tightly in her lap.

"Hey, this is daytime. You aren't flattering me to earn points in the contest?" Jack teased. "Are you?"

"Of course I am," Sydney said with a lighthearted laugh.

Jack laughed too. "If you do win the contest, what would you do with the money?"

"When Philip first told me about the coins, I knew they weren't truly his to give. But if I win our bet, I'd use them to help my family."

"I had a client once who sold ten coins, which, if I'm not mistaken, were similar to the silver 1776 Continental Dollars in the iron box. Only, my client's coins were brass, so not as valuable as silver. "

"Really? How much did he get for the brass ones?"

"An average of half a million. Each," Jack said then

paused. "If the coins had been silver, it would have added an extra million per coin."

Sydney shook her head in obvious shock. "You're the mathematician, financial expert, Jack. How much would twenty-two, 1776 Continental Dollar silver coins be worth today?"

"A cool thirty-three million."

"What? Sydney's eyes widened, and her mouth dropped in stunned surprise. "I considered the stakes high, but this—I had no idea."

"These stakes are the highest," Jack said, thinking that, at least for him, they were. "How would you help your family…should you win the contest, of course?"

"I'd make sure my parents could retire in style." Sydney smiled and, maybe feeling bashful, bit her lower lip. "I'd share with J.D. and Will, my two older brothers. Since they were kids, inventing haunted houses, they've dreamed of building and running their own local amusement park. Neither is married yet because they feel they can't afford families."

"Yet, your father married and had five children, and you turned out all right," Jack offered jokingly, all the while considering their conversation a serious one.

"My brothers and I turned out all right because we have devoted, loving parents just like you did," Sydney replied.

"Our backgrounds aren't so different then, are they?"

Sydney shrugged. "T.J. is studying finance, like you did, and Chuck, my youngest brother, plays college basketball with an eye on signing with a professional team. And I'd include Nellie since she married into the Johnson-Burke family."

"Does that leave anything for you?"

Forty-Two

" I don't know."

Money is not what Sydney wanted out of the contest. She just wanted Jack. But Cammy didn't get Philip, and Sydney deeply feared she wouldn't get Jack. Picking up Camilla Johnson's diary, she thumbed a few pages ahead and read, "'*Malcolm Striker has come forth with the real reason he married me—to insure he would always have a young wench in his bed. He took in his full-time house-keeper and his live-in cook after killing their husbands. He says they do not know this, and he shall kill me should I divulge the truth. He says since my family is accustomed to waiting on customers, he considers me his tavern whore.*'"

Jack growled, "Camilla's father owned and operated legitimate businesses. Striker was a murdering psychopath who bought people and destroyed lives."

Sydney looked over the tops of her glasses at him. "I almost think you're getting as involved in all this as much as I am."

Jack grinned and shrugged. "I play well with others."

Sydney giggled. "Yes, you do."

Jack took the diary and laid it aside. Ichabod hopped

off the Martha Washington chair and moseyed away in the direction of the kitchen. As Jack tugged Sydney across his lap, she took off her glasses. Their mouths met, and Jack's hand strayed underneath her crop top as she wound her arms around his neck. When he slid his fingers up a leg of her panties, Sydney reminded him it was daylight, they were on her turf, and any points won were hers to keep.

"Dammit," he growled and smacked his hands on the sofa.

"Okay now—" Sydney scooted back to her spot beside him, "let's see what else happened to Cammy." When Jack agreed with a groan, she studied the diary, carefully turned pages, and then continued, "'*Striker was furious when he discovered I am four months gone with my beloved Philip's child. He and my father had quite the row. Malcolm accurately accused Papa of knowingly passing off a daughter carrying a bastard child. My father declared I was no longer his problem, but Striker's.*'" Sydney sucked in her breath.

"Sydney." Jack tried to take the diary from her, but she held tight, her hands shaking. "'*Mr. Striker, I have never referred to him as a lord, claims a baby will interfere with me taking care of his needs. He swears if my parents will not take the baby in, which they will not, then the moment it's born, he will kill it. He says the compromise is he will let me live. Philip, trust me, I will not let our child be harmed. But if you can, please come back to me before he or she is born.*'" Sydney felt her throat constrict with pain but forced herself to read to the end of the page. "'*Striker says he will not touch my soiled body until after the birth of the child. Thank you for the five-month reprieve, dear Lord.*'" Jack took the diary. Sydney bowed her head. "Philip will be heartbroken. What am I going to tell him?"

"That Camilla's suffering is long since over." Jack

watched tears trickle down Sydney's soft cheeks. He turned the diary pages ahead five months and read for a moment. As Sydney wiped her tears, he said, "Tell him Camilla got her revenge."

"How? What happened?"

"All alone and nine months pregnant, she ran away from Striker's house in the middle of the night and made her way to Anastasia Island. Relatives there took her in. She had the baby and named him Philip Johnson Burke. She's hiding on the island, and so far, Striker has not been able to find her."

"Good for Cammy." Sydney's teary eyes grew round with happiness and she clasped her hands under her chin. She sniffled and nodded. "I like her."

"Apparently, Cammy had a problem with compromise, just like somebody else I know." He cocked a slashing brow. "Hell, I'll bet Camilla didn't wear a bra, either."

"Of course not. Bras weren't invented until 1913."

"I rest my case," he teased. "You women can be such bad girls."

Her sweet lips brushing his, Sydney whispered, "You men usually ask for it."

"We men usually have to beg for it."

Sydney reared back and laughed. "I haven't heard you beg."

"Then you haven't been listening closely enough."

Sydney wrapped her arms around his neck, and his large hands flattened to the small of her back. He smelled so clean and sexy and male. His muscular embrace hinted of restrained power, and his caressing fingers promised wanton excitement.

"Since you're so wickedly handsome, I won't make you beg."

Jack grinned with boyish charm. "More of your flattery is not going to seduce me on your time and territory."

"I don't need flattery to seduce you," Sydney said. "I know you want me so badly, I can have you naked in twenty seconds any time I choose."

"Uh-huh," Jack agreed absentmindedly and looked back at the diary. He chuckled as Sydney covered the page with her hand.

Sydney raised an eyebrow and warned, "Don't expect me to be easy to seduce tonight."

"By tonight, you'll need me so damn bad, you'll rip my pants off."

"You wish." Sydney laughed incredulously.

"I sure do," he groaned in a husky voice.

"There's a problem—" His ocean-blue eyes smoldered, sending flames to every corner of Sydney's heated body. "With ripping your pants off," she finished, burning to do just that.

"What?"

"We're out of wrappers."

"Right. We've researched and read all afternoon. Let's go out to dinner and stop by the drugstore."

Leaving the diary and Bible open on the sofa, Sydney leaned forward and gently stacked the newspaper clippings into a neat pile on the glass coffee table. She hadn't seen or heard Philip all day. Often, he was wandering the forlorn little pier or searching for Cammy when he wasn't at Jack's house or hers. Philip had waited two and a half centuries, maybe a couple more hours wouldn't matter.

"Last one to my scooter is a rotten egg!"

"You mean the last one to my Harley."

Sydney hopped off the sofa and squealed as the gorgeous man bailed off after her. She raced down the hall and into the kitchen. Ichabod, lying on the window sill, looked unconcerned at yet another wild chase.

Sydney made a grab for her purse, but Jack caught her arm and opened the door. Ichabod darted past them and scampered to the courtyard bench. Laughing as Jack pulled her outside, Sydney ran down the steps ahead of him. He snared her hand, and they passed by her garage on the way to Jack's. He'd left his Harley parked outside, and he let go of her long enough to throw a leg over the seat and start the engine.

She shrieked as Jack started down the drive without her. He stopped, chuckled, and winked. Her heart raced, and she ran to him. Flinging her arms around his neck, she kissed his lips. She loved him so much she wanted the fleeting days of summer to last forever.

Jack sent her back to the garage for the helmets and she came out wearing hers, then threaded her leg between his back and the sissy bar. After Jack put on his helmet, she molded herself to him, and he gave her bare thigh a pat. With helmets in place, he drove to *Seafood and Sunsets*, a waterfront bar and grill that was a favorite of locals. As the sun lowered in the west, they shared a generous platter of salmon, scallops, hurricane shrimp, and snow crab. Then, they headed to the nearest drugstore where Jack parked close to the entrance. Sydney slid off the motorcycle and removed her helmet. Jack did the same and pulled his money clip out of his jeans pocket.

"I'll finance if you do the leg work," he suggested.

"Since you still have my credit card, it's a deal." She placed her helmet over the sissy bar and unselfconsciously held out her hand for the money.

"Hurry back to me."

Forty-Three

J ack watched Sydney's long hair bounce down her crop top to the miniskirt hugging her sexy fanny as she sashayed into the drug store. Out on the main road, a car honked. He saw Patricia Hudson driving past in her Cadillac. As she frantically waved at him, he barely lifted his chin in greeting. But her car slowed, and Jack hoped Sydney returned before Patricia could circle the block and find a parking space. No matter how blunt he'd been, Patricia, both experienced and aggressive, had persisted in trying to get him into her bed. He'd been there years ago. Once. He'd known then there would never be a second time. Sure enough, Patricia backtracked, found a parking spot, and hurried toward him.

"Where have you been keeping yourself, stranger?" Patricia asked upon reaching him. Wearing a business casual blouse and slacks, she placed a hand on his forearm.

"Busy at home," Jack answered.

"You don't look busy now," she said, tracing a finger up his arm to his shoulder. "Let's go to *Seafood and Sunsets*, and I'll buy you a drink."

"Just had dinner there."

"You should have called me."

"Three's a crowd," he said.

The automatic sliding doors of the drugstore opened, and the gorgeous woman, who'd been an innocent virgin and never bought condoms in her life, strolled into view. He grinned at her, and the smile on Sydney's face never wavered as she looked from him to the realtor. Patricia let out a huff of irritation beside him and kept her hand on his arm.

"Hello, Patricia," Sydney said pleasantly.

"I thought you were back in California."

To Jack, Sydney said, "Philip asked me to stay until we find Cammy." To Patricia, she said, "Jack and I made other arrangements."

With a wink, Jack purposely and playfully snatched the drugstore bag from Sydney. Only then did Patricia take her hand off his arm. He peered into the sack and nodded at Sydney.

"Good job, Doc." Jack started the motorcycle and put on his helmet. Sydney did the same, and as the Harley roared, Patricia stepped back while Sydney mounted behind him.

"Goodbye, Patricia." Sydney took the bag from Jack as the realtor stalked away.

"Good riddance," Jack muttered, again not appreciating her rudeness toward Sydney. Wrapping her arms around him, Sydney molded her magnificent body to his. He patted her thigh like always. "Let's go home and do it all night long, baby girl."

They dropped Jack's motorcycle off at his house. He fed Buster, and then, leaving him in the backyard for fresh air and exercise, they made their way across the adjoining properties to the Queen Anne house. By the time Sydney unlocked the door to her house, it was getting dark. Ichabod spotted them and bailed off Jack's half of the bench. Sydney entered the kitchen, and the fluffy white cat pranced in behind her. As Jack shut the back door, Ichabod rubbed against his legs. Sydney giggled as Jack rolled his eyes.

"You're loved, Jack," Sydney said.

"So are you," Jack said as the cat rubbed against Sydney.

They looked at each other for a moment, and then Sydney broke the silence by saying, "If you pour some of that hard cat food into Ichabod's cat dish, I'll go upstairs and find something to sleep in at your house."

"You won't have it on long, but okay."

Heading out of the kitchen to the hallway, over her shoulder, she said, "I think I told you I won't be easy to seduce tonight, and all you might be doing is dreaming."

Picking up a bag of cat food, Jack replied, "And I said I doubt it."

Forty~Four

Tingles raced to every part of Sydney's body. When Jack took a step toward her, she laughed and jogged down the hall. Flipping on the switch to the crystal chandelier in the foyer, she looked back down the hallway in time to see Jack pet Ichabod's head after feeding him. Sydney's heart sang, and then she absentmindedly glanced into the living room while passing it. The glass coffee table grabbed her attention, and she stopped in her tracks.

"Jack, didn't I stack the newspaper clippings into a neat pile on the coffee table before we left the house?"

Swaggering toward her, he said, "Yeah, maybe"

"I know I did." Sydney walked from the foyer into the living room. The newspaper clippings were spread out this way and that. Ichabod had been in the backyard, so there was only one other explanation. Goosebumps crawled up her arms, and she glanced at Jack. "Philip was here while we were gone. He moved the clippings."

Jack followed her and frowned. "Syd-ney…"

"Who else could it be?" Sydney turned on a lamp and sat down on the sofa. Jack stood near her as she put on her glasses. Gingerly picking up the clipping seemingly placed front and center, she said, "Here's proof of what Captain Bledsoe wrote in his journal about Striker being on trial. Guess who testified against him." Sydney's hand shook as she gave Jack the article.

He read the headline aloud, "'*Wife Testifies Against Striker. He Will Hang!*'" Jack sat down next to her, and began reading the article aloud. Though the antique report wasn't as clearly stated as it would have been in current times, it was clear enough. When the newspaper stated Camilla had been holding a three-month-old male child when she witnessed the shooting, Sydney sniffled, and Jack stopped reading. "It happened a helluva long time ago, Sydney."

"Poor Cammy," Sydney choked out. "I can only imagine her joy and fear when she received word the *Sea Phantom* was spotted sailing toward land. She was courageous enough to come out of hiding with her three-month-old son, planning to meet Philip at the pier."

Jack read further and said, "But Striker also heard about the ship and was waiting. The report says a sailor, named Higgins, also testified, saying it was early on a foggy morning when he noticed a woman wearing a green cape in the distance. She was riding in a small wagon hitched to a single horse as Philip Burke rowed their dinghy to the pier."

Sydney and Jack both looked out the window at the pier, and she said, "But Philip has never mentioned seeing Cammy at the pier."

"That fits with Higgins testifying Philip was rowing the dinghy. Philip's back was to Camilla and to Striker when '*Striker charged out of the murky mist and ran down the pier aiming a flintlock pistol.*'"

"Philip was within seconds of being reunited with Cammy and meeting his son," Sydney said. Jack took her shaking hands in his steady ones. "But for an eternity, he has suffered, never knowing what happened to him or to Cammy."

"He might know now." Jack looked back at the article again and then said, "Higgins claims that after killing Philip, Striker pulled a second pistol out of his coat. Higgins dove into the water to avoid being shot. Then, like the coward he was, Striker ran."

Sydney picked up Camilla's diary. "Cammy says while holding the baby she gathered the father, whom he was named after, in her arms and hugged them both on the pier. Her folks became aware of the ruckus and joined her on the dock. But once again they turned their backs not only on her but the baby. Philip's parents wanted to take her and the baby in, but the proximity was too close to her house, so Cammy secretly returned to Anastasia Island that same day. Oh, how sad, Jack."

"I know. C'mere."

Sydney was gently pulled onto Jack's lap. His strong arms closed around her as his muscular legs spread. Her arms wound around his neck as her fanny slipped between his thighs. As he held her, she sobbed for Cammy, Philip, and the baby.

"Look at it this way, Sydney," Jack patted her back, and she gulped, trying to be still and listen, "Camilla nailed Striker in court. He might have been found innocent without her testimony. The sailor, named Higgins, admits he would not have stayed in port to testify against Striker if Camilla hadn't asked for his help."

Sydney nodded. "But, the thought of Cammy and her baby on the dock with Philip dead in her arms, I hate that…" Her voice broke on another sob.

Jack hugged her tightly. "I hate it too."

"Philip knew he'd been shot, but never knew who did it. I told him that his spirit must have been in such shock at the time, he blocked it out. I hope he knows the baby Camilla brought to the dock was his and not Striker's."

Jack reminded her, "Camilla says while holding the baby she gathered his father in her arms. He knows he had a son named Philip."

"Yes, right," Sydney agreed. She crawled off his lap but sat next to him and read from the diary again. "*With Striker in the custody of the authorities and on trial, when Captain Bledsoe met me in court, he surreptitiously offered me coins Philip had earned—*" Sydney stopped and looked at Jack, her heart pounding. "The coins."

Jack took the diary and continued, "*I thanked the captain but couldn't accept the coins because if Striker is found innocent, he could steal the coins from me. Captain Bledsoe said he and Philip agreed the coins should be buried behind the Burkes' house. 'Tis the only place they felt would be safe. Striker hired a horrible man to follow me home from the trial. So instead of leading him to the baby hidden on Anastasia Island, I am temporarily staying in my old bedroom in Striker's empty house.*"

"How gutsy," Sydney said. "But dangerous." She took over reading, "*'Tis rumored Striker expects to be found not guilty. Hence, the horrible man watching me to make certain I do not escape with any wealth Philip may have secreted to me from the British ships. Striker did not think I would be allowed, as a woman and his wife, to testify against him. But the judge kindly allowed it. If Striker hangs, he cannot steal my baby as he stole my beloved.*"

Jack scowled and added his opinion, "Striker was a bastard."

Sydney agreed and read the next segment in the diary, "*This morning Striker was found guilty and hanged by the neck until he was dead. For the baby's sake, I will use the coins to make a grand life for us here in St. Augustine. Now that I am Striker's widow, I am legally allowed to inherit his house and property. Philip's son and I shall hold our heads high.'"*

Jack said, with conviction, "I like a woman who doesn't tuck her tail and run. I guess that's about the same as admitting I believe all this."

But now that Jack had come around to her side, Sydney was too upset to smile back. "If Cammy stayed in St. Augustine, where is her grave, Jack? Why can't Philip find it?"

"We've made a lot of progress today. Let's work on figuring that out tomorrow."

"No, Jack. Tonight." Sydney wiped her teary eyes. She heard him groan as she leaned over the glass coffee table. Ichabod wandered into the living room and jumped onto the sofa as Sydney poured over Cammy's diary and the clippings.

"Go sit in your chair, cat," Jack muttered, but instead, Ichabod lay down on his lap.

"According to this article," Sydney said, picking up another clipping, "Camilla was front and center at the gallows." She looked at Jack as he petted Ichabod. "But it was the last time she was seen alive."

Forty~Five

"What happened to her?" Jack asked. He'd done his best to keep his hands off Sydney, but he didn't think he could do so much longer. "I thought Camilla was going to make a life for herself and the baby in St. Augustine."

"Foul play was suspected. But, with no ransom note and no body, no charges were filed against anyone."

"Surely, her parents didn't send her away at that late date."

"I'll bet Striker's ghost killed her!"

When Sydney whirled around to him, her long hair flew, and Jack saw a wild look in her big green eyes. "Now, Sydney, just calm down."

"Calm down?" Sydney asked and started to get up. "You know that riles me up."

Jack casually slipped his fingers into the back of her miniskirt and tugged her down on the sofa. Ichabod jumped to the floor. "I might believe Striker reached out from the grave and killed her for testifying against him, but—"

"What do you mean reached out?" she asked, turning to face him.

"I figure Striker, who was guilty of who knows how many murders, decided to have her killed for testifying against him. Since no one saw her after his necktie party, I think he paid the guy watching her to follow her home and murder her."

"His necktie party?"

Yeah," Jack grinned, trying to lighten the mood. "His hanging."

Jack watched Sydney worry her lower lip with her teeth. She was so vulnerable and so beautiful, Jack pulled her into his arms and smiled as her arms twined around his neck. He leaned back, letting her fanny nestle between his thighs. He patted her hip and rested his cheek on her silky hair.

"I think you're right. The *horrible man* she mentioned in her diary killed her. What we have found out about Cammy has probably upset Philip more than ever."

"You never promised him the news would be happy."

"True." Sydney leaned back, and he brushed a lock of hair away from her cheek. "But, what if I can't find her grave between now and August 31? September 1 will be here before we know it."

Jack vividly pictured Sydney leaving St. Augustine. Could he take her to the airport, put her on a plane, and wave goodbye? Hell, no. He'd rather take a bullet in the back than watch Sydney fly out of his life forever.

"Jack, let's walk to the pier where they parted and almost reunited. I look at it every day, but you and I have never been there together."

"It's not the original pier from 1776, of course, but it's located in the same spot."

～

With a breeze cooling the night, Sydney wore Jack's green hoodie. They stopped by his house and took Buster with them. Hand-in-hand, they crossed the red brick road and walked down the sandy beach to the dock. The moon lit up the night and shone off the ocean, lapping at the forlorn little pier. Buster sat down on the other side of Sydney as if sensing she needed him. Jack saw in Sydney's glittering green eyes a sadness that made his heart constrict in pain. A wispy wind smelling of the sea blew into the hood of the sweatshirt. Jack gave Sydney's hand a shake and a squeeze.

"It won't be your fault if you can't find out how Camilla died or where her grave is. Maybe her grave isn't around here. After Striker's hanging and knowing the baby was safe on Anastasia Island, maybe Camilla forfeited everything and ran away."

"No," Sydney whispered with conviction. Looking up at him, she shook her head. "Cammy would have used those coins like she said to make a grand life for her son's sake."

"How can you be so sure?"

Sydney put a hand over her heart. "Because that's what I would do for my son, especially if he were all I had left of his father."

"Yes, you would." Jack nodded. Sydney sighed and gazed out to sea. Instead of a horse and wagon carting her away from the pier, Jack saw a cab whisking her away from Magnolia Road. Staring at the ocean, he said, "Painful as it is, Philip had the right to know about his son. I'd want to know if I fathered a child."

Sydney didn't respond as the breeze became wind, slapping up whitecaps on the sea. Jack wasn't sure if she'd interpreted his message or not. If by any remote chance she was pregnant, he hoped she'd tell him. At times like this, he felt his situation with the woman he loved was as uncertain as the choppy waters stretching before them.

"I'd want the father of my child to be involved in raising him or her," Sydney whispered, staring at the water.

"Good." Jack smiled. He turned Sydney to face him and gently gripped her slender shoulders. "We've found out as much as we could about Philip, and we've found out all we can about Camilla. Tomorrow, let's concentrate on Striker."

"We know about that monster." Sydney trembled and glanced around the dock. "I can almost see a sinister, dark figure bursting out of the foggy shadows, running down the pier, and shooting Philip. I'm sure Striker was hoping to get his hands on Cammy at the same time, figuring she would come out of hiding. But it sounds like after killing Philip, Striker was too busy trying to kill Higgins to have spotted Cammy in the distance."

Jack squeezed her shoulders and she looked up at him. "We still don't know where Striker's house was. Let's go to the courthouse or the historical society or wherever we need to go to find out where he lived."

Sydney wound her hands around Jack's wrists and asked, "What good will it do to find out where Striker lived?"

"I'm not sure. But it can't hurt."

Sydney hugged him, and he felt her shiver before she asked, "Wouldn't you rather play basketball at the Y or in your driveway than do research in a stuffy room full of records?"

"Yeah," Jack said as he chuckled. "Tomorrow is Saturday. If you'll play with me this weekend, I'll research with you on Monday."

Sydney tightened her hands around his wrists. "Play with you on a court or in bed?"

"Your choice. Both."

"Bed tonight," Sydney whispered urgently. They turned and followed Buster, who took the lead, back down the pier. "I love history. But, for the first time, I wish I could rewrite it," she said as they reached the sandy beach.

Crossing the red brick road, Jack said, "The past is etched in stone, Sydney. Let's focus on the future."

Her voice quavered, "But, it's no fair, Jack."

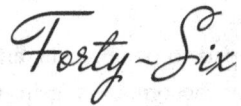

Forty-Six

"**N**o fair, Sydney," Jack said as he laughed the next morning under clear blue skies.

"You don't play fair, either."

Wearing a tummy shirt and short shorts, she had stepped in front of him as they played basketball in his driveway and wrapped her arms around his tapered waist. When he had tossed the ball at the hoop, she'd run her hands over his rear end.

"Foul," Jack said with a chuckling groan. Buster, bounding here and there, barked. "Hell, ever Buster saw that."

"Ooh!" Sydney let go of him and hopped away in a playful fit as yet another basket added to Jack's score. "Call foul on Jack, Buster," she said to the dog as the ball bounced to a stop next to Buster's doghouse. "That makes it forty to zero, your favor, Doc."

"Well, baby girl, I don't know what to tell ya. I've only been shooting with one hand. And half the time, I close my eyes when I take a shot. You said you knew how to play."

"I didn't say I was any good at it." Sydney huffed as

her ponytail swished. She stepped back and admired her opponent. His gym shorts rode low beneath the sexy male navel circled by black hair. "In high school, I was a cheerleader."

"A cheerleader, huh? Let's have a look at your pom-poms."

Jack's eyes dipped to her breasts, and Sydney folded her arms over her bosom. His grin was so boyishly charming. Sydney stuck her chin in the air and looked away to keep from falling under his magnetic spell and lifting her shirt. Even so, his image played in her mind. A sheen of perspiration clung to his naked chest, muscular arms, and powerful thighs. He was totally male and masculine. Her eyes were drawn back to his body and took a bold trip from the soft bulge in his shorts up to his gorgeous face. She met his amused gaze and pursed her lips.

"I quit," she said. As he retrieved the basketball, she threatened, "Furthermore, I'm not going to show you anything but the inside of the courthouse."

"You're not a quitter. If you don't make a basket, you won't be able to concentrate at the courthouse," Jack predicted as he bounced the basketball onto the concrete driveway. "Just like you can't totally concentrate on you and me because of Philip and Camilla." He crooked his finger. "Come here and I'll help you make a basket."

A bit stunned by his insight into her psyche, Sydney went to him without hesitation. "I'm failing at basketball, you and me, Philip and Cammy, and everything."

"Bull." Jack handed her the basketball, twirled her toward the hoop, and clamped his hands to her waist. "Jump!" She did, and her feet left the ground as he hoisted her into the air. She squealed and giggled. "Take your best shot, Syd, just like you always do."

With Jack's help, Sydney made the basket. He stood

her to the ground, and she instantly turned to him. With glances left and right, she lifted her tummy shirt, and with a grin, Jack eyed her naked *pom-poms*. She twined her arms around his neck, and his hands went under her arms. He lifted her up, and her legs locked around his waist. Sydney's heart raced when Jack's hands cupped her fanny as his mouth touched hers. Kissing him, she flattened one hand across his shoulders and ran her fingers through the soft hair at the back of his head.

"Excuse me. I guess you didn't hear me drive up."

Sydney darted a look over her shoulder at Patricia Hudson. She had shoulder-length hair! Extensions? Or a wig? Obviously, the woman was pulling out all stops, and Sydney didn't plan to leave Jack alone with her again. She'd seen Jack send the woman on her way the day of the ruined barbecue and witnessed his cool attitude toward Patricia outside the drugstore. But obviously, she wasn't getting the message. Since the past was etched in stone, Sydney decided to concentrate on the future.

Facing Jack, Sydney quickly unwrapped her arms and legs from around him. He pulled her top back into place and grabbed her hand. Turning toward Patricia, Sydney raised her brows in an innocent expression.

"What can I do for you, Patricia?" Jack asked.

"The other day when I saw you at the drugstore, I'd planned to ask you if you needed any help with the research you're doing on your houses," she added with meaning, "Jack."

"Sydney's in charge of the research. If she needs anything, she can contact you," Jack grumbled just as Sydney's cell phone, lying next to his on top of Buster's doghouse, rang.

"That might be the call we're expecting." With Jack's hand in hers, Sydney gave him a tug. He walked away from Patricia and never looked back. Sydney answered her cell. "Hello?" she said as Jack wrapped his arms around her from behind and molded her to his hard body. It was nearly impossible to concentrate on the caller, with Jack's lips on her neck and Patricia's eyes boring into them, but she managed. "That's wonderful. Yes, we'll be right there."

"Who are you talking to, and where are we going?"

"We can forget the courthouse." Sydney looked over Jack's shoulder, and Patricia glared at her. It was daytime, her hours to win the bet. Might as well take her best shot at Jack in front of Patricia.

"Why can we forget the courthouse?" he asked.

"Because the church is available. By the way, my size five and a half, one-whole-carat diamond solitaire is ready for pick up," she began, knowing Patricia would expect nothing less than a full-carat diamond from Jack, "We're all set." With his back to Patricia, Sydney saw Jack cock a brow as a scolding smile touched his lips.

"Got it." Jack winked conspiratorially before saying loudly enough for Patricia to hear, "Let's go get your ring and rent the church."

Sydney saw Patricia's eyes narrow and knew the realtor wouldn't be back…at least not until she found out Jack was not really getting married. But pangs of possessiveness stabbed Sydney's heart, knowing Patricia would be after him in September. Even so, Sydney smiled at Jack for going along with her. Though she was taking her best shots, in the end, she expected to fail at winning in more ways than just on the basketball court.

Sydney whispered, "It was a member of the National Register of Historic Places."

Forty-Seven

After cooking a late breakfast at Jack's house, Sydney lifted her eyes from the laptop, where she had been compiling and documenting the histories of Jack's six houses. The information was a result of research gathered from the courthouse records, historical society records, and writings in Captain Bledsoe's journal. The most recent was from the National Register of Historic Places. Sun streamed in the alcove window of Jack's kitchen. From over the top of her reading glasses, she glanced across the table at the handsome man she loved.

Jack had *The Wall Street Journal* pulled up on his laptop and was immersed in it. Sydney smiled. His interest in his career had returned. Financially, he didn't have to work. But he wasn't the kind of guy willing to live off family money without pulling his own weight. One of the countless traits Sydney admired about him.

However, if someone had asked her, a few weeks ago, to describe a Wall Street tycoon, she wouldn't have depicted a man who looked and dressed like Jack. His black hair had grown all summer. With length, a gorgeous wave of body had appeared. The sides hid the tops of his ears, and the back touched the collar of his white tee shirt. When he'd ridden his Harley to the grocery store earlier for bacon and eggs, he'd worn a black leather vest over the tee shirt. As he turned sideways in his chair, taking the laptop off the table, he laid an ankle over his knee. That afforded Sydney a glimpse of his snug blue jeans and black leather boots. She was sure if more stockbrokers looked like Jack Malone, more women would invest in the market.

"Something on your mind, Doc?" Jack asked, his gaze on the laptop.

Bringing her eyes up his body Sydney saw him glance at her out of the corner of his eye. "Wouldn't you like to know?"

"Yeah. Tell me."

"I'm glad the National Register of Historic Places had the records you needed on your houses, but we still don't know where Striker's house was."

Jack turned his head, giving her his full attention. "You started from scratch in your kitchen the day Philip appeared. You've made a ton of progress."

"But I haven't seen Philip since Nellie brought that box of information. It's like he no longer gives a fig, as he would say."

"That's not on you. You did your research at Flagler College, you found Nellie on Anastasia Island, and you engaged with all sorts of experts from the museum jail to the historical society. You've done a fantastic job."

Sydney shrugged. "I wouldn't have had the captain's journal and manifest if you hadn't bought them from the antique dealer. It was Bledsoe who verified your property had been a sailor's rest."

"You got Camilla's diary, family Bible, and newspaper clippings. I think the fact that Camilla's family, who owned those meal-serving-taverns, is appropriate since you're such a good cook."

"No more appropriate than the records which said the original owner of your Victorian house was built by the man who started the largest bank in St. Augustine. And that he built the Queen Anne house for his mother and mother-in-law because they were both widows."

Jack smiled and nodded. "Would be great to live here year-round and work next door to the local branch office of the Wall Street firm. Like you once suggested, I'll have it decorated in an old-school style."

"I do like old-school." As they sat at Jack's kitchen table, in her mind, Sydney pictured Jack kissing a wife and child goodbye before walking to his office. If only the wife could be her and the child theirs. "That would be great."

"You don't look like you're convinced it's so great, Sydney."

"Sure, it will be. I can see it all now." Sydney smiled, then shook her head and sighed. "But, you'd think that if the National Register of Historic Places could verify the other four houses here on Magnolia Road were built between 1862 and 1864 by a wealthy attorney whose ancestor came over on the Mayflower, they'd be able to tell us where the house of the infamous Malcolm Striker who hanged for murder is."

"Is that what's making you look defeated?" Jack asked, and she shrugged. "You found out additional information on this block of houses in just the last couple of weeks. My mom hadn't gotten that far, and she'd worked on it a lot longer. Don't torture yourself."

Sydney's definition of torture was not gazing into Jack's ocean blue eyes every day. A sinking feeling weighed the hollow of her stomach, and hot tears stung the back of her eyes at the thought of leaving this man.

"August is almost over. Time for finding out Striker's address is almost up."

Jack closed the laptop and laid it on the table. "On the subject of addresses, the zoning commission is going to let me change the name Magnolia Road to Magnolia Lane based on the information you've uncovered. The addresses which are now 100 through 112 Magnolia Road will return to numbers one through six Magnolia Lane as it was in 1776. I owe you—"

"Nothing." Sydney held up both hands and then clasped them tightly in her lap. She had decided Jack's recent explanation about his maternal family's modest beginnings was to assure her it wasn't because she was poor that she wouldn't win the bet.

She'd never considered Jack to be a snob. She'd just felt unworthy of him. And though she was glad to know he didn't think she was beneath him, she had to get control of her emotions before she crumbled at his feet and begged him to love her. "I told you at the beginning of the summer I thrive on research."

Jack tilted his head and frowned. "Maybe Striker was too infamous."

"What do you mean?"

"Maybe no one wanted to live in his house. If no one inherited the house or kept it up after his death, it would have fallen into disrepair. Like the original houses on this block, maybe it burned, washed away, or was lost during the Civil War. Even if someone eventually did live in it, it wouldn't have necessarily made it into any historical records. And if it wasn't right on the beach like our houses, and vulnerable to hurricanes, it might still be standing."

"You could be right," she said excitedly and then narrowed her eyes in concentration. "Why have you been so persistent in finding Striker's house?"

"That's where we'll find Camilla's grave."

"Dear God!" Shivers shot up Sydney's spine. "Jack, you could be right about that too." Goosebumps popped out on her skin, and she popped out of her chair. Scooting around the table, she seated herself on Jack's lap and hugged him. "What would I do without you?"

"You may soon find out," he reminded her, locking his fingers at her hips. "It's August twenty-fifth. One week from today, on September 1, you'll know if you'll be staying here to teach at Flagler College or are free to go home to Redlands."

Sydney was quiet. Was Jack saying he didn't give a fig about what she did? He'd do just fine without her? The feelings of hopelessness she'd experienced after her breakup with Jack in July ruthlessly stabbed her heart again.

"Ah yes, September 1, the day of reckoning," Sydney said with a soft sigh. "Let's declare a winner of the contest at midnight on August thirty-first. I'd like to know who won the bet before I get the news about my job application."

"Midnight is night-time, my time," Jack grinned and patted her hip. "That bodes well for me being declared the winner and you the loser."

"When Cammy lost Philip, I think her life ended for all intents and purposes," Sydney whispered. "Whether she was murdered by Striker's henchman or died of natural causes, Camilla Johnson had been dead inside for a long time."

Forty-Eight

Jack noticed the sag in Sydney's slender shoulders and heard the regret in her soft voice. He saw the tears glittering in her green eyes. She was worried she wouldn't get the job and maybe even feeling a little guilty for not caring about him the way Camilla had for Philip. What could he do to make Sydney love him body, heart, and soul the way he loved her? If he questioned her comment about Camilla being dead inside, would she admit she felt dead because she could never love him? Maybe. Would he try to come up with reasons why she should? Yes. No. Forget it. He was being too analytical. He couldn't reason her into loving him. Either she did, or she damn well didn't.

Still, he had to ask, "Do you think Camilla realized she didn't love Philip and felt guilty about it after he died?"

"No, not all," Sydney gasped. Her eyes were sharp, and her voice firm. "From the time Philip first told me his story, I knew Cammy loved him totally and completely. I finally have a theory as to why her spirit never found his."

Jack didn't feel any better. Sydney was talking about how much Camilla loved Philip, not how much she loved him. "Tell me your theory, Sydney."

"Doesn't it stand to reason that since he's earthbound with grief that she is too? Couldn't she be trapped by the weight of unfulfilled promises too heavy to lift from her soul?"

"Maybe," Jack said, holding her close. "So you're thinking they're both stuck in a grieving process, like you said I once was?"

"Yes. I'm afraid the reason I haven't seen or talked with Philip lately is because his grieving has worsened. He placed his hope in me, and I've let him down by not finding Cammy's grave."

"If it's any consolation, you cured my grieving, Sydney," Jack gave Sydney the credit due with conviction in his voice. Her smile was filled with compassion as she ran gentle fingers through his hair. She easily stirred a spectrum of emotions in him, ranging from love to desire, worry to joy, and anger to amusement. Why couldn't he have such an effect on her? "Does that mean you think Camilla's spirit is a prisoner in her grave?"

"Possibly. My research on ghosts leads me to believe her spirit is either in her grave or is unable to travel far from it."

"Then we have to find Striker's house."

"But how?"

Jack's cell rang. It was Angus, manager of the Wall Street firm. Jack's eyes followed Sydney as she got off his lap and moseyed back around the glass table. Though she'd worn the bathrobe while cooking, he'd coaxed her into taking it off while eating, leaving her in black satin lingerie. A one piece, it tied around her neck, accentuating her cleavage, and had three rows of black lace ruffles dotted with red bows across her derrière. Her every movement mesmerized him, always making him ache to hold her. Maybe if he'd met her when he'd not been grieving and caught up in a career decision, he'd have made a better impression on her.

"Angus, set up the appointments and have the resumes of the people who are interested in relocating here ready by the end of the month. I'll fly up for the interviews." He listened, then nodded. "Yeah, see you soon." He looked across the table at Sydney and smiled.

"I wondered if you'd decide not to stay in St. Augustine if I got the job at Flagler College. Aren't you taking a risk deciding to stay here, knowing I could be your neighbor?"

Jack had thought just the opposite. Why bother to stay here without her? "Why did you think I'd leave here if you stayed?"

A laugh escaped Sydney as she stood up beside the table. "Because you indicated rather clearly you didn't want to be hassled by a green-eyed nut case from California."

"Yeah, well, I don't mind her in bed."

"Jack!" Sydney laughed and put her hands on her hips.

Standing, he grabbed her and yanked her to him. "Wanna go hassle me in bed?"

"Yes."

How the hell could he say goodbye to this gorgeous girl if she wanted to leave him? He tightened his arms around her, and she rested her head against his chest. He'd taught her how to make love, and she had become an expert. How soon would it be before other men took his place? He felt an ache in his throat. Why not tell her he loved her so much it was killing him? Because the contest would be over and he'd lose the last week he might have left with her.

"It's daytime now," she whispered, looking up at him.

Daytime was her time to compete. But, while he was falling deeper and deeper in love with her, he sensed her pulling back. "Your house or mine?"

"Daytime means my house, my turf, and my bed, my friend."

Jack grinned. "I'll race you over there, neighbor."

Sydney squealed, grabbed her bathrobe from over the back of her chair, and ran across the kitchen to the door. Buster stood and barked as she barreled out of the house.

"Buster, don't let Jack out!" Sydney called over her shoulder.

"Fat chance!" Jack laughed. He and Buster followed Sydney out of the door and down the steps. "Get her, Buster!"

In the courtyard, Buster caught up with her and snared the back of her robe. Jogging behind her, Jack laughed as Sydney boldly let the robe fall. He grabbed it up and said, "You and Buster could do an updated version of the suntan lotion ad with the dog pulling down the girl's swimsuit."

Sydney laughed as she ran. "Tell Buster he'd better not bite my...ruffles, or else!"

"Or else what?"

"I won't let you strip me."

"Buster, go to your doghouse," Jack ordered with a laugh.

As Buster obeyed, Sydney called over her shoulder, "Thank you, Buster! You've become a good friend this summer."

Seeing Ichabod napping on the bench, Jack asked, "When are you going paint my half?"

Sydney just laughed, and he allowed her to stay in the lead so he could watch the ruffles dance across her fanny. As she skirted the courtyard full of forget-me-nots, he wondered how long it would take for her to forget him. Not long. He'd been her first lover, but he wouldn't be her last. She'd always have her choice of men who would want her as much as he did.

Pain cut into his heart as they reached her house. His steps slowed as he followed her through the kitchen and living room. As she headed upstairs, he was just rounding the archway. He took the stairs two at a time and caught her at the doorway of her bedroom.

Sydney pulled free and held up her index finger as she backed away from him. Jack leaned against the door-jamb and watched. Stopping between a full-length mirror and the bed, she crooked her index finger. Damn, she was an innocent little girl one minute and a sexy hot temptress the next. Not only that, this woman could control him using only one finger. He groaned with antic-ipation and heat coiled as he walked to her.

Taking her in his arms, over her shoulder, Jack saw himself and the back of Sydney reflected in the mirror. He ran his hands under her silky hair and along her shoul-ders, then trailed his fingers down her slender back to her small waist. When he touched her bottom, he played with the ruffles decorating her fanny.

Sydney was a flesh and satin hourglass framed by leather and jeans.

Her delicate femininity was so alluring that Jack had to clamp an iron will on himself in order not to rip off her undergarment. She was sensitivity, brains, and sex appeal. She was everything Jack wanted so badly to have and to hold forever.

"Strip me, Jack."

"What's this little number you're wearing called?" he asked.

"Teddy."

Jack's eyes narrowed dangerously. "That's the only

man's name I want to hear come so breathlessly from you." She nodded, and with pleasure, he untied the bow holding up the straps to her lingerie. He eased both sides of the black satin outfit down her body. He looked from Sydney's pink nipples, to her indented belly button, to the vee between her thighs. Jack cupped her beautiful face with his hands and looked into her glittering eyes. "Have I mentioned you're not playing fair in our contest of hearts, Syd?"

Forty~Nine

"On or off the basketball court I never said I play fair, Jackson."

Sydney trembled with relief. She had thought his prolonged silence meant he was not impressed with what she'd worn to try to win him. She slipped her arms around his neck, stood on tiptoes, and touched her lips to his. His arms trapped her to him. Laying her cheek on his chest, she breathed in the leather of his black vest. With her body molded to his, she felt the hard bulge in his jeans pressed to her bare stomach. He wore no belt today, so she brought her hands down his ribs and put her fingers on the top button of his jeans.

There was nothing on earth Sydney wouldn't do to win the contest. For now, she settled on popping open the buttons of Jack's jeans. Hooking her finger into a belt loop, she backed toward the bed and tugged on the magnificent male. His open fly, revealing a path of black hair trailing into his shorts, was loaded with sex appeal.

Sydney's heart raced as he stopped to yank off his vest and jeans. Her knees shook as he dropped his tee shirt and advanced on her. Giddy anticipation coursed through her from head to toe. She backed up another step and met with the side of her mattress.

"Most people think Jack is a nickname for John."

"Philip told me he'd heard your mother call you Jackson when you were a bad boy."

"I didn't think about the fact he was around when I was growing up."

"I think your lingering doubt about ghosts is long gone."

Jack grinned. "Do you know where this bad boy wants to linger for the next hour?"

Sydney gave him an innocent shrug. Her nipples beaded, and she saw a rakish grin on Jack's lips. Taking the weight of her breasts in his hands he gently thumbed the tips. Sydney flattened her hands to his washboard stomach and looked up at him.

"I want us to live together in the same house for this last week of summer, Jack."

Jack brought his gaze up from her breasts and cocked a slashing black brow. "Why?"

Sydney instantly wished she could take the words back. She didn't make another sound as he eased satin and lace past her waist, down her hips, and over her bottom. She ached with longing as he slowly pushed the teddy to her thighs. She loved it when he took control and possessed her body. With a little wiggle, the teddy fluttered to her ankles.

"Because..." Sydney finally whispered, tugging his shorts down his tapered hips. His manhood sprang free, and she closed both her hands around the length of him, trembling with a fierce craving and soul-deep love. "I want this last week of August to be extra happy." She licked her lips, stepped out of the teddy, and hugged herself to Jack's hard, muscular frame. "And because I need all the time I can get with you to make sure I win the contest."

"Move in with me." His smile was charming.

"Okay," she said without hesitation. "Have you lived with a woman before?"

Jack stretched out in the bed and crooked his finger. "No."

Sydney lay down on top of him and whispered, "Then a week is a good length of time. In case you...we don't like it, you won't...we won't be stuck with each other too long."

Sidney was letting him know she wouldn't overstay her welcome. Would he let her bring Ichabod? If so, that might indicate a trace of commitment on his part.

"I guess that cat of yours is part of the deal?" he asked.

"Yes," Sydney purred.

Fifty

Sticking to the contest rules, they'd returned to the Victorian house to spend the night. Waking to a nibble on his neck, Jack wondered if he'd only dreamed Sydney was going to move in with him. After opening his eyes, when his stomach growled, she said she'd make breakfast. They'd played in the shower together first. He'd grinned as she'd reminded him the only clothing she had at his house was the black teddy and robe she'd worn from her house to his in the dark of night. Right on cue, Buster had entered the bedroom with her slobbered-up robe in his mouth.

After breakfast, they decided to go to the Queen Anne house and pack up her clothes and cat. And if Jack had his way, they'd never move out.

Grinning, he opened the front door and checked the mailbox. Nothing. Good. Then he saw Bones ambling down the cobblestones away from Sydney's house. Jack closed the door and, through the cut glass, saw the professor fiddle with the latch on the white picket fence and then head toward Jack's house.

"Hell," Jack grumbled. He didn't see Bone's car and

wondered if he'd walked. If so, he might keep going. No luck. He opened the wrought iron gate to Jack's house, and here he came.

"I'm ready," Sydney said, skipping down the stairs.

Jack turned. She was a magnificent sight to behold. Her wavy blond hair tumbled in wild disarray around her beautiful face. The bodice of her black satin teddy was mostly covered by his black leather vest, which she'd put on after the shower. But he knew the lace ruffling across her pretty bottom bounced in full view. He stopped her descent on the last step.

"Sydney, go back upstairs and find a shirt of mine to put on."

She tilted her head and put her hands on her small waist. "Since Buster slobbered my robe you said I could wear your vest."

"Yes, but—"

"No one but Buster, the clothes-drool-king, will see me cross the back yard to my house, if that's what you're worried about."

"Bones is on his way to the door."

"Don't let him—" Sydney began, he knocked, and she jumped. "—come in!"

"Come in?" came the voice from the porch as the door opened.

Swiveling to face Bones, Jack said, "Don't move, Sydney."

He couldn't let her run upstairs now without Bones seeing her state of undress. Reaching his right hand behind him, Jack scooted Sydney to the center of his back. Standing barefoot on the step above the wood floor, where Jack's booted feet were planted, she was able to peer over his shoulder at the professor.

"Hello, guys," Bones said, seeming a bit flustered.

"Hey," Jack said as the three of them stood in the foyer.

When they were in New York City, Sydney had told Jack that she had never seen him come off as flustered. Her compliment included saying he was a smooth operator in any situation. She'd said from a Wall Street skyscraper to a Florida Victorian mansion, he was never at a loss. In a jet, a Porcshe, or on a Harley, he was always in control. According to Sydney, it was an ultra-sexy quality.

In turn, he'd said it wasn't just her body that drove him crazy. It was her laugh, her personality, and the way she cared about people. From ghosts to her family, she was determined to do her best by them. Innocent girl or tempting siren, she had impressed him as no other woman ever had. Or ever would.

Jack glared at Bones. He wore a tank top, putting his thin arms and bony chest on display. When Jack wore undershirts, Sydney would trace her fingers over his biceps muscles, making him shiver. Her delicate hands always flattened on his chest, and sometimes she pulled his shirt out of his jeans. Surely, Bones wasn't dumb enough to think he'd ever be so lucky to have Sydney touch him like that. This was the first time the guy had appeared in something besides pleated pants. He wore jeans so baggy he could have gotten both legs into one pant leg.

Jack crossed his arms over his chest, and Sydney put her hands on top of his broad shoulders. He instinctively knew that if he was too direct, she'd put the squeeze on him, thereby monitoring the conversation.

"Hi, Leslie," Sydney said. "How are you?"

"Fine, hon—Syd." Bones' Adam's apple bobbed as he nervously glanced at Jack.

"What's up, Bowen?" Jack felt a gentle pressure from

Sydney's slender hands. He grabbed her wrists and yanked her arms around his neck. He was gratified when he jammed his hands into his jeans pockets that she'd clasped her hands at the middle of his collarbone.

Bones looked from Sydney to Jack and answered, "First of all, I wondered if Sydney had decided on her dissertation topic."

"Yes, I have."

"What will it be?" Bones gave her a big grin, and Jack clenched his jaw.

"I'm going to write up the research I've done on Jack's houses, starting with the Mayflower, then the American Revolution, the Civil War, and end with the outcome of restoring this street to its rightful place in St. Augustine history with the historical society's full support."

Hope hit Jack full force. He turned to look at Sydney. Doing so exposed the right half of her body. "You might have to stay past September 1 to do that." She smiled bashfully, and he winked at her. He looked back at Bones and caught his eyes at the level of Sydney's ruffled bottom. Jack faced Bones straight on to make sure Sydney was once again hidden behind him.

"You got your answer," Jack growled, hands on his hips. "See ya, Bowen."

Bones swallowed and fidgeted. "I bought a new car, Sydney. I thought I'd let you know, in case you need any rides anywhere."

Jack frowned menacingly. "You're used to the Porsche and Harley, right?"

"Right and my scooter."

Jack didn't know if that was the truth or not. He figured she was displaying her loyalty to him as he had shown her by not telling Patricia Hudson there was no wedding in the works. Bones smiled longingly at Sydney as she once again cupped her hands to Jack's shoulders.

"Have you made any progress on reuniting Philip and Camilla?" Bones asked.

Sydney slid her hands down Jack's body to his ribs and pressed her breasts to his back. Couldn't Bones see she was too much woman for him? Probably, but it didn't mean he didn't want her.

As Sydney slipped her fingertips into Jack's back jeans pockets, she said, "Jack thinks we need to locate Cammy's grave, but we don't know if we can actually find it or not."

Jack grinned, feeling her palms flatten to the cheeks of his buttocks. Unfortunately, his smile was apparently misinterpreted by Bones, because the professor put his gums on display.

"If you need my help," Bones began, "don't forget that as an archaeologist, I'm pretty good with bones."

"I'm gonna help her, Bone...Bowen." Jack felt Sydney squeeze both cheeks of his rear end. Undoubtedly Bones would keel over in a faint were Sydney to pinch his butt. The picture of a pasty Bones passed out on the floor made Jack chuckle. He realized he wasn't jealous of Bowen. He was just anxious for him to leave so that he could move Sydney into his house.

"I noticed some boxes through the window of the door at your house, Sydney." Bones cast a longing glance at her. "Are you leaving St. Augustine early?"

"I'm moving in with Jack," Sydney replied.

Jack liked her unhesitating answer. The fact she had pecked his cheek after saying it and was covertly caressing his rear end didn't hurt, either. Then, a quick second thought reminded him that she was just repaying him for going along with her in front of Patricia Hudson about the engagement ring and church reservation.

"Yeah, so we're kind of busy today," Jack said.

"Oh, I see." Obvious envy made Bones' long face even

longer as he said, "Well, umm... when did this all come about?"

"None of your business, pal," Jack barked. "I have a suggestion for you."

"Jack," Sydney said warningly.

"I know a gal who's into Cadillacs," Jack said.

"Oh? My Cadillac is used, but new to me," the man answered. "Not Sydney's type of umm... car, I guess." He looked from Sydney to Jack. "Who's the gal?"

"Patricia Hudson," Jack said, then heard a soft laugh escape Sydney.

Sydney eased her grip on Jack's rear end and offered sweetly, "The reason Jack and I are moving in together is to find out if we're totally compatible before getting married."

Bones looked stunned by what Sydney had just said, and Jack wished to God it were the truth. "And she thinks Philip is hiding out in my attic."

Sydney gasped, "I do?"

Jack chuckled. "See? She's practicing her wedding vows."

"Yes, I do. I do!" Sydney exclaimed over Jack's shoulder. "Philip has to be hiding out in your attic."

Jack knew Sydney was worried about Philip and had been giving the matter some thought. He remembered the last evidence of Philip's presence was on the day he and Sydney had poured over Camilla's diary, the Johnson family Bible, and newspaper articles. Sydney threw her arms around Jack's shoulders and, in her excitement, leaned too far to her right. Before he could catch her, she slipped off the stair and landed at his right side.

"Jack, the attic has been Philip's safe place for two and half centuries." Sydney's green eyes glittered as she gave a hop for joy. "I'll bet he's up there right now."

"Probably."

Luckily, Sydney landed facing Jack. He grabbed the front of the black leather vest and yanked her closer. He figured her little hop had bounced the ruffles across her bottom. He looked over Sydney's shoulder and, sure enough, saw the naked lust in Leslie Bowen's eyes as the man riveted his gaze on Sydney's satin and lace fanny. She was nothing short of a hot little sexpot wearing his black leather vest over her skimpy teddy. Jack ripped off his tee shirt and jammed it on over Sydney's head. She shoved her slender arms through the sleeves and he was relieved to see the shirt reached her mid-thigh.

"Jack, please. Come on," Sydney urged, with a pleading look as she grabbed his hand. "I want to talk to Philip before we go back to..."

A blush, as red as the bows on her ruffled butt, stained Sydney's cheeks. Over Sydney's head, Jack's eyes met Leslie Bowen's. Jack didn't say a word. Sydney had all but said they'd just crawled out of his bed and were headed to hers. And Jack didn't mind that one bit. The professor's gaze lowered from Jack's face to his bare chest. Bones swallowed his disappointment and spoke to Sydney with downcast eyes.

"Call me, Sydney, if you figure out where Camilla's grave is. I really would like to investigate it with you... and Jack."

Sydney agreed. Bones opened the door and left them alone in the foyer. Jack locked the door, and then he swung around to Sydney. He clenched his jaw and glared at the gorgeous woman clad in his tee shirt. "Sydney, dammit! I don't want any other guy seeing you dressed in your..." He abruptly stopped himself. He'd almost tipped his hand, letting her know that he loved her so much he thought of her as his.

"Teddy?" she breathed playfully.

Fifty-One

"Yeah."

When Jack casually shrugged, Sydney's hopes that he might be a little jealous plummeted. "Come on. Let's go to my house and get my things."

Clad in Jack's tee shirt, they crossed the back yard to her house. Once she had packed up her suitcases, Jack grabbed them both. She took a last look around the bedroom, where they had made lasting memories. At least for her. With an easy grin, Jack said she'd see this bedroom again. To her way of thinking, that was meant to warn her their week living together at his house was temporary. If she stayed in St. Augustine, she would not be living with him in his house. Pasting a smile on her face, Sydney led the way downstairs and paused in the living room. She walked to Ichabod, curled up on the Martha Washington chair, and petted him, saying that he wouldn't be moving with her.

"Why aren't you bringing your dumb cat?" Jack grumbled.

"Because." Sydney didn't know why that should irritate Jack. "Ichabod's not dumb, he's deaf." Surprise registered in Jack's blue eyes. Or maybe it was relief she wasn't bringing Ichabod. She continued into the kitchen, opened a cabinet, and took out a bag of dry cat food.

"I'm sorry about your cat." Entering the kitchen, Jack set her bags on the floor.

"The majority of white cats with blue eyes are deaf. He was a stray when I found him, and I was afraid he'd be hurt or killed without a home and someone to take care of him." She filled the cat food bowl as Jack leaned against the kitchen counter. Ichabod had followed them and rubbed against Jack's leg. Sydney placed the bowl on the floor and Ichabod wound around her feet before walking to his food. "Even though I'd prefer for Ichabod to stay indoors, he'll always have a streak of feral and want time out in the yard."

"I've seen you talk to him and wondered why he often didn't respond," Jack said, crossing his arms over his chest. "He just seemed indifferent. "Why do you talk to him if he can't hear you?"

"Since he can't sign, he's learned to read my lips," she teased and saw a confused, then endearing smile on Jack's face. She'd given Jack countless signs of her love. Why hadn't he responded? Maybe his *indifference* was his response.

"Or he's learned to read your mind," Jack joked.

"If Ichabod could read minds, I'd have him read yours, Dr. Malone."

"He'd say I feel like a jerk for calling him dumb. I kinda like ol' Ichabod Crane."

Closing the bag of cat food, Sydney shrugged. "I've felt kinda dumb all summer, wondering if I'm as crazy as you think I am," she admitted, filling Ichabod's water bowl. She was crazy for thinking she could win Jack's heart. "Ichabod sensed Philip's presence the very first time he visited."

"Maybe that's a sign that you *should* bring Ichabod to my house at least long enough to take him into the attic," Jack said.

"That's sweet of you." Sydney put the cat food bag away. "But because it's only for a week, I've decided it wouldn't be fair to Buster to move Ichabod in on him. And Ichabod is accustomed to this house. I'll come back to let him in and out and feed him every day."

If only Jack would say he wanted her and Ichabod to move in and stay forever. But he didn't say a word. Then it dawned on her. Perhaps his earlier grumble had nothing to do with Ichabod. Maybe Jack didn't appreciate her continuing to lie to people about getting married. She had done so twice now. No doubt he found her too aggressive. Though she'd like nothing better than to marry Jack, she wouldn't hint at it again, no matter what. Jack didn't deserve that.

Then he asked, "Did you see the shirt and jeans Bones had on? He was hoping to impress you."

Sydney wished the fire in Jack's eyes had ignited because of Leslie's interest. Or perhaps he was warning her not to write Leslie off for the future since her time with him in the present was almost over.

"Leslie couldn't impress me the way you do, even if he had muscles under his shirt. And I couldn't care less what he has...or hasn't got in his jeans." She'd hoped to lighten his mood with that provocative compliment. Jack's eyes smoldered. Maybe her flirting had worked.

"You're as naughty 'n nice as what you're wearing." Jack lassoed her with both arms and molded her to his bare chest. His hug wasn't tight enough to suit Sydney. She wanted him to hold her fiercely as if he'd never let go. Still, within his embrace swirled a magical world all its own. She trembled from the desire of spending the rest of her life in his world. "I like it when you're a naughty girl."

"Well, naughty boy," Sydney hugged him, savoring the feel of his hard body, "you taught me everything I know." When Jack nibbled her neck, she was on the verge of begging him to take her on the kitchen floor when something funny occurred to her. With his lips on hers, she giggled, causing Jack to raise his head and cock his brow. "Speaking of trying to impress someone, did you notice anything different about Patricia Hudson the other day when she stopped by to ask if you needed help with the research on your houses?"

"No." He returned to nibbling behind her ear.

"She was either wearing a wig or had hair extensions."

Jack reared back and squinted in concentration. "Really?"

"Yes." Sydney laughed incredulously. "Patricia has ear-length, straight, brunette hair, remember? But, that day, her hair was shoulder-length, wavy, and light brown."

"You're kidding." Jack threw back his head and whooped. His rich laughter, in turn, lightened Sydney's somber mood. "Hell, I didn't even notice."

"That surprises me almost as much as the fact you suggested Leslie ask her out," Sydney admitted with a giggle. "I was about to compliment her on her hair when my phone rang. After speaking to the lady from the National Register of Historic Places, I got so carried away talking about the phony ring and the church versus your block of houses and research that I..." Darn it! She had just promised herself she'd drop the commitment subject. "Forgot."

Placing his hands on the back of Sydney's neck, Jack

lifted her long hair. She smiled, recalling how he'd said he preferred long hair on women. As he let it spill through his fingers, she wished he preferred everything about her to other women. But this man could literally fly around the world to capture any woman he wanted. Why settle for the one next door?

"Patricia hoped if she looked more like you, and Bones hoped if he copied me, they'd have a chance," Jack replied.

Sydney steadied herself and said, "A *ghost* of a chance, as far as I'm concerned."

She didn't want to presume too much as to how Jack felt about Patricia. She wanted to say a lot more about how she felt about Jack but his poker face shut her mouth. Was he reconsidering an interest in Patricia since Sydney had stupidly pointed out to what lengths the woman had gone to capture his attention? To sidetrack him or maybe herself, Sydney picked up one of her suitcases and handed Jack the other one. He took both, and they headed to his house.

Once there, Jack carted her bags straight up to his bedroom. Buster had followed them, and to make sure he didn't slobber on her clothes, Jack turned around and escorted Buster to the back yard. Sydney changed out of Jack's tee shirt and gave it a hug. Then she traded her teddy for one of the silk blouses Jack had given her and a pair of shorts. She had walked to the door of Jack's bedroom as he reached the top of the stairs.

Did Jack Malone have any idea what a stark contrast in male physique he presented compared to other men? But especially sized up against Leslie Bowen? Patricia Hudson, on the other hand, was pretty, shapely, and worldly. She had a fancy Cadillac, manicured nails, and optional long versus short hair. She had money and was plenty enough woman to keep Jack happy. Sydney worried her lower lip, thinking maybe she should have tried to copy Patricia instead of the other way around.

"Hey you, I asked if you're ready to go to the attic," Jack said.

Fifty-Two

It seemed no matter how hard he tried, Jack couldn't keep Sydney's attention. Yet, his concentration and awareness was fully focused on her. Even in a simple blouse and shorts, Sydney was the prettiest girl he'd ever laid eyes on. No wonder Patricia hoped to copy her.

"Yes, I'm ready," Sydney replied with one of her engaging smiles.

Jack led the way down the hall to the attic door, wondering what Sydney had meant by, *A ghost of a chance, as far as I'm concerned*. Was Sydney hinting there was a chance she cared for Bones? No. She'd said he didn't impress her. Maybe there was somebody who'd impressed her and was waiting for her in California after all. Hell, he wished he could read her mind.

"I need a secret weapon," he muttered.

"A weapon? Jack, no. Philip loves you, and so do…" she cut herself off. "So do not be afraid. He won't hurt you."

"You're the one shaking, baby girl, not me."

She nodded. "I'm excited at maybe seeing Philip." Jack opened the attic door, and she asked, "Do you want me to go up first?"

"Whatever you think. I can stay down here in the hall if you don't want me to go with you to see him."

"Of course I want you to come with me," Sydney said. "Philip's more accustomed to you than he is to me. I think you should go first. Just don't turn on any overhead lights. I don't want to disturb him any more than necessary. Please keep an open mind. Otherwise, you might miss something."

"Okay. Come on." Jack went up the stairs first. He walked to the center of the large attic, and Sydney followed him. They stood quietly and listened.

"Philip?" Sydney whispered. Light filtered in through the dormer windows, sprinkling Sydney with dust particles, making her seem like a dream come true to Jack. That is a dream come true if she fell in love with him. She held tight to his hand and tried again, "Philip, I haven't seen or heard from you for a while. I know you're still here because you spread out the newspaper clippings on my coffee table."

Jack said, "We know it wasn't Ichabod because he was outside."

"Philip, we also know you're angry at finding out Malcolm Striker shot you and maybe had a hand in Cammy's disappearance. And we know you're sad to find out that you had a son you didn't get to raise. But is this where you want to stop? Your goal was to be reunited with Cammy. To make that happen, Jack has an idea." She nodded at him with a pleading look.

"If we can find Striker's house I think we'll find Camilla's grave," Jack said. A small, dim glow appeared. From what Jack recalled, it was the window where

Sydney had said she first saw Philip. Jack couldn't deny the goosebumps he felt or the ones he saw Sydney rubbing on her arms. "Sydney," he said, and nodded at the glow. She smiled at him, obviously thrilled he had seen the light.

"Philip, if you give up now, you'll be losing Cammy when you're so close to winning."

The aura didn't take on a shape, but as it grew larger, Jack sensed how strong Philip's love was for Camilla in order to hold him in place for more than two centuries. Jack heard himself ask, "Where did Striker live?" Though no answer came, the aura remained. Hovering.

"If you can remember, please tell us, Philip," Sydney urged and squeezed Jack's hand. "My time is running short on being here to help you."

Whoosh.

Along with hearing that sound, Jack felt a force surround him, which he could only compare to rushing upward on a roller coaster, except he wasn't moving. He gave himself a shake, and the pressure around him relaxed. His thoughts shifted to the image of his parents in two side-by-side caskets and then his brother's casket. What would it be like to see the skeleton of the person one loved lying in an abandoned grave?

"Don't go to Striker's house," Jack said.

"Who me?" Sydney asked, looking up at him.

"Philip."

"Philip, did you hear Jack?"

Jack felt the strange sensation tighten around him again. "He heard."

"I'll be here for another week, Philip," Sydney advised him. "After that, I can't guarantee anything."

The pressure surrounding Jack swirled. Like a hurricane loose on the sea, it not only pushed forward but from behind and on both sides. Jack stood his ground without moving, but it wasn't easy. Was Philip letting him know what he thought of Jack allowing Sydney to walk out of his life? Without warning, the force dissipated instantly and completely.

"He's gone," Sydney whispered. "How or where, I don't know."

CHAPTER FIFTY-FIVE

Fifty-Three

For the next six days, Sydney existed moment to moment. Each ticking second spent with Jack was priceless and speeding by far too quickly. Certain she was going to lose him at the end of the week, she often found herself on the verge of tears. The Flagler College position, which meant staying in St. Augustine, would hold no interest for her if she didn't have Jack. What would she do when the contest was over and she admitted he won? She'd congratulate him and step out of his St. Augustine life gracefully. Back in Redlands, she'd curl up and die.

"Hey, while I was downtown, I got the black paint for my half of the bench you've been asking for all summer," Jack said with a grin as he stepped into the kitchen on the afternoon of August 31.

Jack's mood was upbeat. At the beginning of the week and again today, he'd left her to run errands. Alone. While he was gone, she'd ridden her scooter to the grocery store, returned, and put a special farewell dinner in the oven. She wiped away a tear before turning to him.

"It's about time you got that paint," she huffed, putting her hands on her hips.

"Is everything okay?" Jack asked and set the paint on the kitchen table. "You look upset. Did you hear from Philip?" She'd hoped he might ask if she'd heard from Flagler College early too. But he didn't. He no longer cared if she got the job or not.

"No, I haven't heard anything from anybody." Picking up the can of paint, she headed to the back door. She desperately needed some distance from Jack in order to hide the love never to be reciprocated. "I keep my promises, so I'd better go paint your half of the bench like I said I would." She fully assumed today would be her last chance. Avoiding his appraising blue eyes, she said, "I don't expect to be teaching at Flagler College at mid-term."

"Expect the best, not the worst, Sydney."

She fully expected the worst to hit her like a hurricane at the stroke of midnight. Telling herself she had to get her emotions under control, paint in hand, she hurried outside.

Jack watched her go, his heart breaking. She'd rather paint that bench than be with him. He'd been about to offer his help, but her quick exit said she didn't want him with her.

Should he tell her that he'd known for a while the Flagler College teaching position was hers? He hoped when he told her that he'd made a trip to Flagler College, prepared to pull strings to make sure she got the job, she wouldn't be angry. But he hadn't had to call in any favors as the former college friend he'd gone to see had confided that Sydney had aced her interview, her qualifications were excellent, and they were offering her the job. The friend had also asked Jack not to share the confidential information. Sydney would be notified via email along with other new hires, as well as those who didn't receive offers.

Painting the bench the second she got the paint was indicative of Sydney's impulsive nature. Jack had feared if she knew she had the job, she'd have flown off to California to prepare for her move. The fact his friend had told him the good news in confidence meant Jack hadn't lost Sydney for the rest of the summer. Now, he wondered if her comment about not expecting to teach at Flagler College meant she was planning to turn the job down.

He sat down at the kitchen table and, through the alcove window, watched her vanish into the Queen Anne house. When she emerged again, it was with a paintbrush and a bucket instead of the paint can. She squatted in the courtyard, putting her back to his house. As she stirred the paint, Jack sighed. He fondly recalled thinking, the day he'd met her, that she was whipping up a brew to poison him. But, she'd indeed mixed up a love potion, and he'd swallowed it all. There was no cure. Now, if only she'd take her own medicine.

Too bad he didn't have a love potion to add to the dinner wafting delicious smells his way. If he did, he'd sprinkle it on her food and make sure she ate every bite. As she swayed in stirring the paint, he pictured her straddling his hips in bed. He'd taught her to make love that way and she was damn good at it. Hell, he was so far under her spell a cure wouldn't work even if it existed.

When his cell rang, the call took him out of the kitchen and into his home office. By the time he returned to the kitchen, Sydney was back and taking a prime rib dinner out of the oven.

"Don't look at the bench until it's dry."

He smiled at the beautiful woman with smudges of black and white on her cheek. If only her feelings for him could be as clear.

After a candlelight dinner, Sydney was having such a hard time holding back her tears that she moved lightning quick in putting leftovers in containers for Jack as he stacked the dishwasher. Using the excuse of checking on Ichabod, she left Jack standing at the back door.

Inside her house, she found the cat curled up on the Martha Washington chair. She picked him up and her tears splattered his white fur. The morning, afternoon, and early evening had flown. She was no closer to having her emotions under control now than when she'd made love to Jack upon waking, ridden her scooter to the grocery store, prepared dinner, stirred the paint, or avoided talking to him while they ate.

A half-hour later, Ichabod jumped out of her lap and wandered to the back door. She followed him outside because she couldn't risk having him disappear the night before her flight. Knowing she had to pack, as she meandered toward Jack's house, Sydney took a look at the bench. With the sun beating down, it was nearly dry. Just in case she was prepared to shoo Ichabod away from it. But she didn't have to. Ichabod stayed in the forget-me-nots.

"Sydney?" came the familiar British accent.

Sydney froze, taken by surprise. "Philip? Where are you?"

"At Jack's end of the bench.

"I can't see you."

"Grief has overwhelmed me. It is an unbearable pain

to have been cheated not only of Cammy but of our son, Philip. I applied all the pressure I could muster on Jack to let him know how I feel about the two of you staying together. He didn't budge, but I am drained of energy. The glow you saw in the attic is now too dim to see in the fading light of day."

Sydney faced Jack's house. "I'm so sorry, Philip. I wish I could do something to ease your suffering."

"You can do something for me. Do not cheat yourself out of a life with Jack."

"Our situation is different than yours." Sydney hung her head and slowly shook it. "He's not in love with me like you are with Cammy."

"I should have eloped with Cammy or stayed here and married her like she begged me to do. I beseech you to learn from my error. Jack is adrift at sea. Claim your bounty. Tell him you love him. Marry him. Have a child with him."

"Thank you for caring." Sydney heard the pleading in his voice, and tears threatened again. "I love you, Philip. I hope you know that."

"I love you, too, Sydney. And so does Jack."

Her head stilling hanging, she asked as she had after she and Jack had broken up in July, "Have you heard him say he loves me?"

"No, but I have been in the attic."

"Brooding," Sydney said gently. "You and Jack are two of a kind. "Have you remembered where Striker lived?"

"Yes."

Sydney's head snapped up. "Philip, that's wonderful. Where?"

Philip sighed. "At 606 Briar Street. But, out of respect for you and Jack, I did as he requested and did not go there."

"I think Jack finally believes in you."

"I think so," Philip whispered. "Sydney, you can be certain you've found Cammy if she is wearing a pink cameo brooch."

"If we can find Cammy, anything is possible. Maybe Jack will be so moved he can find some love in his heart for me."

"That's the spirit."

Sydney's eyes widened. "Was that a pun, Philip?"

"Yes, now be gone with you!"

"Okay! Yes!" With renewed hope in her heart, she said, "I'll put Ichabod back inside, get Jack, and we'll go to Striker's house. You wait here. All right?"

"The first time you and I spoke, it was midnight. Hence, I shall wait here on this bench until midnight."

Fifty-Four

Jack entered the kitchen with one of Sydney's bags from the hall closet. He glanced out the alcove window. There was no sign of her. Without thinking, he looked at the bench. Her half had been white, but his half wasn't black. This evening, the entire bench was gray.

As gray as the gray area of ghosts.

"Sydney," Jack smiled, staring at the bench. She'd had that bucket instead of the paint can because she'd mixed his black paint into her white paint as he'd once suggested. In that instant, she burst out of her house and ran toward his. To hell with waiting until midnight. He would tell her ghosts might be a gray area, but not his feelings for her. He was in love with her, and she had won the contest. He set her suitcase down, opened the back door, and she vaulted into the kitchen. "What's up, Doc?"

"Jack," Sydney gasped. "I have great news!" Her eyes darted to her suitcase. "Am I moving out before midnight?"

"I have to fly to New York. Remember the interviews

for the branch office that Angus was supposed to sched-
ule?" Jack asked, and she nodded. "He did, and he
emailed me about it, but I haven't checked my email all
week. He finally called a few minutes ago to remind me
half a dozen interviews are scheduled starting first thing
in the morning for the team of people to be trained and
ready to get my branch office here up and running."

"Oh right, sure."

"What did you want to tell me?"

"I...umm...finished painting the bench. You can look
now."

"I saw it." He smiled. "The bench looks great."

"Gray, like the gray area of ghosts."

"Right." Jack smiled, happy they were on the same
page. So, no need to rush. At 40,000 feet he'd have her
undivided attention. "There's a jet waiting in Jacksonville." He would tell her that he loved her while flying
high above the clouds. "So get a move on."

"Okay."

"I'll go to the office in the morning, and by the time I
do a couple of interviews, maybe you will have heard
how your interview went at Flagler College."

"Sure," Sydney said, seeming totally detached. "Since
we're discussing plane schedules, I should remind you I
have a reservation to fly back to California tomorrow."

"What?" A knife stabbed Jack square in the heart. "I
thought you canceled that."

"No, I canceled my August 1 flight and rescheduled it
for September 1." Not meeting his gaze, Sydney said, "I
figured if I didn't get the job tomorrow morning, I'd have
plenty of time to pack and get to the airport in Jacksonville by late afternoon. Looks like you already have
one bag packed for me. So, thank you."

"About that job, Sydney...trust me, you won't be on
that plane."

"I *will* be on that plane, Jack." She squared her shoulders and looked him in the eye. "We're going our separate ways as we always knew we would."

"Are you kissing off the Flagler College job?" he asked. *And me too*, he wondered.

"I recently decided," she cleared her throat and shifted from one foot to the other, "that St. Augustine's not for me. I had a nice summer, but I miss my mom, dad, and brothers. I need to go home and get on with my life." Backing away, she placed a hand on the doorknob. "Good luck in New York with hiring a staff for your local office," she finished with a cheery smile.

Jack flinched. "Damn you, Sydney!" he roared. "I knew I shouldn't have gotten involved with you at the beginning of the summer." He plowed his hands through his hair to keep from trying to shake some sense into her. "I told myself to stay away from you when we came back from New York in July. This does it. I'm tired of you jerking me around. Go on! Tuck your tail and run home to mommy and daddy instead of being a big girl and staying in St. Augustine. I'm done!"

Sydney grabbed her suitcase, turned, and raced out the back door. Well, he'd sure made dumping him easy for her. He watched her run from him like the hounds of hell were after her. Then, with a glance at the forget-me-nots and raising her hand, palm out, toward the bench, she disappeared into the Queen Anne house.

～

Sydney didn't stop until she was inside the Queen Anne house. Even when Philip had called to her from the bench, she'd said yes to his question about going to Striker's house but kept on running. Walking into the foyer, she watched Jack's Porsche roar out of the driveway and down the red brick street.

"Goodbye, Jack," Sydney whispered, seeing the tail-lights of his car disappearing around the corner. "I gave it my best shot. But it just wasn't good enough."

Then again, maybe she didn't understand the living, breathing man at all, and just maybe, she should have told him she loved him when she'd had the chance. It would have made no difference, she decided. At least Jack would be in Manhattan tomorrow. She wouldn't have to face him and embarrass herself by begging him to love her. She pulled out her cell.

"Leslie? This is Sydney. I found out where Striker lives. Could you give me a ride?"

Fifty-Five

After a solid forty-five minutes of cursing and speeding down the highway, Jack saw the lights of Jacksonville. Begrudgingly, he remembered Sydney's delight in seeing Friendship Fountain in the center of the town. She was the best friend he'd ever had.

Maybe he should have flown his best friend around the world, taken her on a month-long cruise, or showered her with lavish gifts to win her love. No, she'd pulled back after the short trip to New York City. She was the kind of girl who had to love a man for himself, not for what he could give her. Jack had failed to win her, and there was no amount of money on earth that could buy her love. It was a hopeless, no-win situation. Maybe not for her because she had won the contest and the coins.

When he tapped a button for music, Jason Aldean's *Girl Like You* took the place of Jack's tirade. Like the song, he had never met a girl like Sydney. Yes, she was driving him crazy, and he didn't know what to do. And no, he didn't want to let her go.

Jack had kept an open mind in the attic and perceived Philip. But he'd mistaken Ichabod's deafness as indifference, and he'd not noticed Patricia's new hairstyle. What had he misinterpreted or missed concerning Sydney? Instead of turning a deaf ear to the kind of music she liked, he switched the music in the Porsche from country to pop.

Jack wasn't familiar with Lewis Capaldi, but the lyrics hit home hard and fast. Yeah, he was going under, and there was no one to save him. She sure as hell had numbed all the pain. But she'd pulled the rug, and days would bleed into nightfall.

He had often told Sydney to take her best shot. Had she done so by suggesting they live together? She'd said she wanted their last week to be happy, but he'd detected sadness in her eyes and voice. Had she wrongly suspected her best shot wasn't good enough? He visualized the way she'd hung her head after seeing her suitcase. Had she misinterpreted that? Had he explained he wanted her to go to New York with him? No. He'd yelled at her, and she'd run.

What happened to moving her in and never letting her move out? Was she feeling as unloved as he was? The contest wasn't over until midnight. So, just like in the game of basketball, this game of love wasn't over until the clock ran out. He hadn't taken his best shot at winning Sydney.

"Not yet, anyway."

Jack exited the highway at the airport, made a couple of calls, did a U-turn, and headed back to St. Augustine. He pulled into his driveway far more calmly than he'd roared out of it. The Porsche's clock read 10:45p.m. He jumped out of the car and raced past Buster's doghouse, happily shouting he was home.

"Buster?" he yelled a second time when the dog didn't emerge from his doghouse.

Backtracking, he found the doghouse empty. His

basketball pal, David, was supposed to feed Buster and leave him outside where the dog could relieve himself as needed. Maybe David had taken Buster home with him. Jack would text him right after talking to Sydney.

Running into his house, he plucked a box off the top of the refrigerator. Then he sprinted across his yard and past the courtyard to the Queen Anne house. Finding the house pitch black and locked up, he took his keys out of his pocket and opened the door.

Anxious to see Sydney, he could barely keep from waking her by shouting her name. He was surprised she hadn't called out her window for him to shut up when he'd yelled for Buster. Turning on lights as he passed through the kitchen and hallway, Jack took the stairs two at a time and jogged down the hall. Rounding the corner into her bedroom, what he saw stopped him like a locomotive.

Moonlight streamed in the window, illuminating the empty bed. He'd spent countless hours making love to her in that bed. But the gorgeous girl wasn't there. Memories flashed across his mind, carrying her into the room, laying her in the bed, shedding his clothes, and crawling between the sheets. She was always soft and cuddly and covered him with kisses.

Because she wasn't here, everything felt wrong, out of sync. He called her cell. It went to voicemail. Surely, she hadn't taken a night flight to California. Dear God, could he have passed her on the highway coming home from Jacksonville?

"SYDNEY!" Her name came out loudly enough to wake the damn dead.

The only other time he'd lost control like that was when he'd been told his family was dead. He couldn't get them back. But he had to get Sydney back. He tore through her house, slowing down long enough to glance into the living room. The Martha Washington chair was empty too. He'd left the back door ajar. Had her cat gotten out? Or were they both gone?

Jack raced back to his house, hoping against all odds that she was in his bed. Why hadn't he checked his bedroom first? Had he seen her cat, it would have meant Sydney was still in Florida. He should have made note of Ichabod's second favorite napping place; the kitchen window sill. Again, Jack took a staircase two steps at a time. He reached his empty bedroom as his phone rang. He answered halfway through the first ring.

"Hello!"

"Hello?" came a timid voice. "Jack? This is Leslie Bowen."

"It's too late to be calling."

"I've been calling Sydney for the last hour. She gave me your phone number earlier and said I should contact you in case I couldn't reach her. Look, I just wanted to say that I feel badly about not being able to go with Sydney tonight. But after seeing the way she acted toward you the other day and hearing about your plans to get married, I knew she was a lost cause. So, I asked a certain lady out to dinner tonight. As you know, Patricia Hudson isn't the gorgeous girl Sydney is, but at least she's not in love with another man like Sydney is either. Anyway, I was on my way to pick her up when Sydney called me."

"What the hell are you rambling about, Bowen?"

"You mean about the part about Sydney being in love or where she went tonight?"

"Where the hell is she?" Jack yelled into the phone.

"Philip told her where Malcolm Striker used to live, and Sydney walked over there."

Stunned relief hit Jack like a tidal wave. The other guy who had pulled her away from him tonight was Philip. Best of all, she was still in St. Augustine. Jack closed his eyes in a prayer of thanks. Then his eyes snapped open with concern.

"Dammit!" Jack barked and clenched the small box in his hand. "You let Sydney walk to some strange house? Alone? At night?"

"It wasn't dark when she called," Bones answered meekly.

Jack was furious. "What happened to all the talk about how you wanted to investigate the grave? How the hell could you just write Sydney off like that?"

"Well…because dates don't come my way every day like they probably do yours," Bones said. "I suggested Sydney wait for you. She swore she didn't mind going alone."

"Bull! A man steps up when a woman is putting herself in danger. You should have hauled your ass over here. Hell, I don't have the time for this. What's Striker's address?"

Fifty-Six

"**G**osh," Sydney whispered, clutching the leash fastened to Buster's collar. From the potholed road, under a sputtering street light, she stared at the vacant house—no, ancient, dilapidated shack. Windows were broken, shingles hung at odd angles, and falling gutters hadn't drained rain in eons. "What do you think, Buster?"

"Woof." Buster sounded disapproving.

"When I called Patricia Hudson, right before my phone died, she said she had a date with Leslie Bowen tonight. Buster, she was so busy talking about the fact he has a Cadillac and teaches at Flagler College, I think she'd have given me a lockbox key to any house I wanted just to get me out of her hair or wig or whatever. I'm a chatterbox when I'm nervous, like right now. I wish Jack were here."

Buster barked upon hearing Jack's name. Sydney tugged on the leash, and they walked down a weed-infested path to a drooping porch under rusted awning poles. They climbed rotten steps, and a board broke under Sydney's right foot. Her leg instantly vanished up to her knee.

"Help!" she gasped involuntarily.

There was no one to help her. This hovel sat at least three trash-strewn empty lots away from the only other house which was also a shack at the other end of the forgotten alley. But she *wasn't* alone. Buster slipped his head under her arm. With his help, Sydney pulled her leg out of the gaping hole and stood. Her knees shook, but her foot was okay.

"Thank you, Buster." She looked into the Labrador's soulful brown eyes and petted his head. "I love you."

Buster stayed close. Sydney used the key Patricia had given her to the lockbox, and the front door creaked open. Mold and mustiness assailed her. She fumbled along the wall for a light switch. How could this place even be for sale? Perhaps the land was worth something and a new owner would demolish the house. She found a switch and flipped it.

"Of course, there's no electricity," Sydney told Buster as things remained pitch black.

She turned on a flashlight she'd found at the Queen Anne house. Cobwebs clung to the corners, and monstrous shadows skittered across faded, peeling wallpaper. Far worse, she was sure she heard the scurrying of rats' feet.

"As much as I hate to say it, Buster, I'm certain the basement is where we'll have to go to find Cammy. Patricia said the door to the basement is under the staircase," Sydney said, shining the light along the wall beneath the stairs. "I see the door." Tiptoeing to the door, she turned the knob. She pulled hard, and the door opened. The smell of dirt and blackness loomed. "Come on, Buster."

Sydney stepped onto the first basement stair. The creaking wood reverberated up through her body, reducing her legs to wet noodles. She paused, working up her nerve to go on.

"This place reminds me of the haunted houses my brothers invented on Halloween, Buster," she said to sidetrack herself as they started down the stairs. "J.D. and Will would transform the garage into a place worth charging the neighborhood kids admission." Three more steps. "They blindfolded them and took them on a tour." They descended further into darkness. "J.D. told the kids grapes were monster eyeballs, and Will swore slimy potato peels were dead men's skin," Sydney chattered to Buster and gulped as they reached a dirt floor of the basement. "Speaking of dead men, I hope Malcolm Striker's not earthbound."

Buster growled as something ran across their feet.

"I told Jack that skeletons and ghosts go together. Why am I just remembering that? I didn't realize it would take us so long to get here on foot. I'm sorry it's so late and dark, Buster. I should have come here first and then packed my bags instead of packing first. We'd be done and back home by now. I'm being a motor mouth because I'm not just nervous, I'm scared."

Buster whimpered his understanding.

"Jack thinks I'm a *fearless girl*. But it was his confidence in me that gave me the courage to try to win the contest. Jack's the best friend I've ever had." Sydney patted Buster's head. "No more procrastinating. Spooky or not, let's search for the grave."

Shining the flashlight ahead of her, Sydney scanned the basement. Not knowing where to start, she pulled Cammy's diary out of the pocket of Jack's forest green hoodie.

"I doubt there's any of Cammy's scent left on her diary, but take a whiff, Buster."

Buster sniffed, and Sydney let go of his leash. She reached into her pocket and pulled out the spade she'd once used to plant the forget-me-nots and dig for the coins. She shined the light on Buster as he darted here and there, his nose to the ground. Only moments passed before the retriever singled out a spot and barked. Sydney walked underneath the stairs where Buster dug as if burying a bone...or digging one up. Her heart pounding, Sydney watched and shivered when Buster's claws scraped across something wooden. Kneeling beside Buster and holding the flashlight in one hand, she used the spade to scoop dirt away from the wood.

"Aaahhh!" Despite the fact they were looking for a grave, the instant she realized they had unearthed the upper half of a coffin-shaped box, the scream had escaped her. Falling backward onto her fanny, Sydney scooted away. "Buster, come." Grabbing his leash, she jumped up and backed away several feet. "I'm scared, and I admit it." With a shaking hand, she shined the flashlight on her watch. "It's eleven-fifteen. Jack's halfway to New York by now. But, if he were here, he'd tell me to take a deep breath and stop being emotional. Analytically speaking, I know neither a ghost nor a skeleton can hurt us."

Sydney took the deep breath. This had to be Camilla Johnson's grave. Philip's beloved Cammy. There was no reason to be frightened of Cammy. If it was Cammy in the coffin, that is. Sydney prayed the skeleton was wearing a cameo broach. She forced herself back underneath the stairs, and Buster followed. Sydney knelt down on the ground again and shoveled the remaining dirt off of a pine box. When it was uncovered, she pried at the lid with her fingers. It didn't budge. Taking another determined breath, she tried using the spade to pry up the lid. It was no use. It was nailed shut.

"We need Jack."

Footsteps sounded overhead. She froze.

Fifty-Seven

"Leslie?" Sydney said under her breath. No answer. "Patricia?" she said, none too loudly. Nothing. Buster made a move toward the stairs, but Sydney wrapped her arms around the dog, keeping him safe. "Dear God, please don't let it be Malcolm Striker."

The footsteps stopped.

"Sydney!" Jack yelled.

"Yes," Sydney cried in relief. "Yes!" Buster barked, and when she released him, they both ran to the bottom of the steps. Holding the camping lantern at the top of the stairs, Jack filled the doorway with muscles and a scowl. No matter. He was absolutely gorgeous, and the house no longer seemed scary. "Hi!"

"Don't 'hi' me, Sydney! I'm gonna turn you over my knee and paddle your butt for pulling this stunt all by yourself," Jack growled, holding a crowbar.

He descended the stairs with the lantern light clearly revealing his displeasure at finding her in Striker's basement. She smiled up at him in profound relief as he reached the dirt floor.

"I'm not all by myself. Buster's with me," she said.

Jack set the lantern and crowbar on the stairs. Planting his left foot on the last step, he grasped Sydney's elbow and yanked her over his left knee. His so-called paddling amounted to brushing the dirt off her fanny. Jack let go of her, took her arms, and placed them around his neck. Then his strong, safe embrace closed around her, and he hugged her fiercely like she'd longed for him to do. Oh yes, being in Jack's arms was a wonderful world all its own.

"Buster, good dog for protecting her," Jack said, petting his head.

Standing on tiptoes, Sydney clung to Jack. His scent was cologne and soap. The mustiness of the house was gone. His body was packed with strength. The monsters of the house were forgotten.

"Maybe I'll tell my brothers that you paddled me."

"Do it," Jack whispered. His left arm was a steel band around her as his right hand slid over her bottom. "Then I'll tell them why and we'll see what they have to say."

"No!" Sydney giggled, delicious heat filling her at Jack's gentle squeeze of her fanny. "I won't tell if you won't tell."

"Deal, baby girl." Jack pulled back and smiled at her.

"I don't know why you aren't in New York or how you found me, but I'm so glad you're here."

"I forgot something and had to come back home. I called Angus near the airport and told him to reschedule the interviews. Then, when I got home, Bones called me after taking Patricia Hudson out on a date. He told me where you'd gone."

"Oh." Sydney frowned in concentration, wondering what he could have forgotten. It wasn't his suitcase because he had clothes in New York. He offered no further information. "Well, Buster sniffed out a grave. I'm hoping it's Camilla Johnson's."

"Sydney, let's go home and come back tomorrow."

"No." She couldn't do that. She was leaving tomorrow morning. Reluctantly, she pushed out of Jack's embrace. "Philip's waited long enough. Could you help me pry the lid off the coffin?"

"I brought a gun and a crowbar, not knowing what trouble you might get yourself in," he said and picked up the lantern. "But if you've found a coffin, I guess it's the crowbar."

"There," Sydney said, pointing with a shaking finger.

Jack handed her the lantern, and as he walked toward the wooden casket, she saw the gun stuck in the back of his jeans. Wielding the crowbar, Jack pried the lid off the box. A gasp escaped Sydney as the flashlight and lantern illuminated the skeleton wrapped in a green cape.

"That has to be her," Jack said calmly.

Shining the flashlight, Sydney saw a cameo holding the cape closed. "Yes, it is."

"I'd say Striker paid his henchman to kidnap Camilla at the hanging. The guy dragged her back here, murdered and buried her. The authorities probably assumed Camilla ran away."

Sydney nodded and said, "Her parents had washed their hands of her, and maybe the folks on Anastasia Island had their hands too full with the baby to look for her. Different times back then," Sydney whispered, staring at the grave. "But this was a woman so loved by a man that he couldn't forget her even after two and a half centuries."

"Look around, and you'll find a man who loves you like that."

Spears stabbed Sydney's heart. She would not look around because she would never love any man but Jack. But what had he said at his house? *So, get a move on.*

Sydney swallowed her sorrow and said, "I don't want Philip to see Cammy like this."

"That's why I told him not to come here."

"Cammy, I hope you can hear me," Sydney said. "The son you had with Philip grew up and left a long line of descendants on Anastasia Island." She cleared her throat and continued, "Your beloved Philip has been waiting for you. Even now, he waits in the courtyard that separates your property from his." Sydney paused, looked at Jack, and shrugged helplessly.

"She'll go to him if she can," Jack said. "Tomorrow, the authorities will need to be informed about the grave." He tugged Sydney away from the coffin. "Come on."

"All right." As they reached the bottom of the stairs, Sydney heard a noise like a pebble rattling over wood. She turned and shined her flashlight at the grave. There in the dirt, at the edge of the coffin lid, lay the cameo brooch.

"Wasn't that on top of her cape a minute ago?" Jack asked.

"Yes," Sydney smiled. "I think the grief lifted, allowing Cammy to leave her coffin."

"I think she wants you to have the brooch."

Jack picked it up and held the lantern near the light pink stone carving of a man and woman embracing. He took Sydney's hand and placed the brooch in it. Buster ran up the stairs ahead of them, and they all walked out of the deathtrap together.

Sydney was relieved to see Jack's Porsche parked in the dark alley. It had been a tossup earlier whether to ride her scooter or take Buster. She'd chosen Buster.

On the way home, they didn't speak. Sydney guessed there was nothing left to say. Jack had made it clear she had to look around elsewhere for love. When he stopped the Porsche in his driveway, she let herself out of the car.

She wanted to thank him for...where would she begin?
For everything. But she didn't trust her voice not to
break. She simply waved goodbye.

"Where are you going?" Jack called, getting out of
his car.

Fifty~Eight

In a daze of tumultuous emotions, Sydney blew him a kiss and dashed across his back yard. Nearing the courtyard, she spotted Ichabod snoozing on Jack's side of the bench. How had he gotten out? For no apparent reason, Ichabod arched his back and hissed once.

"Hi, Ichabod. It's just me," Sydney choked out as she reached the outer edge of the bricks encircling the courtyard.

Then she saw it.

A dimly glowing feminine aura was gliding away from the Queen Anne house. Sydney stopped in her tracks. With her next breath, she backed up until she bumped into a solid wall of muscle. She gazed up at Jack as his arm slid around her waist. He looked toward her house as Buster sat down beside them.

Hearing a delicate *whoosh*, Sydney snapped her head back toward her house as well. Within a dozen feet of the courtyard, the glow became as defined and solid as a living person. Clearly, the aura was a beautiful woman with blond hair peeking out around the hood of a flowing, forest green cape.

Buster barked, and Ichabod leaped off the bench, both responding to the glow.

Whoosh.

From the direction of Jack's house, a second dim glow appeared. Buster whimpered again. Jack shushed the dog and focused on the courtyard. Following Jack's gaze, Sydney watched the features of the bronze glow become razor-sharp. There stood a handsome young man wearing a wool cap, navy coat, baggy britches, and shoes with buckles on top.

Sydney tightened her hand around the cameo.

Philip drifted across the dirt on Jack's side of the courtyard as Cammy floated through Sydney's blue flowers. Stopping in the midst of the forget-me-nots, Philip and Cammy met. He swept off his cap, and she ran her fingers through his brown hair. Then he lowered his lips to hers in a centuries' awaited kiss. Twining her arms around his neck, he clasped her to his heart.

Tears streamed down Sydney's face as the couple moved to the bench and sat down. She saw Philip mouth the words, '*I love you*' to Cammy. She whispered in his ear, and they held each other as if they'd never again let go. Profound happiness for them filled Sydney's saddened heart. She sniffled and felt Jack's other arm slide around her.

"Can you see them?" Sydney whispered, looking up at him.

Jack nodded to the bench as Philip and Cammy stood and faced them. Sydney held out her hand, offering them the cameo. Philip smiled, shook his head no, and put his hand over his heart in thanks. Cammy placed her fingers to and away from her lips in a kiss. Then, promises finally fulfilled, they raised their hands in goodbye as their forms began to fade.

"I saw them wave goodbye," Jack whispered. "Philip was right. Camilla did look a little like you, especially when you're wearing the hood of my green sweatshirt around your face like she wore the hood of her green cape. And for just a moment, Philip and Camilla looked exactly like the cameo."

"I'd love to keep your hoodie as a souvenir of this summer." Sydney stepped out of Jack's embrace. She took his hand and placed Camilla's brooch in it. "I'd like you to have the cameo as your souvenir."

"The hoodie is yours, and so is the cameo."

"But, I want the cameo to always remind you of this summer and the green-eyed nutcase who hassled you with her ghosts."

"I'll remember it as the summer a *fearless girl* and a couple of her friends distracted me from death, sailed me through the grieving process, and lured me into wanting to live again."

From where she stood outside the courtyard, Sydney gazed at the forget-me-nots and the bench. Today, she'd told a ghost and a dog that she loved them. Didn't the man before her deserve as much? She'd held her tongue as long as she could.

Sydney whispered, "Life is too short and unpredictable not to tell you something."

"What?"

Sydney was so afraid Jack would be angry or, worse yet, laugh, she kept her eyes on the flowers. "I was mistaken when I said the amount I cared for you couldn't change when we made our bet three weeks ago."

"What do you mean?" Jack put his fingers to her cheek and turned her to face him. "Are you saying you care less or…more?"

Sydney grimaced because he sounded either incredulous...or furious that she would draw this out when he was done. He had tried to make a clean break and now he feared she wasn't cooperating. She moved her face away from his fingers and stepped back. She'd tell Jack how she felt and say goodbye once and for all.

"I...umm... whew!" She took a breath, trying to get the words out.

"You what...Sydney?"

"Well, I might as well just say it." She splayed her hands and then folded her arms under her breasts. She looked down and mumbled, "I'm sorry to tell you that..." She was being a coward not to look him in the eye. She squared her shoulders and met his ocean blue gaze. "I apologize but...I...am—"

"Please just tell me."

"I am in love with you, Jack. I love you more and more each day. That's why I'm flying out tomorrow. I have so much love for you bottled up inside me," she placed her hand over her heart, "I'm about to explode!" Surely, his wide eyes meant he was livid. "But, hey, that means you won the bet. You won the coins. They're in the safety deposit box at your bank, and that's where they'll stay."

"Sydney..."

With the cameo brooch in her left hand, she held out her right hand. But as he had done the day they'd first met, he hesitated to shake hands. He was done making deals with her. She clasped her hands behind her back.

"Congratulations, Jack."

"I want you to have one of the coins as the payment I once promised you for information on my houses." He handed her a box.

"Thank you, but I never wanted or expected a payment. Certainly not a coin worth a million and a half dollars," she said. Sincerely touched, she tried to hand the box back to him, but he wouldn't take it. Clasping the box and brooch to her heart, she said, "Good luck with your houses." *Losers, weepers*. With tears scalding her eyes and fire torching her throat, she turned away from Jack. But she hadn't taken three steps toward her house when such a strong pressure fell over her that she couldn't take another step. "Philip, if that's you," she whispered as the sensation pushed her backward in Jack's direction. "Cammy, if you're trying to help, it's too late."

"Look in the box," Jack urged from behind her.

The strange force held Sydney near Jack. She lifted the lid of the gray velvet box and stared. The pressure around her lessened, and she took the coin out of the box. Her hands shook as she saw what else was in the box. She turned to Jack. His eyes were questioning, and no trace of a smile showed on his lips.

Fifty-Nine

"Jack, what is this?"

"Double or nothin'. You said one carat."

"I don't know much about diamonds, but this is a lot bigger than two carats."

"Yeah, it's four carats. I forgot...I failed to give it to you before I left for the airport, and that's why I came back home. I can write off interviews, but a woman like you doesn't come along every day. I'll never write you off." Jack took the engagement ring out of the box and smiled. "Sydney Crane, will you marry me?"

"Yes!" Sydney threw herself into Jack's arms. She cried into his shoulder as he hugged her. "Yes, I'll marry you. I love you so much, Jack."

Two fading glows grew brighter just long enough to capture his and Sydney's attention before whooshing away in the direction of the pier.

Jack said, "They waited until they were sure we would be together."

"Yes, and they joined forces to make sure of it." Sydney nodded and looked up at him. "I know I can convince you to love me too."

"Convince me?" Jack asked the magnificent woman. She smiled, wiping the tears off her soft cheeks. She was so adorable, he chuckled. "What do you think this is all about?" Sydney bit down on her lower lip and shrugged. "I'm in love with you, Sydney. I had already decided to get you a two-carat diamond engagement ring before you mentioned the *one-whole-carat*." He looked down at the ring between his thumb and index finger. "But I thought you'd turn me down." He sighed. "I was too scared to show it to you."

"You? Scared?" Sydney asked. "You're the bravest person I know. You run a Wall Street brokerage firm, own a skyscraper, drive a Porsche, and fly in private jets. You'll be hailed as a hero for turning this block into a place people from all over the world will visit. You kept going even though you were alone in the world. I was the one so scared I was going to run home with my tail tucked between my legs."

"You're the one who flew across the country to a place you'd never been. As a stranger in town and all by yourself, you faced a ghost. You're the one who rode a scooter to an island, got lost without GPS, and found her way home. You're the little green riding hood who stood up to the big, bad wolf."

"You're my hero, Jack."

"And you're mine."

"What's that noise?"

"I don't hear anything."

Sydney placed her delicate hand over Jack's heart. "Sounds like chains snapping in half around our hearts. What do you think?"

"I think you could snap the last two chains by letting me slip this ring on your finger." Sydney held out her left hand. He glanced at his watch and smiled. "It's midnight. The contest is over, and we both won."

"We did," Sydney agreed as he slipped the ring on the fourth finger of her left hand. "It's beautiful. I *bet* this diamond cost a fortune." Jack shrugged and she said, "This ring *and* the coin are just too much. I'll keep my ring and you keep the coin."

"All of the coins are yours. Share them with your family to prove I'm worthy of you."

"You know that's absolutely ridiculous in this day and age."

Jack smiled. "I think Philip would approve. Share with Nellie too."

Sydney pinched her tear-stained cheek. "I keep thinking I'm going to wake up. You are every girl's dream come true."

"I just want to be yours," Jack promised and hugged her. "I asked the jeweler to make your ring a size five and a half and picked it up earlier today. How's it fit?"

"Perfectly." Sydney's voice shook as she splayed her left hand on his chest. "I'm so happy. Thank you, Jack."

"Thank you, baby girl. You've made me just as happy." He clasped her left hand in his. "Know what fits me perfectly?"

"Me?"

"Yeah. Let's go home and celebrate."

"After being in Striker's house, we need a shower first. So *get a move on*."

Jack grabbed her right hand, and all the way to his house, she held her left hand out in front, admiring her engagement ring. When they reached the back door, Ichabod scampered up and meowed.

"I think I accidentally let your cat out of your house earlier," he said. "Sorry."

"He gets past me sometimes too."

"What do you think about Ichabod, Buster?" Jack asked the dog at his side.

Buster barked. Ichabod heard nothing. Buster sat down, and when Ichabod rubbed up against him, Buster wagged his tail.

"I think Buster made friends with a cat lover and her cat," Sydney said.

"Yeah, well, Buster's bark is worse than his bite."

"Just like his owner's."

Sixty

T he plane Sydney missed on September 1 was long forgotten.

A week later she rolled to a sitting position and straddled Jack's hips. They'd flown to New York City, where Jack had interviewed and hired several well-qualified people. Flattening her hands on Jack's broad shoulders, Sydney recalled the resignation on the faces of some of the females in the Manhattan office as they saw her ring. Concluding the New York business, they'd flown back home with a similar urgency as Sydney's lifting and lowering herself to and away from the hard body under her. They'd spent the majority of the past few days making love and plans for the future. With a husky groan, Jack clamped his hands on her hips and slid her down the length of his erection.

Sydney had poured her love into Jack like the throbs he was spilling deep inside her, which caused waves of pleasure to burst and vibrate throughout her very soul. As their breathing slowed, Jack pulled her down on top of him, pressing her pounding heart to his muscular chest. She smiled with blissful contentment.

Jack groaned, "That felt so good."

Her head on the pillow with his, Sydney sighed, "Yes." Slipping her arms under his neck, she stretched out on top of him, keeping him inside her. "I've enjoyed every minute of our weeklong celebration in honor of my new job."

"Yeah, I like our private parties," Jack said. "I'm proud of you for getting the Flagler College professor position, Sydney."

"It looks like all our goals are within reach. I have four whole months to compile the research I've done and write a dissertation proposal before I start teaching in January. I can't wait for the day when the first tour bus stops at the opposite end of this block."

As he lay within her, Jack asked, "After you teach for a year or two, would having a baby with me be on your agenda?"

"Yes. I can work on my doctorate while I'm pregnant. Let's have at least two."

"Yeah, at least." Flattening his hands on her fanny he patted it, and as she nibbled his ear, he whispered, "You'll be Dr. Malone."

"Our mail will be addressed to Dr. and Dr. Malone."

"Shh." Jack gripped her waist. "Was that a car stopping?"

Sydney sat up again, and still straddling him, looked out the French doors leading to the balcony. "Yes, an airport limousine just pulled up in front of my house."

"Oh, hell. They made better time than I thought they would."

"Who, Jack?"

"Sydney, get off me, quick." Jack didn't wait for her to respond. He lifted her off him and rolled out of bed. Turning around, he grabbed her hands and yanked her out after him. "Where the hell are my boxers? To hell with shorts. Where are my jeans? Put your clothes on."

"Why are you the one racing around trying to get dressed this time instead of me? Who in the world has you so concerned?"

"Your family is here from California."

"My family?" Sydney squealed happily.

"You said you missed 'em."

"They never said a word when I called them after hearing from Flagler College."

"We wanted it to be a surprise," Jack said. "I called them later that day and told them I'd known for a while. I arranged for a jet to pick them up in Redlands and fly 'em back here."

"What?" Making no attempt to find clothes to wear, Sydney stood near the bed and asked, "How'd you know about my job before I did?"

"I've got friends in high places," the gorgeous man told her as he pulled on a pair of jeans. Sydney stood naked, hands on her hips, and one eyebrow arched. He looked at her and said, "I went to Flagler College to pull some strings, but I didn't have to."

Sydney pursed her lips. "Why didn't you tell me?"

Jack yanked a dress shirt out of the closet and put it on before explaining, "Because I was asked not to in fairness to the other candidates." Sydney nodded her understanding. "That worked for me because I didn't want you to go home early to prepare for a more permanent move here."

"I will have to do exactly that."

"Yeah, but now I'll be going with you." Jack said a moment before Sydney hugged him. She was still naked and giggled when he groaned, "Give me strength." Prying her arms from around him, he looked out the window. "Suitcases are being unloaded from the airport limo." He pointed her toward the walk-in closet, and playfully pushed her into it. "Please get dressed."

"They're used to me being late," Sydney said, emerging from the closet in a pair of white jeans and holding one of the blouses he'd bought for her. "They were forever in the car honking the horn on Sunday mornings, waiting to go to church."

"Church?" Buttoning his fly, Jack muttered, "They'll think I've corrupted you."

"I'm the girl who never wears a bra, remember?"

"You're the girl who said she'd wear one when I married her. Sydney, for God's sake, wear one today and make me look good," Jack urged. He yanked a gift bag out of the drawer where he kept his underwear and tossed it to her. "I bought this for you the day I picked up your ring. Look, it's even got forget-me-not-like flowers on it."

Enjoying every second of teasing him, under this tables-turned situation, she took the tag off and said, "We aren't married, yet, so I don't have to wear it."

"I swear—" Jack looked out the window again. "Sydney, hurry up!"

"My bra fits perfectly," she said, after fastening it. Slipping a forget-me-not-blue silk blouse on over it, she asked, "How did you know my size?"

"Hell, you don't know your size." Jack's grin was hot and sexy. "I just cupped my hand around a couple of bras." Voices carried across the yard and in through the window. "Sydney, button your blouse and come on."

"Okay!" Sydney giggled, so happy and so in love with her fiancé. She buttoned the blouse, he grabbed her hand, and they hurried downstairs. He turned loose of her at the front door. "Jack, thank you for bringing them here."

"Of course!" Jack nudged her onto his front porch. "Go!"

Sixty-One

"Hi, Mom! Hi, Daddy!" Sydney called. Jack watched his beautiful fiancée skip down the steps. But when he didn't follow, she pivoted, and stopped in her tracks. She looked back at him and crooked the fingers of her left hand. "Come on, I want you to meet everybody." Jack joined her and together, they crossed his yard.

"Be sure to show them your engagement ring before you tell them I took your virginity," Jack teased in a whisper as they reached the wrought iron fence. He scooped her up in his arms in preparation of setting her into her yard on the other side of the fence. "Because I don't think I could take on your brothers and win today. You wore me out."

Sydney kissed his lips, and when Jack opened his eyes, one of her brothers stood on the other side of the fence. Jack handed Sydney over to a brown-haired man, who indeed looked big and tough. Sydney called him J.D. and he set her feet on the ground a few feet away. After hugging him, she ran to the others. As Sydney's family crowded around her, Jack stayed in his own yard.

A slender woman with dark blond hair curling around a lovely face folded Sydney into her embrace. She admired Sydney's ring and then hugged her again. Jack felt a twinge in his heart, knowing his mother would never hug him again. But, if not for Sydney, that twinge would be a knife. Thanks to her, he'd be okay. He watched Sydney's dad and then her other three brothers embrace her. Jack glanced down, feeling like an intruder. A moment later, a voice similar to Sydney's spoke his name. He looked up and found Sydney's mother walking toward the wrought iron fence.

"Are you the young man who put a bra on my daughter?"

"Well…" Jack thought he might have blushed for the second time in his life. The first time being when Sydney shoved her purse into his hands. He'd covered her up that day because she didn't have on a bra. "Yes, ma'am, I'm Jack Malone."

"Taking care of Sydney isn't an easy job, is it?" Mrs. Crane asked with a lilting laugh. Jack shook his head. "This summer was the first time Sydney ever lived away from home. You don't know how thankful I was to know she was next door to her landlord, who was watching over her. I'm very pleased to meet you, Jack. I'm Kathleen Crane. I hope you'll call me Kathy."

When Jack stuck out his hand, Kathy took hold of it and tugged. He stepped over the fence. When he was in Sydney's yard, Kathy put her arms around him. Jack's arms closed around her as if he'd known her all his life. She wore the same perfume as his mother and kissed his cheek as his mother often had. When Kathy let go of him, she looped her arm through his and hugged it to her as she walked him toward the Queen Anne house.

"Sydney told us you two are getting married," Kathy said.

"Yes, if it's okay with all of you."

"It is. She called home countless times this summer telling us how wonderful you were and how much she loved you." Jack was speechless with surprise. Reaching the cobblestone walk where Sydney, her dad, and her brothers were, Kathy said, "I've got myself another boy."

"This is Jack." Sydney took Jack's other arm and introduced him to the other men in her life, starting with her father.

"Welcome to the family, son," Mr. Crane said as he gave Jack a bear hug. "Thanks for flying us here."

"You're welcome, Mr. Crane."

"Please call me Mike," Sydney's father said.

"Michael was my dad's middle name," Jack told the tall, robust man with gray hair and a friendly smile.

"I'd say Mr. and Mrs. Malone raised a mighty fine fella, wouldn't you, Kathy?" Mike asked and hugged his wife, who agreed.

"Well, Dad, it looks like you've finally got the fifth man on your basketball team," J.D. said as he pumped Jack's hand up and down.

"Sydney told us you like basketball," Will said, also shaking hands.

"She said you have a regulation hoop in your driveway," Chuck said, taking his turn.

"I used to shoot baskets with my dad," Jack said.

"Dad's our coach," T.J., the tallest brother, announced as he shook Jack's hand, then bounced the basketball he'd brought. "We tried to teach Sydney to play, but you've probably found out she stinks."

"She has potential," Jack said. Sydney huffed, and everyone laughed.

Kathy said, "Sydney and I make great cheerleaders."

"Yeah," Jack agreed, his eyes on Sydney. He was going to be okay.

Epilogue

FIVE YEARS LATER—ST. AUGUSTINE, FLORIDA

Jack and Sydney had taken some risks, and life was so good.

September sunshine bathed the backyard, making for a perfect afternoon. Before Magnolia Lane became officially listed in the historical society's directory, Jack had ordered a tall wooden fence built around the backyard. The wrought iron fence kept the estate private in the front yard along the red brick road as the tall wooden fence did with the rear of the Victorian house and estate. The Queen Anne house had been redecorated and made an excellent local branch office of the Malone Building in Manhattan.

The house at the opposite end of the block served as a museum for the other five homes. St. Augustine locals and travelers from around the world were greeted with glorious paintings of the Mayflower and of the Pilgrims coming ashore on Cape Cod, now known as Provincetown Harbor, Massachusetts, on November 11, 1620. Along with artifacts, information, and drawings, the museum told the story of Magnolia Lane's original owner. The man had been a verified passenger on the famous ship but not a Pilgrim. One of the 102 passengers, he was among the group of adventurers and tradesmen onboard who were referred to as strangers by the Pilgrims. Sydney had said Jack was both a tradesman of sorts, and she had been the stranger. They'd shared one heck of an adventure together, and found the original landowner's identity all too apropos for the history of the block.

Along the museum tour, where the Mayflower story left off, the American Revolution began with the explosions of gunfire in Lexington and Concord, Massachusetts, on April 19, 1775. A smaller rendition than the original on display in New York City's Metropolitan Museum of Art, the famous painting of General George Washington Crossing the Delaware on December 25, 1776, welcomed visitors of all ages. Included in the East Florida local history were the St. Augustine star-crossed lovers—Philip Burke, a man who lived in a sailor's rest, and Camilla Johnson, his girl next door in the home of a tavern proprietor. Jack and Sydney agreed they had fought their own battle before the war was settled.

Next, a short documentary introduced visitors to the Civil War, also called the War Between the States. From the first bullet fired on April 12, 1861, by Confederate troops on the Union soldiers in Fort Sumter, South Carolina, to the surrender of General Lee to General Grant four years later, both pain and triumph were depicted.

Destruction of the Revolutionary period houses on Magnolia Lane after the secession of Florida was shared in drawings. Uniforms of soldiers from the North and South were on display in glass cases. In a Currier and Ives lithograph, Abraham Lincoln's assassination was captured in heart-wrenching detail. In sketches, the agony of losing the sixteenth president is shown on the faces of folks who had once lived in the Victorian and Queen Anne houses.

In the final room of the tour were six beautifully framed, current photographs of the houses on Magnolia Lane. A plaque stated the museum was dedicated in memory of the two people who had lived in #1 and #2 Magnolia Lane in 1776. Thus, oil portraits of Philip Burke—clad in a wool cap, navy coat, gray britches, and holding an iron box—faced Camilla Johnson, a beautiful blonde wearing a forest green cape, clasped by a pink cameo brooch, and cradling an infant. There was a framed painting of an ancient pier and sailing beyond it, the *Sea Phantom*. Below the painting stood a fortified glass case displaying Captain Bledsoe's journal and the *Sea Phantom's* manifest. A second case presented Philip Burke's family Bible along with Camilla Johnson's Bible and her leather diary. In a third case were the ancient newspaper clippings from the *East Florida Gazette~Herald*.

Sydney's heart sang when Jack said the museum would have thrilled his mother and father and how proud he was of her for putting it all together. In turn, she would always be grateful to him for helping to make it part of her dissertation.

~

As Sydney sat next to her mother, sipping lemonade, under an umbrella table on a new brick patio surrounded by forget-me-nots, they watched Jack and her father admire the recently acquired, child-sized basketball hoop in the driveway.

"Seriously, what is he going to do with that, you guys?" Sydney asked.

"He's only two," Kathy teased them.

"My grandson's going to learn how to play basketball with this, that's what, ladies." Mike grinned and clapped Jack on the back.

"That's right." Jack smiled down at the toddler standing beside him. The little boy had a head full of thick black hair and ocean blue eyes.

"Basketball," Philip pointed to the scaled-down basketball in Jack's large hands.

"Sydney," Jack called to her, scooping Philip up with one arm. "Did you hear that? Philip said basketball."

"Yes, I heard." Sydney smiled and stood up.

"Grandma heard, too," her mother added, petting Ichabod, who was asleep in her lap.

"You're so smart, Philip," Sydney said, walking to Jack and their son. Jack wrapped his other arm around her. "Your son is a miniature replica of you, just like the big and small basketball hoops."

"That he is," Sydney's dad agreed. "Are you two going to make another grandchild for your mother and me?" Sydney's doctorate was official, and she'd taught for two years. "Or are you going back to teaching at Flagler College?"

Sydney smiled at her dad, kissed the baby's soft cheek, and said, "I want to have another baby before I go back." Just for her husband's ears, Sydney flirted with him, "If it's still on your agenda and if you'll cooperate with me."

"It is, and you know I will, baby girl."

Jack stood Philip on the ground and handed him the ball. The little boy tossed it two feet in the air. Jack chuckled, and Sydney clapped. As her mother joined them, Jack picked Philip up again, and Mike gave Philip the ball. Jack held the baby close to the net, as he'd once done with Sydney, and Philip dropped the ball through the hoop. Jack hugged him as everyone clapped.

"No applause necessary," T.J. joked as if they were clapping for him as he got out of his rental car in the driveway beside Sydney's new SUV.

Thanks to the coins, T.J. had enrolled in UCLA, played basketball for them, and been spotted by the Los Angeles Lakers. After graduating, he'd been drafted by the pro team and landed a lucrative contract.

At Kathy's urging, Sydney's dad had retired at the age of sixty-five. Keeping their California house made it easy to watch T.J. play basketball and see old friends. Her parents had purchased a home in St. Augustine as well, giving them a home on both coasts. Making plans for a world cruise, they had retired in style.

J.D. and Will had made their longtime dream come true by purchasing a floundering amusement park in St. Augustine. Designing a haunted ship ride, called the *Sea Phantom*, it had revived the business, quadrupled both J.D. and Will's investment, and the size of the amusement park. They had married local girls and bought homes within a few miles of Magnolia Lane.

"They're clapping for me," Chuck said, exiting the house holding a letter and an iPad.

Chuck had moved to Florida with his parents and enrolled in Flagler College. Now, he lived in a three-bedroom condo of his own, and T.J. stayed with him when he visited between basketball games. Chuck was a straight-A student studying finance and was already working part-time for Jack in the St. Augustine branch office.

Just as Sydney had once dreamed, every morning, Jack kissed her and Philip goodbye and walked next door to work. He usually came home for lunch and always took her and Philip with him when he flew to Manhattan.

They'd never missed spending the Fourth of July in the penthouse apartment and had already taken Philip to see Friendship Fountain in Jacksonville.

"We were clapping because Philip made a basket," Sydney answered as Chuck handed her the letter.

"Is the letter addressed to Resident?" Jack teased. "I had a tenant once who sent me a letter like that."

"It's addressed to Dr. and Dr. Malone." Sydney laughed and opened the envelope. "It's an anniversary card from Nellie." They had shared the fortune with her and she now resided in a luxury retirement community, drove a spiffy golf cart to and fro, and had lots of friends with whom she could chat. "Nellie says she's the new shuffle-board champ and wishes us all well."

"And since it's your parents' fifth anniversary, Philip," Sydney's mom patted Philip's back as Jack held him, "you have a dinner date with your grandpa, two of your uncles, and me."

"Bye-bye, sweet boy." Sydney kissed the baby's cheek.

"Bye?" Philip asked Jack, clasping his chubby arms around his father's neck.

"Bye-bye just for a little while." Jack cupped the back of the baby's head and kissed his cheek as he thanked God for his family. He and Sydney both did that on a daily basis. "How about if Daddy puts you in your car seat?" Jack suggested to his son, who nodded.

Sydney's father opened the rear door of the first luxury car he'd ever owned, and Jack buckled Philip into the car seat his grandparents had purchased for him. Chuck piled in next to Philip on one side, and T.J. folded his long body into the car on the other side of the toddler.

"Is the anniversary party for the adults still on for tomorrow night?" T.J. asked, having made the trip to the east coast so as not to miss it.

"Yeah," Jack grinned. "Got a girl lined up?"

"They're lined up, all right," Chuck answered for his brother.

Jack laughed, and Sydney rolled her pretty green eyes. Her mom shook her head and laughed as her dad started the car. The car pulled out of the driveway and everyone waved.

Turning to Jack, Sydney said, "I baked a chocolate cake for our private party."

Jack cocked a brow. "You know where I like to celebrate our private parties," he said with a grin and made a fast break.

Sydney giggled and chased after him. Passing Buster, where he sat by the doghouse, Sydney squealed, "Catch him for me, Buster!"

"Stay in your doghouse, Buster," Jack said with a laugh.

Buster barked, and Ichabod ignored them all as he slept on Jack's side of the gray bench in the courtyard blooming with forget-me-nots. Upon reaching the back door, Jack held it open for Sydney, and they kicked off their shoes. Sydney darted past him and grabbed the cake off the kitchen counter. He yanked open the silverware drawer and raced her to the staircase.

"No fair taking the steps two at a time," she warned.

"We proved all's fair in love and war," Jack said, passing her. But being a gentleman, he stopped at the doorway of the master bedroom and let her enter first. Holding the cake, she sat down on the bed with her back to the headboard. Utensils in hand, Jack took his place beside her. He dipped his fork into the cake, took a bite, and swallowed. "Sharing a chocolate cake," he began as Sydney also took a bite, "is where it all started."

Sydney nodded. "All the goals I told you about that day were fulfilled because of you."

"If the next baby is a girl, do you want to name her Camilla and call her Cammy?"

"Yes." Sydney nodded. "I'm so happy we named our son Philip Jackson Malone and if we have a little girl, I want to name her Camilla Jacqueline Malone. We can give her the cameo and tell her it belonged to a sweet girl who lived next door. Someday we'll tell the kids how their grandmother, Jacqueline, intervened on our behalf." Jack sighed, and Sydney asked, "Once a chatterbox, always a chatterbox?"

"That day at the kitchen table, you asked me what my own personal dream was, and I couldn't put it into words. But I was dying for a family. Now, I've got four brothers. The day I met your parents, I had the next best thing to my own mom and dad. And just when I thought it couldn't get any better, you gave me a son. Had someone told me I'd have a wife and family I loved this much or be as happy as I am today, I'd have said they were—"

"A nutcase?" Sydney asked with tears in her eyes.

"Yeah." Jack set the cake and their forks on the nightstand and pulled her into his arms. "I love you, Sydney."

"I love you, Jack. Promise me we'll do bed and breakfast together for all eternity."

"You have my promise." Jack kissed her lips, and a tear there tasted as salty as the sea. He pictured the lonely pier where Philip had left Camilla to search the ocean for treasures. "We learned from Philip and Cammy to face the world together."

"You know what else I've learned?" Sydney whispered.

"What?" Jack asked, holding his treasure to his heart.

"Love made us kindred spirits."

A Look at: Chase Cooper

TRIPLE C RANCH BOOK ONE

Escape to the captivating world of contemporary western romance in this thrilling tale of love, redemption, and untamed passion.

Meet Chase Cooper, the dashing owner of Triple C Ranch-Central, a prosperous cattle ranch nestled just outside the breathtaking landscapes of Colorado Springs. With family ranches adorning both sides of his, and women vying for his attention at every turn, it seems Chase has everything a man could desire. Yet, his heart remains untouched. Believing that the woman capable of taming his wild spirit doesn't exist, he embraces a life of solitude, stubbornly resisting the ties of commitment.

Enter Jade Taylor, a woman whose life is filled with more cracks and crevices than she can repair. After relocating to Colorado Springs a year ago, she finds herself trapped in the clutches of a rigid work contract that denies her a personal life. Fed up with the suffocating control imposed upon her, Jade rebels against the chains that bind her, seeking solace in the serenity of a countryside bed-and-breakfast. It is there that a twist of fate leads her to the doorstep of an irresistibly handsome stranger— a man she cannot banish from her thoughts.

But danger lurks in the shadows, personified by Franco Spatafore, an obsessed plastic surgeon who covets Jade for her flawless beauty. With a chilling determination to possess her, he embarks on a twisted mind game.

Only Chase holds the key to rescuing the woman who has not only captured his heart but also saved him from a life of eternal solitude. Will he find the strength to confront the sinister forces conspiring against them and prevent Jade's disappearance forever?

AVAILABLE DECEMBER 2023

About the Author

Lynn Eldridge is a former president of the West Virginia Chapter of Romance Writers of America and earned an honorable mention in their Golden Heart Contest. Lynn is the author of several historical and contemporary romance novels, including *Desire in Deadwood*, *Remember the Passion*, *Tame the* Wild, and Skyrocket *to Surrender*. Her latest novel, *Hearts and Mountains*, is a 2023 Spur Award Finalist.

In addition to her writing career, Lynn is a licensed clinical therapist and dedicates one day a week in an outpatient behavioral health facility in Charleston, West Virginia.